An excerpt from
My Naughty Minx

She paused, but heard nothing within, so she took a deep breath and began again. "All I want is to be a proper wife. I can't bear this, when I love my new husband so much." She wept as if her heart was breaking, but she couldn't seem to summon real tears in her frustration. At last, August appeared and stood regarding her, one hand on his hip.

"What are you doing?"

"What do you think?" she said. "I'm crying."

"You're faking," he snapped. "Those are false tears. But that can be remedied." He took her arm and pulled her inside. The footman shut the door behind them with an unsubtle bang as August pulled her across the library to his desk. It was her turn to ask, or rather shriek, "What are you doing?"

He sat in his chair and threw her over his lap. "I'm doing what I've wanted to do ever since I woke up a week ago and found you in my arms."

Oh goodness, this wasn't the outcome she'd hoped for at all.

"I won't cry anymore if it upsets you so," she said, trying to squirm off his thighs. "I can be perfectly quiet if I try. I'll go up to bed, silent as a mouse."

"You had your chance to go to bed silent as a mouse. Instead you stood outside my library door and treated the entire household to your ridiculous histrionics."

He flipped up the skirts of her dressing gown, brushed aside her shift, and brought his palm down hard against her bare bottom. He spanked one cheek and then the other, hot, sharp slaps that made her yelp in alarm. "Oh, please, you can't spank a bride on her wedding night! I believe it's against the law."

But then she remembered that Lord Townsend had spanked Aurelia on her wedding night, and that any man in England might spank his wife whenever he wanted to...

My Naughty Minette

by

Annabel Joseph

For Tiffany, who inspired Minette,
and who is one of the most inspiring people I know

Chapter One:
Despicable

England, 1793

August, more formally known as the sixth Earl of Augustine, never expected to spend his twenty-eighth birthday at a tame house party in Berkshire. Since two of his four best friends had married, this sort of thing had become his life.

"Now, Townsend, get your teeth into it." Gentlemen and ladies cried out encouragements as the dark-haired host went underwater again, bobbing for apples in traditional Hallowe'en fashion.

"Open wide," said another. "If you must, use your tongue!"

Perhaps not so tame a party. The Marquess of Townsend and his wife, Aurelia, had gathered a merry crowd of friends and acquaintances to Somerton, their country manor. It would be their last opportunity to entertain for some time, as Lady Townsend expected a child in February. His friend Lord Warren's wife was expecting as well, in March, so the lot of them had gathered for one last hurrah, along with Warren's younger sister Minette and her companion Mrs. Everly, and his friend Arlington, the "Viking duke," who indeed resembled a Viking at times.

August's mother was in attendance too, along with his sisters Catherine and Eliza, and their husbands and children. The Townsends had also invited the Earl and Countess of Colton, whose daughter, Lady Priscilla, was often linked to August in gossip.

Truth be told, Priscilla was practically planning their wedding, with encouragement from his mother, and hers.

During the bonfire at dusk, Lady Priscilla had stood by his side in a wholly proprietary manner, and when the breezy autumn night had blown smoke in their direction, she'd hidden behind him and cried, "Lord Augustine, how heroic you are." He didn't know what was heroic about shielding someone from a bit of smoke. He supposed delicate, china-doll ladies like Priscilla wilted beneath the horrors of flame and soot, which made him wonder why she came down to the bonfire at all.

Priscilla was beautiful and genteel, with her sleek brunette hair and striking blue eyes, but the smallest things she did irritated him. Really, he ought to have stayed in town. He always spent Hallowe'en night—his birthday night—in the company of the famed Dirty Esmeralda. Half-witch, half-wanton, Esme had become his favored outlet for lustful dissolution. When he was in London he visited her three or four times a week, and on his birthday, she always bestowed "special favors."

If he married Lady Priscilla, as he was expected to do, he might have to reduce his association with Esme, or stop seeing her all together. He wondered if Priscilla would find *that* heroic. He wondered if he cared. His only chance at birthday fun this year was the buxom, blonde chambermaid who made eyes at him every morning when she brought his bathing water. Perhaps he ought to seek her out later and have a word with her, though he wasn't sure Townsend would appreciate him sleeping with the help.

"Huzzah!" Cheers rang out from the assembled company, drawing August from these glum thoughts. Townsend had come up with an apple between his teeth. Aurelia laughed and swabbed at his soaked hair and face with a towel. Water dripped onto his shirt; the linen clung to him at his neckline. His cravat and collar had been undone, of course, before he took the first dive. This apple-bobbing ritual provided the younger men the excuse of disrobing—at least partially—before the ladies, and a great many of them waited their turn to experience this masculine thrill. The ladies blushed and whispered behind their fans, and ate ginger and pumpkin cakes, and drank black currant tea.

August sat on the outskirts, leaving them to it. He was not exactly sulking. He was only tired of doing what everyone expected, particularly Lady Priscilla, who doubtless wished him to untie his cravat, take off his coat and waistcoat, and undo his top button so she might simper over him to her friends. Once he'd gotten the apple in his teeth—and he was excellent at this, since he had a big mouth—she would also expect to be the one to dab his black hair dry with a towel. She'd expect him to hand his apple over to her with a smile, bite marks and all. Such a gesture would be tantamount to an engagement announcement.

He found all of this distasteful.

He did not wish to marry Lady Priscilla. At all.

The ginger-haired Lord Robert went next. The amiable young buck had been paying special attention to Minette ever since the house party convened the week before. August searched the room for his friend's little sister and found her sitting near Lady Warren and some other friends. Blast, she was looking right at him. He quickly looked away; he'd long ago learned not to encourage Minette in her childish infatuation. Not that Minette was a child anymore. Goodness, she must be twenty now, if he was turning twenty-eight.

August sighed and stood, and retreated to the other end of the room to sit at the pianoforte. Some of the older houseguests sat at card tables or snored in tufted chairs, keeping their distance from the apple-bobbing merriment on the terrace. His mother smiled at him from a chaise, where she visited with Lady Colton. These blasted Oxfordshire family dynasties, and these china-doll marriageable daughters.

Another great cheer rose from the other side of the room. August sifted through the music at the piano. Bland stuff, suitable for company.

"Play something for us, would you?" his mother asked.

"Oh, yes. Something haunting, in the spirit of the season," suggested Lady Colton with a smile.

August shuffled through a few more selections. "I'm afraid there's nothing haunting here, and besides, everyone's preoccupied with the game at the moment." He looked over toward the terrace, and found that Minette had escaped her group of friends and was headed his way.

"Good evening, Lady Colton," she said. "And Lady Barrymore." Minette embraced his mother warmly. The blonde-curled chit had always been charmingly polite. Since Minette had lost her parents at a young age, many of the Oxfordshire ladies had acted as mother to her over the years. Spoiled her, even. He half-listened as Minette chattered on in her typical happy way about the past season in London, and her brother's marriage to

Josephine, and the Warren baby to be born before Easter. He traced fingers along the keys as the ladies asked after Minette's winter plans. They hinted sweetly that marriage and children should not be far off in her future.

Ah, God. Minette, married with children? It seemed only yesterday Warren was fretting about whether to dress her in ankle skirts. Lady Colton continued to discourse upon the blissful state of matrimony in a voice loud enough for him to overhear. He would not be drawn into the conversation, no matter how loudly they talked. Another cheer from the terrace, and the ladies moved on to the topic of the Townsends' lovely party, the grand bonfire, and the rosemary-pumpkin tarts.

"Well, perhaps Lord Augustine will agree to play if I play with him," said Minette.

August looked up at that. Lord help him, Minette meant to join him at the pianoforte. He might have sent her—good-naturedly, of course—to re-join the other young people, but at that moment he noticed Priscilla and some of her friends heading over. So, instead, he slid sideways on the bench and placed the great, disorganized pile of sheet music on her lap.

"This shall be a treat," said his mother. "Lady Minette has always played so prettily."

Minette did not play prettily at all. August knew this, but he told her to pick something she liked. Of course, being Minette, she liked them all.

"Well, *Flowers of August* might be perfect for the season, and perfect for your name," she said, "but then Lady Millicent sang this other piece at the Denham's dinner and it was beautiful too. It's new and oh so lovely, but it takes rather more of a soprano than I've got. Oh, here is *The Clock Shall Chime*, have you heard it?"

Before he could answer, she went on.

"It's a rather sober piece for a fun night. I don't think it will do. Oh, here is a whole suite of baroque arrangements. The Townsends have the most capital collection of songs, don't they?"

"Perhaps you should pick one," he said in as polite a voice as he could muster. "We can play a duet." Priscilla was hovering, ready to draw him off to some tiresome circle of conversation, and more guests were making their way over from the terrace.

"Here is *Poggle and Woggle*. Oh, that's a dreadful noise, we'll put that one on the bottom. And *Holly on the Green*, but it's not even the holidays yet, only Hallowe'en, and oh!" She turned to him with an accusing gaze. "That means it's your birthday, doesn't it, Lord Augustine? How could we all have forgotten?"

It was too late to shush her, and he probably shouldn't anyway, in front of all these people.

"I say, it *is* your birthday, isn't it?" said Townsend, who had come over with Arlington to the pianoforte. "We ought to celebrate. What would you like? A champagne toast? Some cake?"

August didn't dare think about what he wanted—Dirty Esme. His friends gave him a sympathetic look. They knew where August usually spent his birthday, just as they knew August was only at Somerton because of Lady Priscilla, and parental pressure.

"We must have a song, at any rate, Minette," Arlington said in a brisk voice. "What will the two of you play?"

"Oh, yes, play something," said Aurelia. "A bright song, for celebrating."

Minette smiled and looked up at him, pink cheeked. "It should be *Flowers of August* most certainly, since it's Lord August's birthday."

Everyone agreed that would be lovely, except for Warren, who was giving August dire looks. It wasn't August's fault that Warren's silly sister had nurtured an infatuation with him for the last decade or so. Given the choice between Minette's blushing or Lady Priscilla's aggressive and proprietary hovering, he would take Minette. He scowled back at Warren, shrugged, and arranged the music atop the stand.

"Are you sure you want to play the high end?" he asked, scanning the piece. "It's the more difficult part."

"I'm sure," she said, nodding her head. "I've been practicing my piano."

As soon as they began the piece, it became apparent Minette had not practiced hard enough. There was a great deal of pausing as she searched for the correct notes. Once or twice, August was obliged to reach over her and strike them himself, at which she giggled.

"Tempo, my dear... A little faster," he said when she nearly came to a stop. She did have a lovely voice, strong, melodious, and clear. He supposed her voice got plenty of exercise, with all the chattering she did. She held a sustained note as she searched for the right keys again. Some of the guests laughed, and when August reached around her to strike the chord, there were guffaws and bemused applause.

Goodness, Minette was silly, but it was impossible not to smile when she was around. Although he had learned not to smile at her too hard. Warren was still sending him warning glances.

They muddled through the rest of the song, his shoulder pressed to hers. He joined in on the last chorus, his baritone steady if out of practice. Minette stared up at him, forgetting to play completely until he nudged her hand. They banged out the song's finale, although Minette missed a few of the necessary notes. Their ragged effort was met by enthusiastic applause and wishes for a happy birthday.

Minette's brows drew together. "I never knew you could sing," she said, beneath the clamorous ovation.

"Nearly everyone can sing. And how wonderfully you played."

"Now that is a lie, Lord Augustine." She tilted her head and gave him a look. It unsettled him, for it wasn't the vapid, infatuated look of her childhood, but something aware and flirtatious, and altogether more mature. He looked away, right into the fawning regard of his soon-to-be-bride, Lady Priscilla.

"I must have a turn at the piano now," she said. She was the same age as Minette, but where Minette was flighty, Priscilla was refined. Where Minette was impish, Priscilla was beautiful and confident and...cold. His china doll. "Will you stay and play with me, Lord Augustine?" she asked.

There was nothing else to say. "Of course."

Priscilla leafed through the music and decided on one of the baroque pieces, a difficult work by François Couperin.

"I don't know," said August. "It's a rather heavy piece for the current mood."

"Can't you play it?" she teased in an icily sweet voice.

He could play it in his sleep, but Minette would be mortified when Priscilla performed this showy work just following her shaky attempt at *Flowers of August*. "How about *Poggle and Woggle*?" he suggested.

Priscilla laughed. "You're joking with me, my lord. I love your sense of humor. No, I think we've had enough of such foolishness. The children are all in the nursery for the night."

As she said *children*, her gaze slid toward Minette. It confused him for a moment, this cruel and petty behavior on Priscilla's part, and then he realized the foolish woman was jealous of the girl! Of Minette Bernard, the last woman on earth he'd ever consider courting. Warren's sister pretended not to notice Priscilla's cutting look, turning instead to speak with Aurelia.

"Are you ready to play?" he asked. Priscilla didn't answer, only plunged into the treble part of the Couperin selection. August played the bass. He glanced at Minette as the notes grew in complexity, watching her normally pink cheeks flush a humiliated red. By the time he and Priscilla finished the first movement, his friend's sister had disappeared.

"I hate her!" Minette sobbed as her sister-in-law stroked her hair. "Lady Priscilla is the most despicable creature in the entire known world."

"I know, dearest. I hate her too. We all hate her," Josephine crooned. "You mustn't fret so. Everyone enjoyed your playing with August."

"Everyone laughed at me."

"Everyone laughed *with* you, because it was delightful and fun. Now they're doubtless covering yawns as Priscilla plods away in there, showing off as she always does. I'm sure they much preferred you and your good-natured antics. Even August smiled, and you know that almost never happens."

Minette pressed her handkerchief against her lips. "He smiled? At me?"

"Several times, darling. You would have seen if you were not so intent on the keys. He smiled right down at you as you flubbed all those notes, and no, it wasn't in mockery. I believe he was charmed."

This made Minette cry even harder. In fact, she felt like her heart was going to bleed right out of her body through her tears. "I can't bear this," she wailed. "I can't smile any longer. I can't watch August court Lady Priscilla and pretend I don't care." She grasped Josephine's hands. "You must talk to my brother. Tell Warren we have to leave. Tell him your pregnancy is making you feel tired, or ill, or..."

"I can't lie to my husband. But if we tell him how you're feeling, perhaps he'll agree to leave early. I'm afraid...well..." She gave Minette a deeply sympathetic look. "I'm afraid August and Priscilla's betrothal

13

announcement could come any day. So perhaps it would be best to go, if we can manage it without causing a fuss."

"I just… I can't believe it." Minette paused a moment to blow her nose. "I always knew this day would come, that he would marry somebody, but I can't believe it's finally here. It hurts so much worse than I ever believed. I don't know how I shall stand at their wedding and smile and wish them well. I'll have to manufacture some illness to excuse myself. I'll have to tell them I have the plague."

Josephine held her close and petted her hair. "You could tell them that, but I don't know if they'd believe you."

"I never thought it would really happen. I thought he would break with her. He doesn't love her!"

"I know, my dear. Of course he doesn't love her, but I didn't love your brother either when I married him. And Aurelia and Townsend despised each other before they wed. Now they're deeply in love."

"You're not making me feel better."

"I'm sorry. But if it's August you're worried for, I think he'll be all right." Josephine twisted one of her wavy auburn locks. "I'm more worried about you. Perhaps it's time to move on."

"Move on to what?" Minette cried. "I have always loved August, as long as I can remember. I adore him with all my soul."

Josephine took the handkerchief from her and wiped at her tears. "With *all your soul?* Minette, you're so young. You've plenty of time to find another love, one who is within your reach. August was never meant for you. He thinks of you as a child. As Warren's sister."

"I know, I know. Everyone believes I'm ridiculous, even August, but I can't help how I feel." Minette doubled over, scrunching her hot eyes shut. They would be so swollen and red, she wouldn't be able to show her face. This was so much harder than she'd imagined. She had thought she could be strong and accept Lord August's engagement when it inevitably came. But she was finding it impossible to be strong. "I don't know what I'm going to do. I can't think. I can't eat. I can't sleep. I can't keep up this act anymore. I dream about him and Lady Priscilla. I woke up in Mrs. Everly's room this morning, curled into a ball."

"Mrs. Everly's room?" Josephine blinked at her in concern. "How did you get there? Have you been walking from your bed again?"

"I can't help it. It just happens. Oh, don't tell Warren." Minette clasped her hands together in a gesture of entreaty. "Please, Josephine. He worried so, before."

"And he shall worry now, but your brother would want to know."

"Please don't tell him, Josie. Not yet. It's only the idea of August marrying. It's got me in such a state."

"Dear love." Josephine hugged her close with sisterly concern. "You mustn't be so troubled. You must try to move on. There's some dashing young gentleman out there waiting to sweep you off your feet. I promise, Minette. Your perfect husband is out there. You'll look back at this time and wonder what you ever saw in August."

Minette wished it was so, but she'd never pictured herself with any other man. She'd tried. She'd opened her heart to this one or that, but something was always missing, some connection she felt whenever Lord August was near. It wasn't only his strong, powerful physique or his ebony dark hair. There was something in the depths of his eyes. They were an odd color, somewhat hazel, somewhat brown, and so brooding and mysterious. He was gruff, yet kind. Careless, yet intelligent. Sometimes he greatly surprised her. For instance, she'd never realized he could sing so beautifully. As much as she studied him at every opportunity, there was so much she didn't know, that she felt she must know if she was to be fulfilled in life.

She had always believed Lord August was meant for her, before she even knew about courtship and love, and marriage. How could this be happening? How could he marry someone else?

With a soft knock, her brother entered and shut the door behind him. They shared an abiding affection, in addition to matching light-blond curls and blue eyes. "Minette, darling, are you all right?"

The concern in his voice brought another flood of tears. She would make herself sick if she didn't stop. She had never been the weeping type, but this was an utter disaster.

"Don't cry," he said. He crossed to sit on the other side of her, and gave her shoulders a squeeze. "No one cares that Lady Priscilla can play better than you. She made herself look a right idiot choosing that wretched baroque music to play at a Hallowe'en fete."

"It's not that," Minette bawled. "I'm not crying about that."

She glanced up long enough to see her brother and Josephine exchange a look. Yes, silly Minette, and her childish infatuation with August. None of them understood the chaos in her heart. She wasn't a child anymore, and what she felt wasn't only infatuation.

"My dear," he said gently. "We've talked about this so many times."

"It doesn't matter how many times we've talked about it. It doesn't change my feelings. It doesn't change my love for him."

Warren took her chin and made her look up. "I don't want August for you," he said. "Those are *my* feelings. I know him better than you do. You wouldn't make a good match. What of Lord Robert? He's a steady chap with excellent prospects. He's fun and cheerful, like you."

"He's a ginger," Minette sobbed.

"So?"

"We'll have carrot-topped children, and nothing looks good with that color. What on earth will my daughters wear to their coming out?"

Warren blinked at her. "I don't…know."

"Not only that, but when I talk to Lord Robert, there's nothing to say. When I'm with him, he's cheerful and fun, but he doesn't make me love him."

"And August does?"

"Yes! I've loved him for years, and I've always wanted to be his wife. I feel connected to him somehow. I can't explain it."

Her brother frowned. "I don't think it can be explained. And I don't think there's anything to be done for it. Lord Colton's growing impatient, and August's father is in ill health. So you see, August's under pressure both ways. Three ways, if you count Lady Prissy upstairs banging away on the pianoforte. Listen, mopsy." He squeezed her hand and held it between his palms. "I love you very much. I want you to be happy. Even if August was head over heels for you, I wouldn't let a match proceed. It wouldn't suit either of you. You'd realize it soon enough."

Minette loved her brother, but sometimes she hated him too, like when he was being a know-it-all, overprotective tyrant without any heart.

"You don't understand," she said, pulling her hand away. "You don't feel my pain."

"Warren," said Josephine. "Perhaps we ought to think about leaving early. Very soon," she added, raising a brow. "If it can be arranged."

He sighed. "I suppose the Townsends would understand, but I think it awfully cowardly of you, sis. The party doesn't end for another week."

One more week. By the end of that week, August was sure to be engaged to Lady Priscilla. It was so unfair.

"Please, we must leave," she said, worrying her handkerchief between her fingers. "I'll pretend to be ill. Or you can say you have business to attend to in town."

Warren shook his head. "I'll tell Hunter and Aurelia the truth. They'd know anyway. But we must keep the rest of the guests from finding out the reason, for propriety's sake."

"For propriety's sake?" Josephine rolled her eyes. She tended to scoff at propriety when it suited her. "You speak of propriety when your sister's heart is breaking?"

"Yes, I do," Warren said. "I won't have drama and gossip overshadowing August's proposal to Lady Priscilla. It's going to be difficult enough for him as it is. As for you, my dear..." He looked back at Minette, concern clouding his blue eyes. "My heart breaks for you, too, but you must come to terms with this situation. You must look elsewhere for love. When we return to London for the season, after the baby's born, we'll search until we find a young man worthy of your affections. We'll go on calls and plan dinners. We'll have a ball at Park Street, a lively, grand affair."

Josephine looked heavenward in exasperation. Minette wrung her hands.

"You can throw a thousand balls but it won't make me stop loving Lord August," she said to her brother.

"You may love him all you like," he replied with regretful firmness. "But August shall marry Lady Priscilla before spring of next year."

Chapter Two:
Mary

August retired late into the night, after drinking far more than he should. It was black outside with no moon, an ominous Hallowe'en night. He was another year older, and another day closer to offering for Priscilla. By the end of this week, surely, he must do it. Why not? Who else was there? He'd never courted anyone, or loved any lady with particular feeling. If not for familial pressure, he might have contented himself with several more years of Dirty Esmeralda's talents, and his music, and the occasional bottle of port.

He groaned and drew the curtains of his bed, and fell into a restless sleep, thinking of Esme, and Priscilla, and poor Minette, whom she'd humiliated. Afterward, Minette had disappeared for the rest of the night, and of course people remarked upon it, because Minette was so social. It wasn't well done of Priscilla. If she was his wife—and she would soon be his wife—he might have had sharp words for her afterward, in private. He might have even spanked the spiteful creature, knocked her down a step or two from her pillar of righteousness with a trip across his lap.

But fantasy-spanking Priscilla did nothing for him. His dreams veered in a more satisfying direction: spanking Esme, and then holding her down and showing her just what happened to naughty girls. In the midst of this erotic reverie, a faint sound awoke him. The curtains parted, revealing a white gown and blonde hair. Ah, breasts. The side of the bed dipped and the curtain closed, enveloping them in darkness, but he knew who she was. The alluring chambermaid.

It appeared he was to have some birthday fun after all.

How he'd groused to Townsend and Arlington earlier, that he must spend his birthday alone. His friends must have sent her upstairs to surprise him, or perhaps the lass had come on her own. Either way, he was happy for the company, and not at all too drunk to perform. His cock stirred at her scent, her warm acquiescence as she snuggled close beside him. He knew from her glances the past few days that she found him enticing, and he planned to give her a good show of it, out of gratitude as much as anything else.

He stroked her hair, finding it soft and curly, sprung loose from her staid servant's cap. He couldn't see her face in the darkness but he remembered a pert nose and saucy mouth. He breathed in her sweet, flowery scent and caressed her soft skin. Esme had soft, fragrant skin like this. He might even pretend this girl was Esme if he wished it. One willing body was very like another, especially at this dark hour, on this witching night when he'd been born so many years ago.

"Have you come to be my special treat?" he whispered, drawing her pliable body closer. "Oh, but you smell pretty. You're kind to visit me."

She made some soft, sleepy sound in response. He knew he must be gentle with this young trollop. She'd be experienced—she wouldn't have come to his bed otherwise—but he had to remember she was a Berkshire maid, not a London whore. He traced the curve of her waist and hips through the thin cotton of her night shift. She gave a light, breathless sigh, arching against him. She was petite but beautifully feminine, with great, round breasts and a bottom that filled his hands.

"How sweet you are," he said, chuckling at her cuddlesome manner. "Will you give me a kiss? It's my birthday, you know."

She didn't answer. These servant girls could be so shy around proper gentlemen. He cupped her chin and tried to kiss her, but he ended up grazing her nose in the darkness before he found his way to her lips. Her kisses were shy too, but her fingers crept up his shoulders and curled in his hair in a decidedly welcoming way.

"You want to be here with me, don't you?" he asked, just to be sure. "You didn't get lost on your way back to the servants' quarters?"

She went still, and he thought for one moment that she'd rise and leave him there, aroused and unsatisfied. But then she said, in a soft, whispery voice, "Yes, I want to be here."

The way she said it had him rock hard. "I'll make it good for you, my little pretty," he promised. He kissed her again, entranced by her freshness, her reticence even as she pressed her body closer to his. "We're going to have a fine time together this Hallowe'en night. You're not afraid of ghosts and goblins, are you?"

She whispered in that same soft voice, "No, milord. I'm not afraid."

His fingers played over her knee and then trailed up the bare skin of her thigh. She wasn't bold and brassy like Dirty Esmeralda, but she was equally luscious in her way. He caught the hem of her shift and bunched it in his palm, drawing it upward. "I'm going to take this off. I want to be able to touch you everywhere and make you feel good."

"That sounds...nice."

He went by touch rather than sight, inching the garment over her head, though she tried to grasp it back at the end. "It's all right," he said. "I'll lay it right here so you can find it later. I'll let you back to your bed by dawn, so you don't risk the housekeeper's wrath."

"Oh. Thank you. That's very important."

The formal, polite way she said this made him smile. "You're a funny one, aren't you? Silly girl." He drew her closer, not to maul her or anything. He wanted to enjoy her for a while, trace her curvy waist and squeeze and suckle her bounteous breasts. She made the most erotic sighs as he caressed her. She twitched and tensed, and grasped his shoulders, giving herself up to sensation as they lay together in the dark. His mind wandered to thin, icy Lady Priscilla. No, he didn't want to think about her now, not with this willing, warm angel in his bed. He stroked his palms up and down the maid's back.

"What's your name, missy?" he asked.

Silence again. The little imp. Did she think he wouldn't recognize her in the light of day? Did she think he didn't very well know who'd been making eyes at him all week?

"Mary," she finally said. It was probably a false name, but that was all right. He'd call her whatever she wished as long as she spread her thighs for him and helped dispel some of his frustration this dreary night. Her feminine scent compelled him, and the feel of her curves made him want to thrust his cock inside her. *No, not yet.* The night was young and she was fun to play with, with her squirms and her little sighs. He petted her, stroked her, made soothing sounds as he dropped kisses upon her lips and down the column of her neck.

"Mary," he murmured. "How I love your breasts." He helped himself to a handful of one tit, and locked his lips around the other, nibbling gently at her nipple. He wasn't the type of lover to spout poetry. He preferred to let his fingers and lips make the poetry, and she didn't seem to mind. His hand tightened on her waist as he teased and licked the pointed peak. She panted beneath him as if she'd never experienced such sensation before. He suckled the other breast to hear the sound again, a moan of shock and discovery. Poor lass. Her previous partners must have been quick and neglected her pleasure. All the more reason to take his time.

"You like that, do you?" he asked.

"Yes," she whispered in the darkness. "It feels wonderful."

He paid court to her gorgeous breasts until her nails dug into his back, until her nipples were so hard and tight he could trace their contours with the tip of his tongue. He bit down on one rather hard, just to see what she would do. The nails dug deeper and her hips bucked; a ragged mewl escaped. How delightful these servant girls could be. He generally stuck to a small circle of working women in London. They were marvelous at their art, but tended to stay detached at the end of it. This lovely blonde lass had an open, uncontrived manner that charmed him, that made him think of softness and playfulness, and comfortable things.

He squeezed her rounded bottom, traced down her thighs, then eased her legs apart to explore her feminine folds. He delved down into her soft fluff of curls and palmed the heat of her pussy. She tensed, going still in his arms.

"No, don't fret," he said. "Open for me, Mary. Let me see if you're feeling naughty or nice."

She trembled a little, so he kissed her until she calmed and then he pressed his fingers deeper, into her sleek, secret place. "Oh, what's this?" he teased. "You're feeling naughty indeed. I'm glad." He smiled against her lips. She was so hot and wet, and so responsive. He decided he couldn't go through the rest of his life without knowing the taste of this novel creature, so he ducked beneath the covers, from darkness into more darkness.

His little angel gasped, and reached down as if to stop him. Goodness, didn't these country boys know how to properly satisfy their partners? "Let me do it," he said, pressing a kiss against her belly. "Open your legs and let me kiss your pretty pussy."

Some of the tension left her as she ceased to resist. With a satisfied growl, he parted her quim with his thumbs and licked across slick folds until he found the little nub of flesh that made her jerk in reaction. His entire world was her scent and her trembling, and her soft, throaty sighs, which he had already memorized by heart. How exciting, to explore and experiment without sight. He was obliged to learn her needs through his other senses, which proved to be a rousing endeavor. She tasted piquant and sweet, and innocent and wicked. Noises filtered down to him beneath the covers, more groans and muffled moans. She needn't be so quiet, he thought, for the heavy bed curtains provided them an impermeable fortress from the world.

With time and patience, and the gift of his big mouth, he eased the shaking in her limbs, and had her arching to him instead. Lick and stroke, nip there, suck here. Eventually, she forgot about being quiet and became rather vocal. His cock swelled, aching to be inside her, but this was so diverting. She was going to come for him, he could feel it. He eased a finger up inside her, mimicking the sex act, pushing it in and out in rhythm to her jerks and pleading breaths. It would be good to have her well primed before he mounted her.

"Yes, that's it," he whispered between grazing nips of his teeth. "Yes, naughty girl. Is it good for you?"

Her legs tensed again, pressing against his ears. He concentrated on her pearl, teasing licks and then more pressure, and was rewarded with an abandoned cry. She even sounded like an angel when she came. He chuckled against her skin and gave her one last lick for good measure, and found his way back up in the dark by way of lingering kisses. Hips, belly, breasts, shoulders, neck. Ah, there were her lips, moist and slightly parted. He licked and kissed them, wishing he could see the expression on her face, but not wishing to disturb this dark, mysterious intimacy.

"That was a lovely way to begin," he whispered. "Don't you agree?"

Begin? Minette thought. *What else are you planning to do?*

She lay in his arms, replete, appalled, and rather hellishly conflicted. She knew she must stop this, but at the same time, she wanted to see what other wonders August might be able to perform. After all, who ever imagined a man could pleasure a woman in such an outrageous fashion? Who ever imagined the rush of warmth and completion he might give her as his mouth and hands played over her body?

She'd dreamed so many nights of lying beside Lord August and basking in the warmth of his embrace. She'd dreamed of him touching her and kissing her with lustful abandon. In fact, she had wished for it so badly that when she awakened to find it happening, she thought herself still in the throes of a dream. Long moments had gone by when she was half asleep and half awake, long moments before she became aware that she was actually, in true reality, in Lord August's bed.

Her blasted sleepwalking. She ought to have confessed to her brother that it had started again. Warren would have locked her in, or asked Townsend to station a footman at her door.

Then you wouldn't have had this.

But she *shouldn't* have this. My goodness, he was making free with her person in a very licentious way, and he wasn't finished yet. In his defense, he thought her a kitchen maid, and she let him believe it, because otherwise she would have to go away, and it was August, whom she had loved and idolized for so many years...

Oh, he was so warm and so large and so *real* next to her, and had apparently gone to bed tonight without any clothes. In her folly, she'd allowed him to undress her too, and give her all manner of caresses, things she hadn't even read about in romantic novels. At least she didn't think she had. The language was often flowery and nonspecific.

While she lay there trying to think back to some of the more instructive passages, August stroked her skin, and fondled her breasts and put his mouth upon them, teasing her nipples with his teeth until she shuddered in a helpless kind of trance. Minette knew she ought to stop him. She *really* ought to stop him and leave. But it felt so good, and she would never, ever have another chance to feel this way, especially once he was betrothed to Lady Priscilla.

And so she dithered and sighed, and clutched his thick, dark hair that was so much softer than she had ever believed. She wished she could see him, see his warm, muscled body lying beside her. Of course, she'd memorized every aspect of his hands, and his face, the only parts of him that showed outside his clothes. If only she could see the rest of him. If only this encounter between them was real, and not some dream-launched caper that would only lead to misfortune.

"Mary," he sighed.

Yes, Mary. She was Mary for this hour. She'd stay an hour and then she'd tell him she had to go back to the kitchens. Servants rose at early hours. She was Mary, a naughty, wanton servant girl who'd crept into the Earl of Augustine's bed to warm him on his birthday night.

Minette Bernard, this has gone on long enough. You're playing a dangerous game.

Just a half hour, perhaps, and then she'd find the strength and opportunity to go. It was only so pleasant to be hugged and touched and caressed by the long-time lover of her dreams.

"You're very quiet," he said. His fingers found her face in the dark, and traced down her cheeks to her parted lips. "What now, my angel? Would you like a chance to use this pretty mouth?"

"To kiss you?" she asked. She tried to use a different tone and inflection, the way the servants talked. If he discovered her identity now...oh, what a terrible scene.

"Yes, to kiss me." He knelt up in the bed. She could hear his movement in the darkness, and feel the mattress dip. She could just make out the outline of his body. So large and strong. He reached and groped for her hand, and pressed it downward along his torso.

Oh, my. He placed it on a hard, hot shaft of flesh, and moved it up and down. She didn't know if she was touching him or...well. What else could she be touching? But this part of his body was so big and stiff, so much larger than it looked tucked in his breeches. Not that she spent a great deal of time studying men's breeches. Only August's breeches, when he wasn't looking at her, of course, and she knew she'd never seen anything this large outlined beneath the fabric's surface. Thank goodness it was dark so he couldn't see her flushing in shock.

"Go ahead and kiss it," he said. "Don't be shy."

He brushed fingers into her hair and drew her face right down to him, to *it*. She felt panic. Kiss it? The way he had kissed her down there?

"I— I'm sorry, milord, I don't know how," she said in a shamefaced whisper.

He laughed. "Country girls. If you don't want a chance at it, I suppose it's all right. I'm not going to last much longer anyway."

Oh, thank goodness. Minette believed things had gone rather far enough. If this interlude was nearly over, well, she would miss the pleasant closeness of it, but it was probably for the best.

He drew her down beside him and pressed his great, distended shaft against her hip. She still felt troubled by this unfamiliar aspect of his body, but then he caressed her again with deft, knowing touches that made her melt inside. He kissed her, his warm, sweet breath tasting faintly of brandy. She felt transported by his strange roughness that also felt like gentleness. *Thank you, Mary, naughty servant girl, for giving me these moments.* She hummed in approval as he parted her legs and began to stroke her in that singular way. Her body grew even damper than it had been before.

"Oh, yes, you like that, my sweet. I know." She could feel his smile against her lips in the darkness. She took his face in her hands and scratched her fingers through his stubble, and brought his lips back to hers. He groaned against her mouth, but she was the one who wanted to groan, for the pleasure of this intimacy, and for knowing the feel of his stubble and skin, and the fresh, spicy scent of him. How many times had she wished to kiss his lips just this way?

His groan roughened, and he pressed a finger inside her slick, sensitive place, where he had fondled her before, and then shifted so he was over her with their hips aligned. It felt lovely to lie this way, with his weight against her but not against her, since he braced himself on his arms. She stared up in the darkness as he leaned to kiss her. Oh, to see him in the light, to see all the beauty and strength of him overlying her. She placed her hands against his chest and then, before she quite knew what he was about, he surged forward. Her cozy, contented feelings exploded into pain.

She cried out. She didn't know. She hadn't expected this. He had forced his big, thick shaft *inside her body* and it felt like she'd been split in two.

"I'm sorry," he said. "I know. I'm hung like a bloody Scotsman." His voice sounded strained. "Blast, you're so small. Give it a moment, it will go easier. And I won't come inside you, so don't worry about that."

25

What on earth did he mean about not coming inside her? He was already there, stretching her wide and hurting her terribly. Minette felt a sort of chagrin, an indignant shock that he was doing this to her. It had been so comfortably blissful as he caressed and kissed her, and then... Her stolen moments playing the kitchen maid seemed to have taken an unexpected turn. A turn which really *hurt*.

Now what was she to do? She couldn't reveal her true identity, not now with August pushing his thing inside her in this bizarre and ardent way. She lay beneath him, flabbergasted. She'd never imagined this was what he had meant to do to the poor kitchen maid.

"Don't you like it?" he asked. "Move with me, and take your own pleasure. It's more fun for me if you enjoy it too." He changed the rhythm of his thrusting, and slid his pelvis against hers in a way that brought a jolt of arousal amidst her terror and shock. Oh, but she couldn't enjoy this. She was fairly certain she was ruined, that this was not something that happened to a proper lady outside of her marriage bed.

And it was all her fault, for she was not a kitchen maid, but had let August believe she was. Her brother would kill her. At best, he would whip her. At worst, he would toss her out onto the streets. The idea of his wrath brought a sob to her lips.

"Here now," said August. "What's this? I know I'm a big fellow, but I'm trying to make it good for you. Do you have regrets now? Do you want me to stop?"

Did she have regrets? Oh, she had a thousand regrets, but she clutched at him when he would have drawn back. "Please, milord. I'm only a bit...frightened of you."

"You mustn't be frightened. No harm can come of pleasure." He cupped her face and kissed her, a long, lingering kiss that felt completely different from the others, because he was pressed so deep inside her. She clenched a bit around him, and was surprised that it felt rather...good. *No harm can come of pleasure.*

He wrapped his arms around her and cradled her, moving inside her slowly, sensually, until she began to experience a mounting sense of need. Now that she had fallen this far, perhaps she ought to fall the entire way, and enjoy these moments—however long they lasted. How long would this last? The more he kissed and grasped her, and moved inside her, the less she cared. She felt tender where they joined, but also hot and excited in some way. *I don't understand*, she wanted to say. *Please help me understand this.* But he thought she was Mary, a kitchen maid who crept into gentlemen's beds for this sort of congress all the time.

"Yes, that's better," he said as she moved with him. "I told you you'd grow accustomed to my size." Once she was in the rhythm he wanted, he leaned back and lifted her into his lap, holding her tight as he moved her up and down on his thick length. She clung to his shoulders, burying her face against his neck and breathing in his smell. It was a very hot, sweaty, energetic business, but she felt so close to him now that they were connected in this way. When she gasped or sighed in pleasure, he answered with gruff, masculine noises of his own.

She tried to reach that same apex of squeezing, aching release that she'd achieved earlier, but she found it all so odd, and so distracting when he groped her or pinched her or—my goodness—spanked her bottom.

"You're too delectable, my dear," he said at last. "I can't hold off any longer."

"Hold off what?" Her question was lost in his ragged groan. He lifted her off his staff, his groan transforming to a drawn-out growl as hot liquid dripped upon her belly. Before she could come to terms with this stunning development, he'd swiped it away with his palm and collapsed atop her. He let out a long, contented breath.

How strange and mysterious he seemed to her now. She had known August as long as she could remember, but she'd never known this side of him, this sweating, kissing, licking, thrusting part of his nature. How comfortable he was in such activities. Why, she believed he was falling asleep on top of her.

"Milord," she whispered, stirring. "Please, I must go."

"Not yet." He moved a little off her, so she could breathe again, but he kept her trapped beneath one arm and one muscular thigh. "I don't want you to go yet. Just a little while and I'll let you up, and send you back to bed with a bit of sweetness for your trouble."

Sweetness. What did he mean by that? Money? Tears pooled in her eyes. Oh, she'd done an unforgivable thing. She'd gone from a kitchen maid to something more like a whore. She knew that men weren't perfect, especially men like August who were reputed to be fast with women, but she'd never expected to be confronted with this side of him so…intimately.

She had to get away.

"Please, milord." She tried again to squirm from beneath him.

He caressed her arm. "No, not yet. You smell so sweet, and you're soft and warm. And it's my birthday, did I tell you? Just a few minutes more."

All right. A few minutes more. The last few minutes, because then she'd have to leave this bed and never, ever tell a soul about what had taken place. She'd have to see Lady Priscilla on August's arm, and exchange words with the two of them, for August was one of her brother's closest friends. Meanwhile, in her mind she'd be remembering August's scent and the feel of his naked skin. She'd helplessly recall the scratchiness of his stubble beneath her fingertips, and the firm hardness of his...

Oh. No.

A tear slipped down her cheek. She brushed it away before it could alert him to her distress. What a colossal mistake she'd made. Warren had always fretted that her sleepwalking would be the death of her. He would probably prefer her death to a situation like this.

But for these last few minutes, she would soak in everything sensual and compelling about August, because she would never be this close to him again. She would remember the feel of his body against hers, his tender kisses and grasping hands, and his heavy satisfaction. She would tuck it away in her memory for the future, which, in her case, had come to look terribly bleak.

Chapter Three: Minette

August stretched and tightened his hold on the delectable female beneath him. The subtle musk of lovemaking still lingered in the air, along with the scent of her soft, alluring hair. They must have fallen asleep after their sensual exertions. He needed to rise and fetch her a *douceur* for her willing company, and send her on her way.

In a moment. First he groaned and pressed his cock against her. He was rigid as a rail. A small voice responded, "Oh, no." It wasn't Mary's voice, but a voice he recognized.

He just didn't understand why he was hearing it in his bed.

His eyes wrenched open. The serving lass squirmed beneath him, only she wasn't a serving lass. August blinked, then blinked again. His cock wilted with tremendous speed as he stared down at Minette's terrified blue eyes and mussed blonde hair.

"I'll just— Oh, bother. I fell asleep," she said. "If I could just get my shift—" She wiggled back from him and tumbled right over the side the bed.

"Jesus. Minette." He sat up to help her, and then he saw the blood. It was all over the sheets, all over her shift.

All over him.

No. This wasn't happening. He'd taken a servant girl to bed, a melting, shy, pleasing servant girl, who at some point had inexplicably transformed into his best friend's sister. He reached down and caught her arm, and saw more blood between her thighs. He knew some virgins bled, but it looked like he'd slaughtered a goddamned animal.

He hauled her to her feet and helped her pull her night shift over her head. Her fingers scrabbled at the laces, drawing it closed about her neck. She wouldn't meet his eyes, and he...he couldn't get the sight of her bloodied thighs out of his brain. Her gaze dropped to his waist, and lower, to his half-erect cock. Didn't his body understand this crisis? He pulled the sheets up over his randy organ and wished himself to the devil.

What the hell was he to do?

He couldn't go back. He couldn't make this different. He had done this thing—bedded his friend's sister on a cursed Hallowe'en night. He would have to marry her now, to preserve her honor, and his. Not that he had much honor to cling to in this whole mess. Good God, *Minette*. He'd taken her virginity, and he hadn't been respectful or tender about it. He'd bedded her exactly like what he thought she was, a saucy servant girl. August lay back on the bed and covered his face with his hands.

"This can't be happening," he muttered. "I was supposed to marry Priscilla. I was to offer for her this week."

"You still can," Minette said. "I'll go. We'll just...forget this ever happened."

He caught her wrist before she could skitter away. "You can't go. I've been inside you. I've had your virginity." His gaze returned, along with hers, to the stain between them on the bed. "I thought you were the goddamned kitchen maid. Why didn't you stop me?"

Minette stared at him, wringing her hands. "I don't know. I was asleep in the beginning, and then it began to feel rather pleasant and..." She clutched her night shift closer across her chest. "I had no idea what you intended to do at the end."

"No idea?" He threw out his arms in disbelief. "I did exactly what happens when ladies slip into gentlemen's beds in the middle of the night, you blighted innocent."

"I didn't mean to slip into your bed. I was asleep! I always sleepwalk when I'm troubled."

"Did you have to sleepwalk to *my* room? I thought you were someone else."

Tears shimmered in her eyes. She blinked and they careened down her pale cheeks, sparkling trails of grief he'd caused her. He'd utterly debauched the girl, his best friend's sister, the woman he'd long looked on as a sister of his own. He took her hand, because he couldn't bear to touch any other part of her.

"God, don't cry. We have to think about what to do."

She wiped her tears away, but more overflowed. "Let me go to my room, August. I'll wash up. We can hide the sheets somewhere, or burn them. You don't have to marry me. Let me sneak back to my bed before the entire house is up."

"I'm not talking about the marriage part, dear girl. I'm talking about Warren. Your brother will call me out for this, if he doesn't murder me where I stand."

"He'll never know," she insisted. "I won't tell him. I swear, I never will! I ought to have stopped you. I wish I had stopped you!"

August yanked back the curtain on his side and searched for his breeches. Very well for her to wish that now, when it was far too late for either of them. He'd have to marry her, or spend the rest of his life knowing himself for a detestable villain. How was he to manage this debacle? His mother wouldn't understand. Lord Colton would be livid, and Warren would think he'd lost leave of his senses when he offered for Minette.

Minette. God save him.

He needed to clothe himself. He felt dirty. Dastardly. At the exact moment he located his breeches, a knock sounded at the door. He and Minette locked eyes. Another knock followed, and men's muted voices, and then the door swung wide as Warren, Townsend, and Arlington strode into the room.

"Wake up, Augustine. You've got to help us look. Minette's gone walking in her sleep again and we haven't been able to find—" His voice cut off mid-sentence. August saw the scene, for one sickening moment, as Warren must have seen it. August drawing on his breeches, the blood on the ivory bedsheets, his sister's stricken, tearful look.

"Oh God," Warren breathed. "I don't... I can't understand what I'm looking at."

"Get out, will you?" August pulled the curtain closed to hide Minette. Warren whipped it open again, staring between the two of them. A scarlet flush crept into his face.

"Get out," August said again. "For God's sake, Warren, leave." He pulled up his breeches as fast as he could, and stuffed his cock into the front with shaking hands. "Get out and let us make ourselves presentable. Send the others away."

Warren emerged from his stupor then. Fury replaced shock. He lunged for August's throat and gripped his windpipe, and shoved him against the bedpost. "My sister. August. You filthy whoreson. I'll kill you for this."

"Listen to me," August rasped with what little breath he could draw into his lungs. "Let me explain."

"You were my friend. A brother to me. I've trusted you all these years." He let loose a string of blistering oaths as Townsend pulled his hand away from August's throat.

"Look to Minette," Townsend barked to Arlington over his shoulder. "She's going to faint."

While August sucked in air, Arlington wrapped a blanket around Minette and sat her on the bed, and flicked up the sheets to cover the bloodied spots. Townsend forced Warren to meet his gaze. "Be quiet, would you? Shall we make the whole house aware? It's just the four of us here. No one else needs to know."

"He ravished my sister," Warren said, jabbing a finger at August's face.

"You must let him give his account," insisted Townsend. "I'm certain there's some reasonable explanation. August's an honorable fellow."

That Townsend would say so while Minette sat trembling on a bloodied bed spoke volumes about the depth of their friendship.

"I didn't know Minette was Minette," August said. "Obviously, I had no idea, or I'd never have..." He turned to Warren with a pleading look. "It was dark, I was half-drunk, and I thought you'd all sent a present for my birthday. I thought she was that damned maid with the curly hair."

"I was the one who came to his room," Minette broke in. "It's not his fault. I ought to have told you the sleepwalking had started up again. I came here and climbed into his bed while I was asleep."

"But you didn't sleep through the whole thing," said Warren. "Surely you didn't sleep through...everything."

Minette squeezed her hands in her lap as a heavy silence settled in the room.

August wished there was a way to protect her from this shame. "Don't blame her," he said to Warren. "She didn't realize what she was doing."

"And you didn't either?" he asked in a bitter voice. "Excuse me if I find that difficult to believe."

"It was dark behind the curtains," said Minette. "I know he didn't know. I know from...from the way he behaved. He thought I was a maid named Mary."

Warren spun on her and held up a hand. "I've heard enough from you, Minette Bernard. Just sit there and be quiet."

Arlington frowned at Warren. "Let your sister speak. This involves her also."

"No," August said. "She shouldn't have to speak. The dishonor is mine. The blame is mine."

"It's not," cried Minette. "It's mine. Even when I came awake, I didn't stop you. I didn't leave as I should have."

"Because I wouldn't let you."

"Don't tell them you restrained me, or did this against my will. I won't let you, August. I won't let you take the blame for this when it was clearly my fault."

"It's not your fault," he said through gritted teeth. How could she have known the consequences of staying, innocent and sheltered as she was? He remembered the way she'd tensed and cried out when he entered her. He had thought it shock at his size. "You wouldn't have stayed if you understood what I intended. You're a good girl, Minette."

"No, I'm not." She burst into hysterical sobs, shaking so pitifully that Arlington steadied her and handed over his handkerchief. "I'm not a good girl. I stayed because you made me feel so warm and happy. I meant to leave, I just never did. I knew it was wrong, but it felt so lovely when you held me and kissed me. "

Warren clapped his hands over his ears. "No more. Don't say any more." He glared at his sister so harshly that August felt glad Arlington had taken up a position of defense on her behalf. "You ought to be beaten to within an inch of your life for this," he said. "After all my care for your reputation! After all Aunt Overbrook's efforts to bring you up and make a lady of you."

33

"Minette is a lady." The men all turned at the heat in August's voice. Minette stared at him with big eyes. "I have said the blame is mine and I'll not allow anyone to say otherwise, nor will I allow you to punish your sister for something that was entirely my fault. I'll marry Minette as soon as can be done. I shall make things right."

Minette sobbed into Arlington's handkerchief. Warren passed a hand across his mouth, as if he'd eaten something that made him ill. "But then you'll be her husband," he said.

August wanted to protest the words, and the condemning look on Warren's face. He wanted to say he was not so bad a fellow, but to do so would lay the blame back on Minette. And even if everyone knew it was Minette's fault, even if August also ached to beat her to within an inch of her life, it wasn't gentlemanly to come out and say it. It wasn't gentlemanly to shame ladies, ever, especially when the lady in question was sister to your friend.

Or former friend.

There was a tap at the door, and the buxom, blonde morning maid flounced in with a bowl and pitcher. "Your hot water, milord." She stopped as she noted the four men, and the tone of gravity in the room. Warren and August both moved to block her view of Minette. "Can I get you anything else, milord?"

August couldn't speak. Townsend piped up after a moment. "Go tell the housekeeper to bring Lady Townsend at once. Someone has fallen ill."

She bobbed a curtsy. "Yes, milord."

The maid's eyes sought August's before she left. He gave her a hard look and her gaze slid away. Perhaps it was all the maid's fault, for giving him those glances that made him expect her to visit. Perhaps it was no one's fault. There was certainly no way to fix things back to the way they'd been, and now that the initial shock had cleared he was forced to face all the uncomfortable particulars of his situation. He would have to jilt Lady Priscilla, who was both headstrong and prideful. She'd do her best to drag his reputation—and Minette's—through the mud. He'd enrage her powerful father and break his mother's heart. The woman was already overwhelmed dealing with his father's failing health. Speaking of failing health, news of this unexpected engagement might just finish the old man off.

But the worst, most awful thing of all was that he would have to marry a woman he considered a sister, a woman he couldn't bear to take to bed.

You've already bedded her, you beast.

But he could never, ever do it again. He could barely look at her now, after the way he'd used her last night. And he wouldn't be able to go elsewhere to sate his needs; Warren would cry foul if he tried to take a mistress. Since Warren and Towns had fallen in love with their wives, they'd become insufferable about marriage and fidelity.

In short, August could look forward to never having sex again.

Damn Minette. She had always been trouble, had always been an irritatingly persistent burr beneath his blanket. Even so, he never could have imagined her destroying his life, his prospects, his friendships, his entire world so completely, and in just one night.

Thanks to Lord Townsend's meticulously run household, a great tub of steaming water was waiting for Minette by the time Aurelia secreted her back to her bedroom. Minette begged to be left alone, so Aurelia wouldn't see the garish blood stains on the insides of her thighs. Minette was so ashamed, and so numb she could barely feel the warmth of the water as she sank into the tub.

Once the blood on her body was gone, she set about trying to scrub the traces of blood from her night shift, to no avail. She ended up throwing it into a sopping ball on the floor. She couldn't bear to wear it again anyway. The blood reminded her of the pain, and of August pressing inside her in that forceful, smarting way. It reminded her of his large, hard body and the shocking ways he'd touched her.

And then, in morning's light, how horrified he'd been. How confused, how angry...and yet he had defended her before all of them, even before her furious brother, who very well knew what a muckling addle-brain she was. August had announced, *I'll marry Minette as soon as can be done. I shall make things right.* He'd asked to marry her in her dreams a thousand times, but in her dreams it had been out of love and desire for her, not an unwanted consequence of her stupidity.

So she couldn't be happy about it, not yet. Maybe someday, if August forgave her, and her brother got over the fact that she'd humiliated him in front of all his friends. She didn't know when that day might be. At the moment, it felt very, very far away.

"Minette?" Aurelia poked her head in the door as she was drying her hair. "Are you done bathing? May I come sit with you?"

"Yes, I'm done." She'd washed and washed, although she still didn't feel clean. Her friend's sympathetic expression nearly started her crying again.

"Please don't look at me that way," Minette said. "As if I am someone to be pitied. I did a horrible thing. I am a horrible person who ought to be scorned."

Aurelia embraced her and led her over to an upholstered divan. "I'm not going to scorn you. You're my friend, and friends stick together when things like this happen. And truly, everyone realizes you didn't do it on purpose. Hunter told me what happened, that you'd sleepwalked into August's bed, that you'd done such things since you were a girl, and never had any control over it."

"I could have left once I woke up." Minette pulled in her knees and laid her forehead against them. "I ought to have left, but it felt so good...up until... Oh, dear." She looked ruefully at her friend. "I didn't know." She felt ridiculous to say it, but Aurelia nodded in an understanding way.

"Believe me, Minette, I had no idea either. The first time Hunter and I..." A flush rose in her cheeks. "Well. Ladies ought to know more than they're told. We oughtn't to be left to discover these matters at the point of crisis. The Townsend wedding night was an absolute nightmare. I didn't want to be there, and I didn't want to be married to him."

"Did he hurt you?"

Aurelia studied her a moment. "Did August hurt you?"

Minette didn't know how to answer. "He did, I suppose, but I think it would have been very hard for him not to. It was a matter of..." She made some helpless gestures with her fingers, pantomiming his largeness and the rather small space he'd put it in. "I don't think he meant to be rough, but there was blood afterward."

"Don't worry about the blood. I've already had the housekeeper throw the sheets away, and she won't tell a soul. But it's frightening to see it there, isn't it? I assure you, it only happens the first time."

Tears pooled in Minette's eyes. "The thing was, it felt so good before that."

"I'm glad. Good for August. I suppose Hunter tried to make me feel pleasant on our wedding night, but I was a shrinking wretch." She pulled a face of wide-eyed terror that made Minette giggle through her tears. "If August didn't throw you over his lap and spank you, then you've already had a better first experience than me."

"Lord Townsend spanked you on your wedding night?" Minette was aghast. "Whatever for?"

"For resisting him. I had no intention of letting him anywhere near me with that..." It was Aurelia's turn to sketch a poking, thrusting male member in the air. "It was a jolly scene, I assure you. Him flailing away at my bottom, and me crying and threatening to tell my father he'd been so bold as to try to"—Aurelia erupted in giggles—"consummate our marriage. I was a very prudish lady back then."

"Did he still...consummate the marriage...after he spanked you?"

"Yes, he certainly did. I realize now how patient and careful he was, but at the time, I felt terribly abused. I cried myself to sleep afterward, as I remember, crouched under the bed sheets so he wouldn't hear me. He slept in another room."

Minette could barely imagine the scene. Lord Townsend and Aurelia were so close now, as to seem two halves of the same person. "I cried too," said Minette. "Not because he hurt me or spanked me but because..." Another sob broke loose. "Because I'm ruined. Now I can't have a proper wedding night. I always pictured it would be so romantic, with flowers and sweet talk, and gentle words of longing, and gazing into one another's eyes."

"And scolding and spanking, and crying one's self to sleep." Aurelia gave her a wry look. "Wedding nights are hardly ever as perfect as we wish them to be. It's all right. You must look on the bright side, and think of all the lovely things to come. My goodness, Minette. Lord August is going to marry you. Isn't it what you've wanted your entire life?"

"Yes, but not like this." Minette couldn't seem to get a grasp on her emotions. As soon as she started feeling better, some vision or memory of the night before assailed her peace.

"Oh, my dear girl." Aurelia dabbed at her tears with a hanky and then went to answer the soft tap at the door. Josephine entered and flew to her side, and gathered her in a warm, fortifying hug.

"Josephine," sobbed Minette, burying her head against her sister-in-law's neck. "What am I to do?"

"Everything's going to be all right," she answered briskly. "You're not to cry anymore. Townsend and Arlington would die before they'd breathe a word to anyone about what happened. Even Mrs. Everly is not to know. She slept through the entire incident, thank God. Everything will be fine."

"Except that August has to marry me!"

Josephine drew back and regarded her with confusion. "Last night you were weeping about the loss of him, and now you're weeping because you're to be his wife?"

"He doesn't want me for his wife," Minette wailed. "Warren's making him marry me against his will, and I'm sure he'll hate me for it. This is such a coil."

"It's not a coil, and I can't imagine anything so outrageous as August hating you. The two of you have been friends for years. And Warren isn't making him marry you. August is marrying you because it's the proper, respectful thing to do. I spoke to him, dear. His only concern is your well-being. He asked me to come here to be sure you were all right."

"I'm not all right," she said.

Josephine pulled Minette's hands from her face and held them tight. "Certainly there will be some uncomfortable moments in the interim, but you and August will soon be happily wed. You only need to find that bright, cheery woman you normally are, and bring her back to face all this upheaval. You must smile and hold your head high and be the Minette we all know."

Minette returned her sister-in-law's concerned squeeze. "How is Warren?" she asked.

Josephine smoothed a wrinkle in Minette's dressing gown. "He's upset, of course, but he'll come around. You know how he gets when it comes to his little sister."

"He wants to punish me, I suppose."

Josephine sighed. "He probably does, but I doubt he will. The truth is, you rather belong to August now."

Aurelia and Josephine exchanged a look. Did they wonder if Lord August would punish her for trapping him into marriage? She had a sudden vision of herself bent over his lap while he walloped her on the bottom with his big, strong hand. She pressed her fingers against her eyes and willed the vision away. "I hope my brother does not stay angry very long," she said instead. "I feel awful to have disappointed him so badly."

"He's not angry or disappointed as much as he's worried about you," said Josephine. "He's looked after you so long and now he has to let you go. I think that's what upsets him most. This was so...sudden. I'm not sure he was ready to lose you." She traced one of Minette's blonde curls. "I know *I* wasn't. I've grown used to your company, and I'll miss you terribly when you're off at Barrymore Park being Lady Augustine."

Lady Augustine. How many times had she dreamed of having that title? "You're going to have a baby to keep you busy," she pointed out. "You and Aurelia both."

"And you'll have one too, soon enough," said Josephine. "All our children can be playmates and grow up and be fast friends like the three of us, and like the gentlemen. You'll see, Minette. Everything will be well."

"Yes," Aurelia concurred. "It doesn't matter how things begin, you see, but how they develop over time. Don't give another thought to last night's proceedings. Smile instead, and look to the future. Think about it this way—you could be Lady Priscilla, about to be cruelly jilted."

"She deserves it," said Minette, "for playing that awful baroque recital last night. Everyone will assume that's the reason, don't you think?"

Aurelia and Josephine burst into laughter and Minette managed to laugh along with them. That was her talent, after all, her gift to the world, as people often told her: to smile and be amiable, and make everything bright.

Chapter Four:
The Thing About Swans

The necessary public actions were slated to take place that afternoon, with Aurelia's help as hostess. She planned a tea party outside for the house guests and insisted that everyone must attend, since the weather had blessed them so majestically.

August wandered about the picnicking tables with a sense of dread, waiting to play his part. He would need to approach Minette in full hearing of Lady Priscilla—and as many other house guests as possible—bend over her hand, and ask her in an attentive and lovelorn way if she would accompany him on a walk around the lake. Such a bold invitation would signal to everyone that his affections were now focused on Warren's sister, not Lady Priscilla.

If he was to marry Minette, he needed to quickly and publicly dash Priscilla's expectations, as much as it would infuriate the girl.

At least he had not yet officially proposed to Priscilla. If they'd been betrothed, things would have been a hundred times more wretched, for to break an engagement was the height of crass behavior for a gentleman. As it was, he would make some powerful enemies for choosing Minette over Priscilla. The one mercy was that no one—save his closest friends—knew the reason why.

Arlington approached him with a glass of iced punch. "Something to shore up your courage," he said quietly.

August accepted the drink, grateful for his friend's support. Warren hadn't spoken to him since he left the room that morning, and Townsend was busy helping Aurelia oversee the party. Arlington looked at him closely, without judgment. "Holding up, old man?"

"Yes, of course. But ask me again later, when this business is done."

"Aurelia's got all the young ladies sitting together. If she can get Lady Colton in the general vicinity, you had better make your move."

August grimaced and took a sip of punch, then coughed as it burned down his throat.

Arlington smiled. "I added a little brandy to it. I hoped it might help."

"I thought Aurelia was starting a new fashion in garden party beverages." He took another sip of the adulterated punch, and let out a long breath, holding the glass up as if in a toast. "Thanks. My last drink as a free man."

"You haven't been a free man in a long time. We all know that."

The friends fell silent. August gazed at Minette, wondering how she managed to look so happy and carefree after last night. But of course, it was an act, just like the act he was about to perform. He knew her well enough to see the faint tension in her brow and the restless movements of her fingers. "Tell me it's going to be all right, Arlington."

"It's going to be all right. Minette already loves you, of course, and Warren will come around and forgive you some day. Colton's going to cause trouble for you where he can, but never forget, you've got powerful friends too."

His Grace the Duke of Arlington was one of those powerful friends. At thirty-one, he'd been in control of a sprawling network of interests for over a decade. Townsend was in line to be the next Duke of Lockridge, while Warren was a wealthy earl with excellent Parliamentary connections. And, of course, August would inherit the Barrymore marquessate from his father at some point. Some very near point, now that the French pox had advanced to ravaging the man's heart and mind. Yes, August was not powerless or friendless.

Only very disappointed in his recent behavior.

"I suppose I'd better go. There's Lady Colton sitting down right between the two of them." August drained the rest of his drink in one swallow and handed it back to his friend.

41

"Godspeed," said Arlington. "Remember, you love her. You've always loved her. You just haven't been able to express yourself until now."

"It's a ridiculous story, isn't it?" August ran a hand through his hair and straightened his cravat. "No one will believe it."

"Enough people have seen Minette pining over you these last ten years. Perhaps you've only just become aware of her as a woman, rather than a girl. I don't know. Something like that. Go now, quickly. Aurelia is giving you looks."

August set off across the lawn. One foot in front of the other toward the two women, one dark and regal and haughty, the other like a blonde, fluttering butterfly. He could see Minette trying very hard not to notice him approaching. *Perhaps you've only just become aware of her as a woman, rather than a girl.* Yes, he'd become aware last night, when he'd filled his hands with her delectable arse and traced the curves of her waist and her magnificent breasts. As soon as he remembered, he pushed the memories away.

Lady Priscilla looked up expectantly as he approached. Perhaps she thought this was the moment of his announcement. Perhaps she believed his friend Lady Townsend had planned this idyllic party so he might finally declare himself. Her round, unblinking eyes regarded him with utter possessiveness. That he might be approaching another—the idea would not even occur to her. She smiled and tilted her head as if to address him.

August stopped instead before Minette. *Remember, you love her. You've always loved her.* "Lady Wilhelmina." His voice caught on her formal name, for nerves. Perhaps it would make this seem more realistic. "How pretty you look today. I wondered if you might honor me with a walk around the lake."

"Oh." Minette made a choked sort of giggle, as if she were surprised. "Why, I suppose that would be fine."

"There's a great deal of pretty scenery." *Pretty scenery? Shut up, you dolt. Minette, move!*

She put down her cup and fiddled with her fan, and pushed back her chair. It took perhaps ten seconds but to August, it felt like an hour. All the conversations in the immediate vicinity halted. He might have heard a gasp. In his peripheral vision, he could see Lady Colton's lips drawn tight across her teeth, and Priscilla's smooth dark hair beneath her light-colored bonnet. He managed a clumsy look in their direction, in fact, smiled at all the ladies at the table as any gentleman might do.

"Thank you so much," said Minette as she came around the table and offered her hand to be placed upon his arm. "I've been wanting to walk about the lake for some time now. I've been sitting too long eating too many cakes." Her sparkling laugh sounded perfectly natural. How he admired her for it. He looked only at her as they walked back across the garden, past a bank of flowers and shrubs, to the stone stairs that provided access to the foot path.

It was a perfectly proper thing to do, of course. The picturesque lake was in full view of the entire garden party. He only had to make sure he looked at her like a man falling in love, which was rather difficult, since she was prattling on about geese.

"What are you talking about?" he asked, exasperated.

"I was just wondering if geese and ducks hatch their young in the same season. Do you know if they do? Because I thought I saw a goose down here a few days ago, or perhaps it was a duck, and it looked smaller than the others, and I wondered if it was a baby. Or, you know, a younger one."

"We're far enough away now that you don't have to make up mindless conversation."

She gave him a confused look. Of course, she hadn't been making up mindless conversation. She'd only been being Minette. "I don't know if geese and ducks hatch in the same season," he said. "Perhaps we can ask Townsend's groundskeeper." He tightened his hand over hers. "Not right now. Right now we make everyone believe we're falling in love with each other."

She looked up at him, a quick, shy look he couldn't interpret, then out across the lake. The banks hummed with insects, and yes, there was a great family of geese, some larger than the others.

"You have always called me a goose," she said, turning with him onto the path.

"No, Warren calls you a goose. I've always called you a nuisance, which you have been. Thanks to you, Lady Priscilla is probably back there planning our demise, along with her mother and father's help."

"Do you think so?" She looked at the ground, then off to the trees, then out into the distance. Anywhere but him. "Will you be terribly sad not to marry her?"

August shrugged. "I never liked her. You know that. But I never wished to marry my sister either."

"I'm not your sister."

"You might as well be. I did all the things for you that I did for my own sisters. Sat at blasted tea parties, carved dolls for you, rescued you from trees. Come to think of it, I did rather more for you than I did for my own sisters. You've always been a scamp."

She made a protesting noise that ended up in tinkling laughter. "You did rescue me a great deal, didn't you? Do you remember the time the dog bit me?"

"It didn't bite you. You only thought it did."

"But you swept me up in your arms and shooed the dog away." She had a faraway gaze, as if she were remembering the moment. "I thought you were the most heroic fellow."

"I was what? Fourteen? Fifteen years old? I thought myself a heroic fellow too."

How things had changed. He remembered the day that dog had chased Minette about the garden because she was covered in sticky sweets. She had quickly gone hysterical at its jumping and licking, and when August lifted her up, she'd sobbed in relief and clung to his neck. His own sisters were older and treated him like a paltry young knob. At that age it had pricked him to madness, and here had been a young, defenseless cherub whom he could rescue and protect. He'd envied Warren his little sister for years, until Minette grew up and started mooning over him in her determined fashion. Then things had become decidedly awkward, since he couldn't think about her in any romantic way.

Even now, as he looked down at her delicate hand on his arm, and her blonde curls peeking from beneath her bonnet, he thought, *What the devil am I going to do?*

The answer to that was nothing. He would do nothing. He and Minette would have a marriage in name only, until and unless the day arrived that he could see her as something more than an innocent child. It didn't help that she was back to chattering about baby ducklings.

"Why don't we sit down?" he asked, steering her toward a weathered wooden bench. He brushed away the leaves, and then they sat together, rather closer than they'd ever sat before.

"And then," said Minette, "well, you would never believe it but this little duckling nipped its brother on the tail, or perhaps it was his sister, it's impossible to know, and the other turned around and gave a hilarious, tiny sort of snarl. I'm telling you, I'd never heard a noise like it. And it was the cutest little duck, all fuzzy and furry, you know, just before its feathers had come in. And Lady Julia and I just watched and laughed, wondering if a full row would break out. It didn't, you'll be pleased to know, but we still talk about that snarling little duck. Why, perhaps it was rabid."

August gazed into her eyes in what he hoped was a lovelorn fashion. "Perhaps it had only had enough of the other duck poking at it."

"You know something I learned recently? I forget who told me, some gentleman, but he warned me in no uncertain terms that swans were unpleasant creatures and that one should never approach them if one can help it. No matter how pleasant and graceful they look, he said they could be excessively violent if they were in that mood. Which is sad, because I always thought it great fun to feed bits of food to the swans when we visited Lansing Grange. They had black and white swans, and even these sort of grayish in-between swans." She thought a moment, putting the tip of a finger to her chin. "Although perhaps they were only white swans in need of a good scrubbing."

"Minette." He took her hand, surprised to find it shaking. "Let's not talk about geese anymore, or ducks, or swans, or anything else to do with water fowl."

She looked down at her lap, then looked back at him. "Of course, if you prefer not to. What else would you like to talk about?"

"Did I hurt you?" he blurted in a rough voice.

He hadn't meant to ask it. He had meant to bring up some safe and offhand topic, but Minette's fingers were trembling, and he couldn't bear to think why.

"Do you mean...?"

"Last night. Did I hurt you? I want you to know that I won't— That we needn't—" He sighed. "If I hurt you, I swear I didn't mean to, and I won't do any such thing again."

"I know you didn't mean to," she said. Her hand had gone limp in his. She opened her fan to flutter an insect away. "The thing about swans, whether they be black, or white, or—"

"Minette."

"I was going to say that I wanted swans at my wedding for the longest time, but I don't anymore. Warren says you're going to get a special license and marry me next week. So there won't be any time for swans, or a great deal of planning. But now that I know more about swans and their unpleasant dispositions, I don't want them at the wedding anyway."

August sighed. "If you want swans, you shall have them."

"I don't," she said, looking up at him. "I'm absolutely sure that some pretty flowers and music shall be quite enough. I'd hate for anything to ruin our day, particularly swans, because they aren't as sweet and romantic as everyone thinks."

He looked away first, but not before he saw the anxiety in her gaze. "Doves would be nice at a wedding," he said. "They're very peaceful."

He was not surprised when Minette launched into an animated monologue about her many adventures involving doves. If it eased her fears to chatter about inane things, August was happy to let her talk, although he couldn't remember conversing about birds for such an extended period at any point in his life before now.

The important thing was that the people across the lake at the tea party saw him holding her hand, and gazing into her eyes like a dazzled fellow who was falling in love.

Chapter Five:
The Worst Wedding Night Ever

In deference to her brother's wishes, Lord August married her the following week, just after the house party ended. They recited their vows in the picturesque chapel at Marble Grove, a sleepy village bordering the Warren estate. Many Oxfordshire families attended, but others stayed away, most notably the Coltons and their set. Lord Barrymore, August's father, did not attend either due to illness. Minette wondered if that was true, or only an excuse.

Minette studied August throughout the ceremony and the small wedding breakfast at Warren Manor, trying to discern if these absences upset him. He smiled when he ought to smile, and held her hand, and conversed with the guests like a pleased bridegroom, but there was some tension underneath, some simmering darkness. Minette did her best to maintain a merry mood, although she bawled like a child when she said goodbye to Warren and Josephine and Mrs. Everly afterward. Even worse, she had to share the coach to Barrymore Park with her new mother-in-law, who frowned at her the entire way.

Oh, there was nothing for it. Her wedding day had been a disaster, nothing like the sort of day she'd hoped.

Now she was Wilhelmina Anne Randolph, the Countess of Augustine, married to Method Edwin Randolph, which was such a strange name for a person they'd always called August. Method? A method for what? Who would name their child such a thing? At least she knew Barrymore Park well, having been there on more than a few occasions with her brother. It wasn't really August's house, but his parents'. Lady

47

Barrymore introduced her to the housekeeper as Lady Augustine and both the women's noses seemed to pinch in distaste. Minette was then ensconced in a rather distant wing, pending refurbishments, Lady Barrymore said. When they nearly "forgot" to fetch her for dinner, Minette had the lowering suspicion she'd been placed in the distant wing by design.

Do not lose your nerve now, she chided herself. *You must be a pleasant, amiable wife, like Josephine is with Warren, or Aurelia with Townsend. You must smile and bring happiness to your husband's home and your husband's world.*

And yes, she would go to bed with him, even if the process puzzled her. Even if it hurt. She waited in her prettiest night dress for him to come to her after dinner, but the hours ticked on into evening and then nighttime, and he didn't come.

Perhaps he imagined she wouldn't welcome him, after their awkward encounter Hallowe'en night. Perhaps he'd gotten lost on the way to her rooms, as she was so far removed from the main areas of the house. Well, she had never been one to shrink about and allow matters to go awry. They were married now. At the very least they ought to say good night to one another, and if there were other words that must be said, Minette was not afraid to say them.

She pulled a robe over her night dress and proceeded into the hall. A footman stood just down from her door. "Will you take me to my husband?" she asked. "Lord Augustine," she clarified hastily, in case the servant was not well informed.

They began the great trek back toward the main house, and once they arrived, the footman took her downstairs to the library. Why, it was nearly eleven o'clock, but Lord August was there, laboring over correspondence. "Lady Augustine," the footman announced, before turning on his heel and shutting the door.

Goodness, these haughty servants. She turned to August with a smile. "Are you working tonight, on your wedding night?"

"I had a few matters to attend to." His face revealed new lines in the lamplight. He did not put down his pen.

Minette tried to think of something to say that might soften the tension around his eyes. She found her voice had left her for the first time in a while.

"How are your rooms?" he asked.

Distant, she thought. *Like your expression.* "They are very well, for temporary rooms," she said aloud.

"Yes, temporary. We'll find you something better. There were plans for refurbishments, but no wedding was expected until next year."

"Oh." She swallowed hard. "I want to thank you for...for your sacrifice today. In marrying me."

"Let's not call it a sacrifice, as that sounds rather grim. I married you out of duty, and respect for your honor. And so your brother wouldn't kill me," he added as an afterthought. "We shall attempt to make the best of things."

"Yes," she said, seizing on his words. "I want to make the best of things. I want you to know I'm completely recovered from our... Well. I want you to know that I won't shrink from my marital duties."

A corner of his lip quirked up, not that he looked very mirthful. "Such noble bravery won't be necessary. You're doubtless tired after our busy day, and I must finish this correspondence before I leave for London in the morning."

"We're going to London in the morning? No one informed me."

"I'm taking my mother to London," he said. "You'll be staying here at Barrymore Park. My father is very ill, you see, and his physician is in London. I won't be able to spend much time with you until he's through this latest spell, so it's better if you stay here in Oxfordshire, near your brother and Josephine. If you like you can even stay at Warren Manor. I leave that up to you."

Be pleasant. Be amiable. Even if your composure is about to break. "Why would I stay at Warren Manor now that we're married?" she asked.

"My father is very sick and the London household is in upheaval at the moment."

His expression was closed, inscrutable. She didn't understand why he distanced himself from her, even within his house. He'd put her in the far wing, and now he intended to journey hours away from her and stay there for some indeterminate amount of time. "I'm sorry your father is ill," she said. "Perhaps I might come and help."

"You're not coming."

Now he had said that very rudely, almost in the tone of a scold. "But I should really like to come," she said.

49

"And I would really like you to go to bed, so I can finish what I need to finish."

"But it's our wedding night." Her anguished voice rang out in the silence of the library. The tall shelves seemed to tower over her like bleak, dark wraiths. "A groom is supposed to go to bed with the bride on her wedding night. He's supposed to kiss and romance her, and hold her in his arms."

"And there are supposed to be swans and flowers and music. I know. But we've already established that our marriage is not the conventional sort." His fingers tightened on his pen. "I'm sorry, Minette. You're charming and sweet, but I'm not of a mind to bed you. Not tonight."

"When?"

"Later," he said evasively. "I have things to do in London, as I've told you." He looked back down at his letter and began to write. Minette realized she'd crumpled great handfuls of her silk robe in her fists. She let it go and smoothed the fabric.

"Do you think you can be rid of me so easily?" she said. "Warren will bring me to London if I ask him."

"I wouldn't do that. You'll be happier staying here."

"Living on my own in this cavernous manor? For how long?"

"Until things settle down."

"And what if I don't agree with this 'living apart' plan?"

He threw his pen down on the desk. "It's not up for discussion." His voice sounded taut, like the crack of a whip. "Will you go to bed as I asked, or will you stay here and continue to argue with me?"

"I'm going to stay and continue to argue with you," she said. "I'm going to whine and nag until you agree that I must accompany you to London."

"Then you'll be whining and nagging a long while, for I've made my decision."

He picked up his pen and hunched back over the desk. He was in waistcoat and shirtsleeves, his handsome gray wedding coat strewn carelessly over a nearby chair. She went over to twitch at it, and straighten the folds lest it wrinkle.

"What are you doing?" he asked after a moment.

"I'm seeing to your coat, in the absence of your valet. I bet you'll be taking *him* with you to London."

"Yes."

"But not your wife."

He looked up at her with a dark expression. "I'm going to lose my temper in a moment. I don't want to, but I will if you keep this up."

It was really a very scary look he gave her, but if she capitulated now, he'd go away and leave her in this vast, lonely house for God knew how long. "I wish you would put down your correspondence and listen to me for a moment. It's only that I believe, after many years of reading romantic novels, that there's a certain way married couples ought to go on. Of course, as a man, you've never read a romantic story. Let me tell you, the couples in those books have problems all the time, but over the course of the book, through adventures and misadventures, they come to love one another, you see?" He stared at her as if she was daft. She threw up her hands. "My Lord August, how are we to have our adventures and misadventures and fall in love if you're miles away in London and I'm back here in Oxfordshire?"

He gave a great sigh. "Come here, if you please. I would like to show you something."

There, his pen was down. Now he would listen to her. She went to stand beside him at the desk as he reached inside one of the drawers and drew out an oblong white box tied with ribbon. He opened the lid to show her an engraved wooden plaque of some sort resting on a bed of satin.

"What is it?" she asked, picking it up.

"Your brother gave it to me today as a wedding present."

She tilted her head to inspect the word inscribed into one side. "WAR? Whatever does it mean? What an inappropriate thing to inscribe on a wedding day plaque."

"They're your new married initials. *W.A.R.* Wilhelmina Anne Randolph, and it's not a plaque, it's a paddle."

"A paddle?" She took a step back.

August nodded at her, tight lipped. "A paddle with your initials on it."

Minette gawped down at the thick, polished thing. Yes, it was long and rectangular, with a perfectly obvious handle she hadn't noticed before. "Is it...is it a paddle for cooking? For taking tiny loaves of bread out of the oven?"

"It's not a paddle for tiny loaves of bread." He took it from her and turned it over in his hand. "I think you know what it's for."

Minette narrowed her eyes. "What a despicable present for a brother to give on his sister's wedding day."

"I believe he meant it as a lark. Nonetheless, it's a very fine paddle and I'm very close to using it." He put it on his desk and drew her close. "Now, my dear, I'm going to give you a kiss good night, and then I'm going to go back to work on my letter and count silently to ten. When I look up, I expect you to have disappeared completely. Are we clear with one another?"

"How quickly are you going to count?"

"Minette."

"It's only that I don't know how quickly I'll need to walk. You have a big library."

He cupped her cheek, and when she lifted her lips to his, he kissed her forehead instead. Oh, this whole situation was maddening.

"Are you counting now?" she asked when he released her.

"I'm already nearly to two."

She took a look at the paddle—damn Warren—and turned for the door. She opened it so forcefully she nearly bowled over a footman. She felt sorry for the man but she was so very angry. She ignored him, took a few steps down the hall, and leaned against the smooth mahogany paneling. This was not how things ought to go at all. She wanted to cry. Well, she began to cry a little, but she quickly realized nothing would come of tears.

Or, rather, nothing would come of *quiet* tears.

She looked over to be sure the door was still ajar. The footman had been so offended when she knocked into him he hadn't remembered to shut it. She broke into her best theatrical cry, the one she used when the stakes were highest. They'd never be any higher than they were now. When she got no response, she cried louder. She thought she saw the footman's eyebrow twitch. When he moved as if to shut the door, she gave him an awful look so he froze where he was and turned to face front.

"Oh, I can't believe I'm to be left alone here," she wailed in melodramatic grief. "I can't bear it. I'll start sleepwalking all over again. I'll probably walk off a tower or something, and dash my brains all over the cobblestones below." She paused, but heard nothing within, so she took a deep breath and began again. "All I want is to be a proper wife. I can't bear this, when I love my new husband so much." She wept as if her heart was breaking, but she couldn't seem to summon real tears in her frustration. At last, August appeared and stood regarding her, one hand on his hip.

"What are you doing?"

"What do you think?" she said. "I'm crying."

"You're faking," he snapped. "Those are false tears. But that can be changed." He took her arm and pulled her inside. The footman shut the door behind them with an unsubtle bang as August pulled her across the library to his desk. It was her turn to ask, or rather shriek, "What are you doing?"

He sat in his chair and threw her over his lap. "I'm doing what I've wanted to do ever since I woke up a week ago and found you in my arms."

Oh goodness, this wasn't the outcome she'd hoped for at all.

"I won't cry anymore if it upsets you so," she said, trying to squirm off his thighs. "I can be perfectly quiet if I try. I'll go up to bed, silent as a mouse."

"You had your chance to go to bed silent as a mouse. Instead you stood outside my library door and treated the entire household to your ridiculous histrionics."

He flipped up the skirts of her dressing gown, brushed aside her shift, and brought his palm down hard against her bare bottom. He spanked one cheek and then the other, hot, sharp slaps that made her yelp in alarm. "Oh, please, you can't spank a bride on her wedding night! I believe it's against the law."

But then she remembered that Lord Townsend had spanked Aurelia on her wedding night, and that any man in England might spank his wife whenever he wanted to. "I'm sorry," she said instead, trying a different tack. "I ought to have gone to bed, but I wanted to tell you—oh—*ow!*"

The more she talked, the more he increased the intensity of his spanks. She threw a hand back to cover her smarting bottom. "Please! Please stop!"

"Move your hand."

"I can't."

"Move your hand, or I'll spank you with your paddle and it will feel considerably worse."

"It's not *my* paddle," she said peevishly.

"It has your initials on it," he replied. "And I can see why. I asked you very clearly to go up to bed and let me finish my work. Instead you've annoyed me until I have no choice but to discipline you. Now answer me. Do you want a paddling or not?"

Tears welled in her eyes at his heartless scolding. His hand rested on her scorched skin, warm and large. It reminded her of his touches, his caresses. He had been happy to caress her when he didn't know who she was. "I don't want the paddle," she said, sniffling.

"Then move your hand. You won't be warned again."

The paddle looked evil, but August's hand was pretty awful too. She jerked and squiggled as he resumed her punishment. No matter how she struggled, he only collected her tighter, spanking her steadily all over her bottom until the whole of it throbbed. The only way she could stop herself throwing her hands behind her was to make them into fists and press them to her mouth. Tears of indignation flowed down her cheeks.

"This is the worst wedding night ever," she cried as she kicked at an especially smarting blow. "And you are the meanest, most horrible husband in the world."

"That's probably so," said August. "Because I won't tolerate stubborn and annoying wives." He paused, and then Minette felt a whoosh and an explosion of fresh, stinging pain from the paddle.

"*Nooo*," she screamed. "That hurts too much."

She looked over her shoulder to see him regarding the implement with admiration. "It does pack a wallop. Do you need any more spanking, or have you finished being naughty for the night?"

"I've finished, I promise."

He put the paddle down and hauled her to her feet. She could still feel the rectangular outline of the paddle across her bottom cheeks. Worse, she couldn't seem to stop sniffling and crying like an infant. He tipped her face up and made her meet his gaze. "You've had that coming to you, young lady."

It upset her to be lectured like a child. She wasn't a child. She was his wife, and she wished to be treated as such. She wished he might kiss and embrace her, and fondle her, and do those outrageous things he'd done to her Hallowe'en night. She wasn't a 'young lady.' She was a woman. A woman who didn't appreciate being spanked on her wedding night.

"I'll go to bed," she said in a trembling voice, "if you'll come with me."

He stared back at her, his face set in authoritative lines. "I'll come with you, but I won't stay."

"Then I won't go."

Something in his gaze flickered. "You are very brave to say that just now." Before she knew what he was about, he'd swept her up in his arms the way he'd done that day when she was terrified of the dog. She wasn't terrified of dogs anymore. No. She was more terrified of loveless, sham marriages, where one party stayed in the country while another stayed in the city, and everyone gossiped about them behind their backs. It appeared she had entered into one of those marriages. And when August went to London, he would probably go visit his lady of the night, and pay her to do the things he wouldn't do with her.

But I'll do them for you. I would do anything you wanted.

August carried her up the wide staircase and down the series of corridors, while Minette tried to think of the words that might thaw him. She was considered a gifted conversationalist, but she came up empty this night. She felt so very frustrated and tired, and oh, her bottom hurt. She laid her head against his chest, against the soft, fresh-scented silk of his waistcoat, and cried a few more tears before they reached her far-flung room.

A footman—a different one now—opened the door for August to proceed through it. Once inside, he passed through her dressing room to the bedroom and tossed her on the bed. He sat beside her, but not in a fond way. He sat on the edge of the bed with his hands on his knees. He also looked very frustrated and tired.

"You must understand..." He paused and ran his fingers through his hair. "This is the way things have to be right now. I need time, Minette. I have a lot of other pressures, a lot of things going on. My father's very sick and he's not going to get better. I have duties in London. I have fences to mend and preparations to make."

"Preparations for what?"

"My father's death." He said it in a very hollow way.

She wanted to comfort him, to embrace him, but she was terrified he'd push her away. So she only stroked the side of his arm, up and back, in a tentative gesture. "I'm sorry. I'm sorry your father's going to die. I never really knew my parents so I don't know what that feels like. Very bad, I suspect."

"It does feel very bad, and you needn't be there in the middle of it, trying to be my new wife with sadness all around. Give me some time to get used to everything that's happened, please, darling. Give me a little space."

"If that's what you want," she said. "I love you, August. I always have."

He let out a sharp breath. "Why? Why have you loved me for so long? What do you even know of me, Minette?"

"I know enough. I know that I love you," she said staunchly. "Please, let me come to London. I won't addle you, I promise."

He placed a finger over her lips. "I know you won't mean to addle me, but you will. I'll send for you when things have calmed down, all right? I'll see you at the holidays, at least."

"The holidays are six weeks away," she said past his finger. She wanted to bite it, he made her so furious, and if he gave her another of those chaste forehead kisses, she believed she would fly into a rage.

But he didn't give her a forehead kiss or any sort of kiss. He squeezed her hand and pressed his cheek to hers, then stood and walked out of the room without so much as a backward glance.

Chapter Six:
Inquietude

London was dreary as hell in mid-November. So dreary, in fact, that August occasionally questioned his decision to leave Minette in Oxfordshire, but at the end of it, he had no choice. Barrymore House was already full to bursting with his father's illness and his mother's grief. He wasn't sure the mausoleum walls of their town residence could expand enough to contain Minette's chatter and liveliness, and if she came here, she would expect him to sleep with her.

Which he couldn't possibly do.

He tried to imagine it sometimes, tried to move his mind past his childhood memories of Minette, and his brotherly regard for her. If he thought about it enough, perhaps it would wear down those uncomfortable, incestuous barriers, but no. The uncomfortable, incestuous barriers were still there.

Damn him. He had no idea how he'd get heirs on her. The two of them would eventually need to have children, so at some point he'd have to overcome these reservations. *Just pick a night with no moon, and have her creep within the bed curtains...*

She was easier to spank, because there were so many reasons to spank her. The marriage, first of all. Colton's censure, for another. Priscilla's powerful father had sent August a scathing note letting him know exactly what he thought of his manners. Now Priscilla would be out again next season, at every social event, and every time he saw her, she'd heap guilt upon his head. She'd whisper things about Minette, who was too sweet and good-natured to fight back.

He stood and walked out of his study to the back of the house, and the balcony that flanked the entire floor. He needed air. Maybe he needed Minette. He wasn't sure. He'd been a week now without her, and he hoped she'd gotten over her anger at being left behind. He'd written to her the day he arrived, a polite and cheerful note for his polite and cheerful bride, sending his wishes that she was well. She'd never written back.

He thought he might go see Esme. Warren wasn't in town to complain about it, and August could easily skulk in through the back door. Esme would take his cares away for precious moments. An entire evening. He'd never gotten his birthday favors, by God. A breeze blew, strangely warm, with only the slightest chill of autumn. Sun shone on his face as he squinted through his lashes. No, he wouldn't go see Esme. Maybe someday, but not yet. His mind wasn't in the right place, and his manhood had taken a blow this past week, when he'd mistaken innocent Minette for that serving maid. Blast, but he ought to have known.

The breeze picked up, ruffling his hair, airing his linen shirt sleeves now that he'd abandoned his coat. Why did he feel like he was waiting? What was he waiting for? A new year. A new season. His father's death. A letter from Minette. Something. Anything. Someday things would get better and he wouldn't feel this restless unhappiness.

The breeze died back and August heard voices in the house, in the grand main room that stretched from front to back. An older lady's warble, and a younger lady's bright, cheerful tones.

"Why, of course she shall be happy to be shown to her rooms," the older lady said. "This is her home now, isn't it?"

"But I should like to see my husband first." Minette used the ingratiating tone she always affected around the servants. "If Lord Augustine is not terribly busy, would you tell him we've arrived?"

It was as if he'd conjured her with his thoughts. He took one last look at the lush serenity of the back garden and stalked through the door and into the house.

"August!" Before his eyes could adjust from the brightness outside, he was nearly bowled over by a barreling bundle of energy. Minette embraced him, all ivory skirts and blonde curls, squeezing him in her arms. He looked over her shoulder at the gargantuan hat and formidable bulk of her aunt and thought to himself, *I am not dressed for company.*

"Minette." He tried not to growl the word as he disengaged himself from her. "And Lady Overbrook." He sketched a bow toward the smiling matron before turning back to his wife. "What on earth are you doing here, darling? I thought you were to stay in Oxfordshire." His voice strained with the displeasure he felt.

"It was too dull in Oxfordshire," said Minette. "I went to stay with Warren and nothing was happening there, except for Josephine getting rounder and both of them mooning at each other all the livelong day."

"Minette," her aunt chided.

"Well, it's true. When my auntie wrote that she was coming to London, I knew I must come along too so I might set up here at Barrymore House for the winter. You don't mind, do you? Oh, and Warren has written a note." She poked around in her reticule and extracted a folded page. Behind her, servants unloaded trunk after trunk of female belongings, hauling them through the foyer and to the stairs.

August flicked open the seal on the embossed notecard. *I'll make this short so I'm not tempted to go on about what a blighted coward you are*, it read in Warren's handwriting. *She's your wife. You live with her.*

He closed the note and rubbed his eyes. The harried housekeeper arrived, bearing a hastily assembled tea tray.

"How wonderful," said Minette. "I'd be delighted to take tea. Won't you put on your coat and join us, August, and visit with Auntie before she's off to Marlborough Square? Is your mother here? I'd love for her to join us too."

"Mother is resting."

Minette was already headed toward the front parlor. "Do you still take tea here on the flowered sofas? They've always been my favorite."

The flowered sofas were still there, but he hadn't taken tea with anyone the last seven days, and hadn't planned to today. He went to the library for his coat, feeling unbalanced and stressed. By the time he met them in the parlor, Minette and her Aunt Overbrook were balancing tea cups and saucers on their laps, and asking for sandwiches. Such was her charismatic power that the overworked servants complied with nary a frown, and produced a tray of tea cakes and finger sandwiches in record time.

"I'm so glad to be out of that carriage," said the Dowager Overbrook. "And how smart Barrymore House looks, Lord Augustine. I haven't been to visit your mother in so long."

"She'll be sorry to have missed you," he said. "She spends her afternoons at rest."

"Of course. We're terribly gauche to arrive at tea time and trouble you."

"It's no trouble at all," August assured her, the only feasible response.

"But is your mother well?" asked the dowager. "And Lord Barrymore?"

"I told you he's been ill, Auntie," said Minette. "And Lord August has been here handling everything, and leaving me to my leisure in the country. But I ought to be here helping however I can." She looked at him over the rim of her tea cup. He'd forgotten how small and delicate her hands were, and how blue her eyes. "It was nothing at all to come from Oxfordshire. Warren and Josephine would have come too, but she's feeling awfully tired."

"I would have liked to see your brother and his wife," said August. *So I might punch Warren right between the eyes*, he added silently. What was he to do with her now that she was here? He couldn't very well send her back, since her aunt had come to stay for some time, and he couldn't spare the time to take her back himself. All he had in these hectic days was the predictability of his schedule and the quiet of the house, both of which Minette was already disturbing. She gave him a wide, happy smile he was hard pressed to return.

"I only wish you would have stayed in Oxfordshire a while longer," he said.

"Is your father's illness contagious?" asked Lady Overbrook.

"What? No." August put down his tea. "Not contagious. Only very...unpredictable. One never knows how he'll feel from day to day."

"It was like that with Lord Overbrook's gout," said the dowager, shaking her head. "Rest his soul. Some days he was sprightly as an imp, and other days he could hardly rouse himself from bed. Does your father suffer the gout?"

Lady Overbrook scrutinized him with acute attention. She was clearly dying to know what ailed his father, being the gossipy sort. "No, he does not have gout," said August. "He has a...progressive illness."

"Tell me it is not the consumption!" she cried. Minette's eyes went wide.

"No," he assured them. "It's not consumption, although some of the symptoms are the same. The physicians tell us my father cannot be cured. It's been very difficult for my mother."

Beneath Minette's sympathies and Lady Overbrook's continuing questions, August could hear the distant strains of his father's ravings. He looked toward the door. In the bustle of bringing the tea trays, someone had left it open.

"I'm going out," his father shouted in a ragged voice. "You'll not keep me prisoner here."

A footman ran by, and then his father in his invalid's clothes, night gown and stockings, since he ripped off anything proper they dressed him in. His features were grossly disfigured by the telltale ulcers of advanced syphilis.

"I've a horse to ride. And a tree," the man cried, flailing his arms.

"Yes, my lord," came an attendant's weary voice. Countess Overbrook and Minette had both gone very still. There was a great pounding from the area of the front door.

"My horse," said his father. "Bring my horse. I'm going to the theater. Fairies. There are fairies, what? On stage. I have a tree. I'm under the tree, I tell you, and they're all around. You don't believe me!"

"To bed, my lord, please," another attendant pleaded.

His father howled a string of lewd oaths. This at last propelled August to rise and shut the door, but a footman shut it first from outside, so August was left stranded halfway across the parlor. He flushed red, his hands in fists. On the other side of the door, he could still hear his father cursing and railing as they corralled him back to his private wing of the house.

"Well," he said, turning back to the women. "This is obviously one of my father's worse days. I apologize."

The dowager fingered her fan. "I am so sorry, Lord Augustine. I am sorry for his...inquietude."

August nodded to acknowledge her sympathies. Minette looked pale. She touched her cup, picked it up and put it down again. "Yes, I'm sorry too. It's terrible to feel so agitated and out of sorts when one is sick. I remember smacking my nurse once when I had a fever. Well, I don't remember, I was very young, but apparently she tried to make me take some broth and I was not at all in the mood for it. I hit her and upended the bowl all over the poor woman. I was the very worst handful as a child."

You are still the very worst handful, August thought. She'd come here against his express wishes, dragging along her aunt so that the society maven might see and hear his father's demented ravings. Doubtless the woman would tell everyone she knew that the vaunted Marquess of Barrymore was dying of the pox.

"I ought to go and be sure my father is all right," he said.

The dowager stood very quickly for a woman of her age. "Then I shall thank you for your hospitality before I take my leave. I promised Lady Metcalfe I would dine with her and her family this evening, and I know my niece wishes to settle in to her new home."

Hands were squeezed and air kisses were exchanged. Lady Overbrook sailed out and climbed into her waiting carriage, now emptied of Minette's things. He half considered ordering them repacked, and sending her off with her aunt. It would serve her right for defying his wishes. *She's your wife. You live with her.*

Yes, Minette was his wife now, and as such, obliged to obey his commands.

Minette focused on unpacking and arranging her things, rather than the edge in August's voice when he'd instructed her to await his company in her rooms. Why, there was so much to be done. Her private sitting room wasn't aired, the bed wasn't made, and the dressing room was rather smaller than the one back home.

But then, she hadn't brought all her things. Some were coming behind, in a hired baggage coach. Oh, it was all very sudden and disorganized, but when her aunt said she was coming to town, Minette knew she must seize the opportunity or resign herself to being stuck in the country for a tiresome amount of time. Her husband wasn't happy about it. Yet. She would soon show him that she wouldn't be any sort of nuisance at all, that, in fact, she could make his life much more pleasant with her company.

Yes, even pleasant in *that* way. She'd had some enlightening talks with Josephine over the past week, about men and their desires, and how to keep them happy. Josie hadn't been terribly explicit—and Minette was grateful for that, since the lady was married to her brother—but she had given her advice about tenderness and courage, and allowing men to express themselves, and being willing to give oneself up to their deepest desires, even if those desires seemed strange or frightening on the surface.

Minette didn't intend to be frightened. She would do whatever she must to develop a closeness with August, and she certainly couldn't develop this closeness unless she was living in the same household with him.

So she would not fret about his reproachful looks or that disquieting edge to his voice, because she was exactly where she ought to be, and if he didn't know it now, he would know it soon enough. He was probably only at ends due to his father's illness, which was not the sort of illness she had envisioned. She had pictured Lord Barrymore sniffling and sick in bed, not stalking about the house in bed clothes, raving about trees and fairies and being kept prisoner. Poor August. Lord Barrymore had clearly lost his mind, and her husband must have thought such outbursts would trouble her.

But the only thing that troubled her was the idea of August bearing these burdens alone, without his caring and supportive wife by his side. And in his bed. My goodness, she really couldn't stop thinking about bedroom things now that she'd been confronted with him again, now that she'd remembered anew how large and masculine and handsome he was, with his thick, tousled ebony hair and those dark hazel eyes that held her gaze with such intense focus.

She shivered and arranged her primping things upon the vanity table with her maid's help. The best way to calm her nerves was to settle in and remember her purpose here—to provide companionship to her husband in his time of need.

Still, she jumped when the strident knock came at the sitting room door. She passed through the comfortably appointed room to open it, hiding any misgivings behind a brilliant smile.

"There you are, August. I'm just helping Mercer put away the last of my things."

Bother, that frown. And he always looked so formidable when he wore dark clothes. "Send Mercer away," he said brusquely. "You and I are going to have a talk."

Oh, no. She did not believe this would be the sort of talk she'd enjoy. The sort of talk, for instance, where he might thank her for coming to London against his wishes because he really hadn't known best, and because she belonged here and might help him, and all of that. It looked more like the sort of talk where he might scold her and turn her over his knee for being disobedient and stubborn.

There was really only one practical way to handle such a discussion. Minette ducked and slipped past him, and broke into a run down the hall.

She heard his outraged gasp, his order that she stop and return to him immediately, but she was not so foolish a woman as that. Barrymore House was a great big domicile, and there must be plenty of places to hide when one was in crisis. She must go downstairs, to the kitchens or the stables, where lots of people were around, and where August would not want to seem an insensitive husband before the staff. She took the stairs two at a time, nearly tripping on the landing, for she heard his steps right behind her.

Why, it wasn't dignified for a husband to chase his wife when she clearly didn't wish to be caught. She ought to have made Aunt Overbrook stay until she knew August's feelings on her unexpected arrival. He would have behaved in front of her aunt, she was sure of it.

Goodness, he could really run fast.

He caught her arm and drew her to a halt, and tossed her, without so much as a by-your-leave, over his shoulder. "What a capital idea," he said, only slightly winded. "Let's have this discussion in my study, since I happen to have your paddle stowed in the desk."

Minette froze in the midst of her squirming. "You brought the paddle from Oxfordshire?"

"Indeed I brought it, so you wouldn't be tempted to dispose of it in my absence." He took hold of her legs to arrest her kicking. "I'm glad I thought of it. If you ever deserved a paddling, it's now."

"But what have I done? I've only come to be with you," she pleaded. "I was lonely."

He strode into the study, hauling her past a duo of footmen with her bottom and skirts flailing in the air. It was not well done of him. When he set her down, she faced him with her hands on her hips.

"Do you know what? You are terribly confused about how to be a husband. You're not doing anything right. You're not being kind or warm, or caring. You decide that you ought to leave me in Oxfordshire when everyone knows husbands and wives should be together. Now you're dragging me about your home in front of all the servants in this humiliating and ignoble way."

Rather than see her side of things, his frown only deepened. "Are you finished?"

"No, I'm not finished," she said, tossing her head. "I can go on another twenty minutes or so about all the things you're doing wrong in this marriage, not that I think you'll listen, since you seem a very stubborn person indeed."

His brows rose. "*I'm* a stubborn person? I told you in no uncertain terms that I didn't want you to come to London, and here you are. You brought your aunt with you to be sure that gossip of my father's illness spreads to the greatest group of society possible."

"I brought my aunt with me so I wouldn't have to travel alone. And she is not a gossip."

"I beg to differ. Every one of her friends is going to learn in short order that the Marquess of Barrymore has gone mad, and it's your fault. Not only are you stubborn, Minette, but you don't consider anyone else's wishes, only your own. You wanted to come to London and so you came, completely disregarding my instructions to the contrary." He took her arm and marched her over to the desk, and jerked open a drawer to withdraw the horrid paddle. "As a consequence, you're going to receive a very harsh spanking."

"But it's not fair." She began to tremble out of shock, out of fear, out of dread that she wouldn't survive an entire spanking with that painful implement.

"Not fair? Did you disobey me, Minette?"

"I disobeyed you, but only because—"

"I don't care why. I only care that you learn not to disobey again. Bend over the desk."

"Please, no," she pleaded. "I don't want to be paddled."

65

"And I didn't want you to appear here this afternoon with your Aunt Overbrook. You see how these things work." He pressed her down over the desk and drew her skirts up, holding her in place with one firm palm. "If you don't want to be punished, don't countermand my orders. Now be still," he barked as she kicked at him. "You're getting a dozen smart cracks with this paddle."

"Why don't you just give me a stern lecture about things? *Owww!*" She jumped and cried out as the first stinging stroke landed upon her bottom. "Husbands shouldn't spank wives. A scolding would work just as—"

Her voice cut off with the hot explosion of the second stroke. She reached back to impede him; she knew it wouldn't be allowed but it hurt so badly she couldn't help it. He took her hand and pushed it back down to the desk. "Place your hands beneath you and keep your feet on the floor. I'll add more strokes each time you impede me."

His strident tone left no question that she must obey. A dozen strokes to bear, and she was dying after only two. She mustn't earn any more. The next smack landed, sharp and crisp. She kicked her legs, but put her feet right back on the floor again before he decided to make good on his threat.

"Oh, no," she whispered as the fourth one landed, harder than any of the three before. "I can't bear this."

But she had to bear it. She pressed her cheek against the desk, balling her hands into fists beneath her breasts. Five, six, seven, eight, steady, painful cracks without any respite. She wiggled and tensed her arse cheeks, for all the good it did. It was so hard to bear the throbbing, stinging pain. "Please, I'm so sorry."

"I'm glad to hear it, because if you ever go against my orders again, you'll be spanked until you can't sit down. Do we understand one another? You are to obey—" *Whap!* "—your husband—" *Whap!* "—in all things."

She put one of her fists in her mouth to stay the sobs that erupted with each progressive blow. She bit down on a knuckle, but that pain was nothing compared to the scorching torment he was visiting upon her bottom. Warren would be sorry if he knew she was suffering this way because of that paddle. Or perhaps he wouldn't feel sorry. Perhaps he would agree that August had the right to discipline her. Goodness,

Warren would have spanked her silly for a stunt like this, for using Aunt Overbrook to get around one of his decrees.

The idea of her brother's disapproval and sympathy with August made her cry even harder. Warren had spanked her, yes, probably even harder than this for her worst offenses, but this was August who was displeased with her. August, her love, her idol, who was disciplining her in this cold and authoritative way. The last two strokes were the worst. She wailed so loud that all the servants doubtless heard it, including the two footmen outside the door. Her bottom ached so hotly she could feel it in her pulse and in her trembling legs.

She lay still with her eyes shut tight. She heard him walk around the desk, heard the drawer scrape open and heard him drop the paddle inside and shut the drawer again. What now? Would he send her back to the country? Would he punish her further?

She felt his hand on her arm. "Stand up," he said.

She obeyed, but she couldn't meet his gaze. She stared at his neckcloth instead and tried to speak through her shuddering breaths. "I'm s-so s-sorry. I suppose I've brought nothing but irritation to your life."

He watched her a moment, then reached in his pocket for a handkerchief. "I asked you to stay at Barrymore Park for a reason."

"Will you send me back?" She brushed at her cheeks. "I don't want to go back, but if it will make you less angry, I suppose I will bear it. Because, oh, you hurt me just now."

"It was a punishment. You disobeyed me, Minette. You went against my express wishes."

That brought more tears, a veritable fountain of them erupting all over his handkerchief as she balled it against her eyes. She felt his arms come around her, and she leaned into his embrace, as much as she disliked him at the moment. Spankings had never factored into her dreams of wedded bliss, although she knew Warren spanked Josephine when it was called for, and that Lord Townsend spanked Aurelia too. Somehow Minette had believed she would be too perfect a wife for such consequences, especially married to a man she loved so much.

"I'm sorry," she said again. "I wish you wouldn't send me back. I won't get in your way. I won't disobey you again, not in anything."

He drew away from her and took the handkerchief, and dabbed it against her cheeks. "I'll have to think about what to do. In the meantime,

I've duties to attend to which your sudden arrival has put in disorder. You may go to your room and stay there for the remainder of this afternoon."

It was an order, not a request. He still sounded so angry, so cold. She wondered to herself if her stunt had been worth it, to be closer to him. Because sometimes you could be standing a foot away from a person and feel like there were acres between you to be crossed.

Chapter Seven:
Minuet

August dined alone, after Minette sent down a tersely worded note that she was feeling "unwell."

He wasn't feeling so well himself. He'd punished his wife for disobedience, which was his husbandly right. However, he'd also punished her because she wanted to be with him, which didn't seem husbandly, or right, at all.

But that wasn't the most disturbing aspect of this afternoon. The worst thing was that he'd gotten aroused while paddling her, a perverse reaction that troubled him in the extreme. Like any English chap, he loved to spank women in the course of naughty games, but he also had a firm grasp of the difference between play and discipline. So why had he gone hard in the midst of paddling Minette, when he only had discipline in mind?

Perhaps it was stress, or his recent lack of sexual outlet. He thought for the hundredth time that he must go see Esme, and realized for the hundredth time that he wasn't going to do it, especially now with Minette in the house. He went to the ballroom instead, where he could pound out his frustrations at the pianoforte.

As he crossed the vaulted and echoing space, not a velvet curtain stirred, nor chandelier tinkled. Utterly, hauntingly still. He lit a few lamps in the corner, enough to see the music, but not much more. He didn't like to look around at the ornately beautiful ballroom because it depressed him, and reminded him of times gone past.

How long since this great hall had housed dancing and merriment? Too long. When it was his ballroom, when he was the Marquess of Barrymore, Minette would want to organize balls every year and invite everyone. He could see it so clearly, her bustling about and conversing with all the guests, a proper marchioness. Well, he wasn't the marquess yet. For a moment, he had a sensation his father was in the room with him, watching him with an accusing gaze. The skin prickled on the back of his neck. He left off playing and turned around, but it wasn't his father watching.

Minette hovered in the doorway, in a night dress and prettily embellished dressing gown. Warren had always outfitted her like a perfect little doll. August supposed he must do the same, and order her a full wardrobe for winter and the season coming up. Sometime soon, she would need black gowns for mourning...

"How long have you been standing there?" he asked.

"Long enough to hear your beautiful playing," she said in an awed voice.

He didn't want her to be awed. He wanted her to be sullen and cross from her spanking. He wanted her to revile him and wish to avoid him, but here she was, gazing at him in adoration. "You ought to go to bed," he said. "It's late."

"I couldn't sleep."

There, that was a hint of reproach. Just a little hint. She crossed the parquet floor, watching him as if she feared he'd send her away. He wanted to. This room was full of sadness and ghosts, but she appeared to sense none of that. In fact, the closer she got to him, the more she brightened, until she stood beside him like a pretty, beribboned flame.

"That song was lovely to listen to. Crashing and full of drama. If anyone would recognize drama, it's me, wouldn't you say? What composer wrote that?"

He looked at the music, then down at his hands. "No one you would know. Some obscure fellow."

"It sounded so strong and complex, and yet melodious, like when someone feels very angry, but then they can't help seeing some pretty thing and being almost angry at how pretty and nice it is. And you want to compose poetry at the same time you want to take the thing and throw it off a cliff, or pluck off all its feathers if it's a bird. Because there are a lot

70

of pretty birds out there if one looks for them, but when you're angry, you feel like you want to wring their little necks. Do you ever have that feeling?"

He looked at his wife in exasperation. "Yes."

She sat beside him on the bench, not quite touching. She did a little trill amidst the treble keys. "How silly you must have thought me at the Townsends', picking out our little duet. I never realized you could play with such talent. I wish I wasn't a disaster at everything I try."

"You aren't a disaster at everything you try."

Minette made a delicate pout. "I can't play any instruments, I can't sing well, I make a muddle of anything I embroider, my poetry never rhymes, my letters always ramble in a most regrettable fashion, I step on my partner's toes when I waltz, unless that partner is an exceptionally strong dancer who can guide me where I need to go, rather like you did that time we danced at Warren and Josephine's ball—"

"I could give you lessons at the pianoforte if you like."

Minette left off her list of shortcomings and clasped her hands before her chest. "Would you? That would be wonderful. Does that mean you will allow me to stay?"

He looked back at the keys, picking out a somber melody. "I suppose you must stay. Warren has written that he and Josephine and the Townsends are coming to London in a couple of weeks, to make some purchases for their nurseries, and to visit the both of us."

"Yes, I suppose there are tons of things they'll have to buy before their babies come. Little gowns and blankets, and silver rattles, and lacy caps, and soft, tiny stockings for the babies' feet. Do babies wear stockings? But they must, don't you think, especially babies born in the winter months when it's cold?"

Before he could answer, she continued on with the list of items Aurelia and Josephine simply must have, to include things like books and toys and oh, perhaps, a little pony if they bred them small enough for toddling boys and girls, not that she had ever gotten very good at riding horses...

When she was a child, August used to dread her endless, rambling monologues, and avoid her when she was in a mood to prattle. But there was a sweetness in them too, when one wished to forget about troubles and become lost in a pleasant, gentle voice. You never knew what Minette might say. As she chattered on about babies and children, he gazed at her and thought, for the hundredth shocked time, *she is my wife.*

And she was beautiful and charming, and exquisitely formed. He didn't want to think of her like that, but it was rather hard to avoid it when she sat next to him in fetching evening clothes. Eventually he would make babies on her, and she would hold them on her lap, and blather on to them in this same way she blathered on to him. Perhaps she would tell them nursery rhymes and fairy tales. Perhaps she would sing silly songs made up of her poorly-rhyming poems.

He turned away a little, so he couldn't look down the front of her dressing gown and see the curve of her breasts. How terrifying to imagine her bearing his children. If anything happened to her in childbirth, Warren would kill him. Were they still friends? He ought to write back to Warren but he didn't know what to say. The man's letter had been to the point, almost brusque. Of course, that's how they'd always written notes to each other, in plain, concise language. What could he say in a letter? *Your sister and I are well.* That would be a lie. *I don't really want her here. I don't know how to deal with her. I still can't believe I had to marry her.* All of those were true, but probably the wrong things to say.

He certainly couldn't write that he dreamed with plaguing regularity of the night he'd lain with her, or that he'd gotten an aching erection the last time he'd paddled her heart-shaped bottom.

"August? Did you hear my question?"

She gazed at him, sweet, chattering Minette, and he felt like the world's greatest pervert for the lurid direction of his thoughts. "I... Forgive me. What did you say?"

"I asked if you knew the age at which children begin to walk. Because then, of course, they would need proper shoes. I'm sure Aurelia and Josephine will figure it out long before the shoes are actually needed. I'm ever so glad they're having children first so they can teach me everything they learn."

August watched her, uncertain if he was still expected to respond.

"So you don't know when they begin to walk?" she asked after a moment.

"I'm afraid I don't know much about children. I was the youngest growing up."

"But your sisters have children now, don't they? You're an uncle, and my goodness, I suppose I'm an aunt now. You must tell me all my nieces' and nephews' names and ages, and what they look like, and what manner of children they are, whether they are timid or bold, or silly or serious, or bookish or adventurous, oh, and we must know their favorite foods for when they come to visit."

August twined his fingers together in his lap. "I can't remember all of that off hand. My sisters never trusted me to be around them much."

"Whyever not?"

He turned to her, this cheerful, winsome wife who must delight all children without so much as lifting a finger. "I'm not the type of man who knows what to do with children."

"Don't you like them?" Her face clouded at his tone. "Don't you want to have children of your own?"

"Of course I do, eventually." But having children would mean bedding Minette again, repeatedly, in fact, until she fell pregnant. And when he thought about bedding Minette, a great conflict of feelings roiled in his brain until he couldn't think about anything at all. "I only wonder if now is a bad time for it," he said in a hedging way. "Perhaps we ought to practice being an auntie and uncle first, until things settle down. You're very young. We've plenty of years yet to start a family."

"I'm not so young. Not *very* young."

"You seem very young to me." And he felt old, so old and corrupt compared to her. He played a couple of grimly dissonant chords. Minette sat up straighter and seemed to shake herself from the pall of his pensive mood.

"Well, thank you for letting me stay here at Barrymore House even though you didn't want me here with your father's illness and whatever else has got you down. I'll try not to be a nuisance, although I would love some piano lessons, so I might be a nuisance about that. Which is a shame, because I know you're very busy, and I've already inconvenienced you just by being here, which I am so sorry for, even though you've punished me already and therefore gotten us back on an even keel—"

"How about now?" he asked, interrupting her. He leafed through some music on the sideboard until he found the piece he sought. He put it on the stand and slid to the left so Minette would have better access to the keyboard. "Play this piece for me as well as you're able, so I can see where you are in your training. It's a simple piece, a minuet. It's good for learning notes and keeping a steady tempo."

"What did you call it again? A Minette?"

"A min-u-et," he corrected, before he realized she was making a joke. An impish smile broke across her face, bright humor in this dim sepulcher of a room. He didn't intend to smile back, but he did. She had a devilish ability to make people grin even when they didn't want to. With effort, he composed his features and pointed to the keys.

"Come, we must be serious if you want to learn."

"I will try my best to play it," she said with a nod. She began to plink at the notes, a laborious process, since she looked up at the notation and then down at the keyboard nearly every measure. He let it go on a while, and then he tapped the page.

"No, look up here. This is where the notes are. An accomplished pianist never looks down at his or her fingers."

She paused on a ragged chord. "But how can I play the right note if I don't look at the keyboard?"

"You must come to know the keys by touch. You must learn to see them with your fingers." When he was a child, too young to light the lamps, he'd played the piano in the dark with his eyes closed. He couldn't tell her about that, about those frightening, dark nights. He thought instead of the dark night when he'd touched her and explored her, and taken her virginity. He'd done all of that by touch alone. "It's something that comes with practice," he said in a tight voice. "Try to feel the keys without looking at your hands. You know middle C. The others follow in a very predictable fashion."

She tried to do it, but quickly grew flustered. When she fumbled and looked at her hands, he tsked and made her raise her chin again.

"I can't," she said. "I suppose I'm a failure before I've even begun."

"Do you want to give up?"

She blinked at him through tears. "Would you have left Lady Priscilla in Oxfordshire if you had married her?"

Her question, so abrupt, so heartfelt, made him wish he had a pistol at hand to take his own life, or at least injure himself badly enough that he needn't answer. He thought for a long moment, then told her the truth. "I wouldn't have married her until after my father died."

"He's going to die for sure?" she asked in a trembling voice.

"Yes, he's very ill. He rants and raves and goes into convulsions. He must be constantly minded, lest he wander about and come to danger."

"Like my sleepwalking?"

"It's nothing at all like your sleepwalking." Minette shied back at his sharp tone. He brushed away her tears, despising himself a little more again. He knew she didn't mean to be a ninny. She understood so little, and she was so innocent that August loathed to explain. "My father's heart and mind have been ravaged by this...disease."

"What disease?"

Did Minette know about the French pox and how one acquired it? Did he wish her to? "It's a disease gentlemen get if they consort with the wrong sort of women," he explained. "That's really all I'd like to say. It's nothing to concern you, and nothing you can catch by being around him. They've tried to treat it with various remedies but it's only gotten worse."

"Oh."

"For my mother's and father's privacy, I don't want anyone to know. Although I suppose your aunt will spread the tale now, or at least awaken speculation."

"I'm sorry," Minette said, wringing her hands. "I'm so sorry about all of this, about angering you and bringing my aunt here, and disturbing your peace. I suppose I deserved that paddling today, although I wish you hadn't brought that horrid block of wood to London. If I had my wish, you'd fling it into a fire, a very hot, very consuming fire so it would be instantly incinerated, but I imagine that's not going to happen."

"No." He gave her a warning look. "No one is going to fling it into a fire."

She held his gaze longer than he expected, before she blushed and looked away. "I don't want to give up."

"What?"

"The pianoforte." She looked at the music and determinedly set about to play again. August felt slightly muddled, the way he often felt around her, with her flighty conversation and changes of subject. He also felt a strange enjoyment at her playing, although she missed half the notes or more. Or perhaps he felt enjoyment in her company this bleak night, when he was not at all sure of his thoughts or his yearnings. He slid closer to her, and put an arm around her so he might cover both her hands with his.

75

"Close your eyes and feel the music," he said.

"I can't close my eyes and read the notes."

"I'll do the notes, you feel the tempo and melody of the minuet. Relax your fingers. There, that's good."

This exercise brought them in close contact. Perhaps too close. He could smell the sweetness of her hair, and feel the tickle of it against his cheek. Her fingers were so small, so warm. He'd written this minuet, just as he'd written the music he was playing when she came in. He wrote so much music, none of it especially meaningful, but he thought he'd always remember the feel of her fingers and the scent of her hair when he played this piece.

"Oh, that's much better," she said with a nod. "It's easier when you help me play the notes."

"Music isn't supposed to be easy. You have to learn and practice. You must have a hunger to get better, even if it means hard work. Perhaps the reason you're a 'disaster' at everything is because you don't try hard enough."

Her hands lost a little of their energy beneath his. Why was he scolding her, for God's sake? Minette was Minette. He couldn't change her capricious ways now. They were a great part of her charm.

What were *his* charms? He couldn't imagine anything in his taciturn nature that might attract a blithe spirit like Minette. What was it about him that had ensnared her affections so many years ago?

"Try on your own now," he prompted, once he'd finished guiding her through a particularly complex passage.

He could see the effort in her tense fingers, and the set of her shoulders. She wanted to please him. She loved him, and he couldn't imagine why, except that she'd gotten it into her head that it was true. He didn't dare ask *why do you love me*, because she'd answer with some long-winded nonsense about sun-tinged clouds, and rainbows, and frolicking squirrels.

When she finished and looked up at him, he said, "You did that very well," and her smile blinded him. Her eyes... How had he never noticed the seductive shape of her eyes, and their deep blue color? He didn't know her anymore, which unsettled him greatly with all the other change upending his life. He shuffled the music around to have something to do, something to look at besides her adoring gaze. "If you continue to practice, you shall make excellent progress," he said. "But tonight you ought to go to bed. It's very late."

He rose and took her hand, and guided her up from the bench. She clutched the front of her dressing gown and looked toward the stairs. "I'm not sure I can find my room."

"I'll walk you there."

He went ahead of her, setting a brisk pace. He wished he could have handed her off to a footman. When they arrived, he made a little bow and stood staunchly on the hallway side of the threshold. "I hope you pass a restful night."

She looked at the floor, then met his gaze, blushing pink. "Are you going to come to my room tonight? Perhaps a bit later?"

"I think you had better get some sleep. You've only just arrived and it's been a long day."

She'd still have the marks on her bottom from when he'd spanked her. He couldn't deal with that, not least of all because it might arouse him, and then what? Would he make love to her like a husband did a wife? Or like a lofty lord made love to a whore, or a servant girl named Mary?

"Will you come to my room some day?" she asked in a quiet voice. "Because I wouldn't mind."

"Yes, some day," he said, "but not tonight." He forced a smile, pecked her on the cheek, and retreated to his study for a much-needed drink.

Chapter Eight: Tempt and Tease

Within a week, Minette had much improved at playing the minuet. However, she'd had absolutely no success in tempting her husband to her bed. It tormented her that he refused to consummate their marriage. Well, she supposed it had already been consummated, but not in the proper way, that is to say, after they were legally married, with full comprehension of who the other person was. It seemed a terrible, careless omission, something that ought to be done without delay, but her husband politely declined to do it, because he hadn't wanted to marry her, or thought her too much like a sister.

She hated to think he purposely avoided her, but on a typical day she only saw August at dinner and piano lessons, both of which were often cut short due to some crisis with his father. As for other company, August's mother made it clear with scornful glances and freezing conversation that she would have preferred Priscilla as a daughter-in-law. Sometimes Minette wished she'd obeyed her husband and stayed at Barrymore Park. By the second week, she had started sleepwalking again, drifting down the stairs and wandering the halls as if trying to find her way back to Oxfordshire in her sleep.

Perhaps the reason you're a "disaster" at everything is because you don't try hard enough.

August's words resounded in her head each time he turned away from her, each time Lady Barrymore frowned at her, each time Minette crawled into her cold bed alone. She would not give up on her marriage, not ever, not until the day she died. If she must fight for her husband's affections, she resolved to fight with every weapon at hand, and try anything, even lowering and risky schemes, and so here she was on Garrett Street on an unseasonably cold morning, creeping down the alley from the milliner's shop she'd just pretended to enter after convincing her maid she must stay in the coach.

In her years-long effort to collect tidbits of information about August, she had learned that he often visited a woman named Dirty Esmeralda, who resided in a rose-colored house on Garrett Street. Minette didn't remember at what age she had first learned about August and Dirty Esmeralda. She had been young enough, in her covert eavesdropping, to believe the woman's name was related to a lack of baths.

Now that Minette was older, she understood the nature of his visits with Esmeralda. The "quality" side of her wanted nothing to do with such a low person, but some other, more desperate side understood that this Dirty Esmeralda would know precisely what August liked in bed. What might tempt him and make him crazed with desire, crazed enough to overcome this silly view of her as his sister. She pulled her great, obscuring cloak and hood around her face and mounted the back stairs of Esmeralda's respectably tidy domicile. Thank goodness there was only one rose-colored house on Garrett Street. Minette knocked as hard as she could, trying to shore up her waning courage.

The door opened. A sagging, wrinkled woman squinted out, looking her over from head to toe. "What do yer want? This ain't an hour for callers."

Oh my. Dirty Esmeralda was nothing like she'd expected. She tried to picture her husband...and this woman...

"Who is it, Antha?" came a strident and slightly accented voice.

"Some fine lady." The old woman turned back to Minette with a scowl. "If you come to ask Esme to leave off with your husband, you'd best take it up with him yourself."

"That's not why I'm here," said Minette. A statuesque woman appeared behind the crone. She was stunningly beautiful, with wide brown eyes and copious amounts of wavy black hair.

"Why are you here then?" She was in a pale pink dressing gown, with a cup of tea. "This is my resting time, you know."

"Are you Dirty Esmeralda?" Minette asked.

"I might be. It depends on who's asking."

"Oh." Now that she was face to face with this doe-eyed, enchanting creature, she completely lost her nerve. If this was what August preferred, she had no chance at winning his attentions. "You'll think I'm silly," she blurted out. "I've only come to ask your advice on how to... Well, this is terribly humiliating, but my husband and I have been married for three weeks now and he hasn't... Well." Minette looked around. "Perhaps I ought not to have come. I'm sure you are in great need of...of rest."

She turned to leave, but the voluptuous woman stopped her with a hand upon her arm. "It's cold as blazes today. Come inside a little while, and have some tea."

The old woman shuffled off, and Esmeralda led her into a cozy sitting room with deep pink velvet-paneled walls and a roaring fireplace. She offered her a seat on a luxuriously embroidered divan, and perched upon the chair opposite. Antha took Minette's cloak and brought her some tea as she stared about the parlor in wonder. These ladies of the night lived rather like royalty. A white ball of fur jumped in Minette's lap and rubbed a cold nose against her chin. After a closer investigation—and a sneeze—Minette identified the creature as feline.

"I've never seen a cat like this before," she said, putting down her tea to stroke its long, wispy fur.

"I got it as a gift, from a place called Persia. Shoo her away if she bothers you, but I'll tell you she doesn't often sit in people's laps. She must like you."

"I like cats." Minette scratched it behind the ears. "Unfortunately, they make me sneeze."

"Go on then, Salome," she said to the cat, lifting her from Minette's lap. "Go to the kitchen and ask Antha for some cream."

Minette sniffled and brushed the cat fur from her fingers. "I don't have much time, so I suppose I must be very bold and wade right into matters. I need a favor. A great, desperate, very important favor, which I will do my best to repay if I ever have the chance. Oh, I ought to have said my name is Minette."

"You can call me Esme." The woman watched her in a rather amused way. "You've recently married Lord Augustine, haven't you?"

"Yes." A flush rose in Minette's cheeks. "And I know you know him. Please, I'm not angry. Well, I'm rather sad, and I want to cry and tear out my hair when I think of him in your arms, but that isn't your fault, so let there be no tension between us. I'm entirely aware that...gentlemen will... Well... To return to the topic... Oh, this is a wretched thing to admit, but Lord Augustine finds me wholly unappealing. In fact, I would go beyond that, and confess that I repel him."

Esme's brows drew together in a dark line. "I'm sure that's not true. He married you, didn't he?"

"There's an entire story behind that, and I haven't time to tell it. Just believe me when I say he doesn't feel attracted to me in the least. We grew up in a very close way, like brother and sister. Now that I'm his wife, he feels...incestuous about the whole thing."

"Oh. That's unfortunate." Esme's sharp eyes studied her. What did she see? The blonde curls, the blue eyes, the pretty, ladylike features? What Minette would have given to possess Esme's bold coloring and sensual bearing, if it would make August feel passionately toward her.

"What am I to do?" Minette cried. "I love him to madness. I adore him, I always have. I want us to have a true marriage, with closeness and romance and babies, and passion and affection. I want him to kiss me because he can't bear not to, and give me those smoldering looks that gentlemen give the ladies they love. I want him to be content and happy in our marriage. You see, I've cared for him forever, for years and years. And so I thought, perhaps, if you would not consider it too much a betrayal of his confidence, that you might tell me the things you do with him that make him want to be with you. Because then, perhaps, I can try to do them and capture his attention in the area of...bedroom matters."

Somewhere over the course of this outpouring, Esme had propped her chin on her hand. "Bedroom matters. Hmm. Are you a virgin then?"

"No. He...we..." Minette could never explain how she'd lost her virginity without sounding daft. "We coupled together once, but he thought I was someone else. It was dark and he was a little drunk."

"I see."

"This necessitated our marriage."

"I had already worked that out. So, you need some advice on how to entice your husband?"

"Yes. Perhaps if you have any pamphlets on the matter, it would be less awkward all around." Minette's cheeks were so hot she thought she must resemble a beet.

"I'm afraid I don't have any pamphlets, excepting some on the prevention of venereal disease." At Minette's blank look, Esme chuckled. "I don't suppose you know what those are. Good for you. But my dear, there must be a little awkwardness, or I should say, vulnerability if you are to get anywhere in 'bedroom matters.'"

"I don't know what you mean."

Esme thought a moment, and took a sip of tea. "I suppose what I mean to say is that desire is not a nice, neat thing, like a pamphlet. It's something that must be poked and fed and tended to, like a fire."

Minette could not hold her gaze. She was so much wiser, this woman. She knew everything about desire, while Minette knew almost nothing, except that she desired August above all things. "And how do you...poke that kind of...fire?" asked Minette.

"You wish me to tell you, 'caress him here,' or 'kiss him there' or 'whisper this in his ear,' but I can't say what will melt the ice between you and your husband. You must come to know him yourself. You must observe and experiment until you discover what he likes."

"But you already know," said Minette in despair. "He's been coming to you for years. How can I ever catch up?" Tears rose in her eyes, and she dabbed them away as furtively as she could.

"Don't get upset," Esme said, refilling her tea. "Yes, I know what Lord August likes from me. That doesn't mean he won't want very different things from you. If you behave just as I do, and mimic the tricks I do with him, then Lord August will feel as if he's lying down with Dirty Esmeralda rather than Lady Augustine."

"You do tricks?" Minette threw up her hands. "It's hopeless. I can't do any tricks at all. I suppose he'll continue coming to you since I can't ever hope to attain your level of expertise." She got to her feet, and set her tea cup on the tray. Tears spilled onto her cheeks. "Oh, this is terrible. I shouldn't have come. I feel even more discouraged than I felt before. No, I'm not angry at you," she said, as Esme rose and came to her. "You're so much nicer than I expected you to be. I don't blame you for refusing to help me. It's only that I love him so much, and I want him to want me. What on earth is to be done?"

Through all this blathering and crying, Esme set Minette back down, and sat next to her, and took her hand.

"I'm not refusing to help," she said when Minette had calmed a little. "I suppose it wouldn't be amiss to teach you a few erotic tricks. What do you know of the more adventurous side of lovemaking? Do you read the right sort of books?"

Minette blinked at her. "I read romantic novels."

"Romantic novels won't teach you what men really need. I have a better sort of book which I can loan you, about the sublime art of pleasuring men. And finding pleasure yourself, which is also important. Do you ever stroke yourself, Minette? Stroke your kitty?"

Minette thought a moment. "I stroked your kitty. That lovely white one."

"My dear, that is not the kitty I mean. I'm speaking of the pussy between your legs. Do you play with it and make it purr now and again?"

Minette flushed as she remembered her night with Lord August, the way he'd stroked and kissed her there, and made it feel so hot and tingly. "I... Well..."

"There's nothing wrong with admitting you do. At least to me."

My goodness, this conversation had rather taken a turn. "I suppose I have become a bit more aware lately of...that kitty."

"When you are near Lord August? When he glances at you, or smiles at you?" Esme looked pleased. "That's an excellent harbinger."

"A harbinger of what?"

"Marital bliss, my dear. If he makes you feel excited, that's half the battle. The other half is making him feel excited."

"Yes, that's the reason I'm here, even though August would kill me if he knew. You won't tell him, will you?" she asked in an aside. "He can be awfully unreasonable when it comes to my behavior."

"He spanks you, doesn't he?"

Minette felt embarrassed to confirm such a fact, but Esme obviously knew. "Yes, and I don't like it very much."

"He probably likes it more than you do," she muttered under her breath. "But let's stay on topic, shall we?"

"Yes, please. There must be a way to seem less sisterly to him."

"Oh, there are many ways. Let's start with your face."

"My face?" Minette had never thought of one's face as a very erotic thing, but perhaps that was the problem. Esme's face did communicate a certain lavish sensuality.

83

"When you speak to your husband, particularly just before bed," she said, "you should meet his gaze very directly, and make your eyes soft. Tilt your chin a little, so you seem a bit more saucy." Esme watched as Minette attempted this. "No, don't clamp your lips together. Leave them soft, like your eyes. Leave your mouth partly open."

Minette attempted this too. Esme shook her head and laughed.

"Not wide open. That will suggest something else altogether. No, just slightly open. Tempt and tease. This must be your new motto, Minette. Slightly-open lips might tempt your husband into a kiss. Tease him with a sigh and a shiver, and he won't be able to resist. No, not quite so dramatic a sigh, and you have lost the softness about your mouth. You must make your lips loose and kissable."

Minette tried to follow her instructions, but she felt rather ridiculous.

"It takes practice," said Esme. "You must work on it in your looking glass. Once you have the expression right, then you can move on to sending the correct signals with your posture and positioning. You know how you have always been taught to sit up straight, and keep your knees together, and preserve a proper distance between you and a gentleman?"

Minette nodded.

"In the case of your husband, you must disregard all of that. You see"—Esme sat up very straight, away from Minette—"this is a proper distance." She slouched closer to Minette, so her bosom brushed against her arm, and her lips were rather alarmingly close to Minette's. "This is an improper distance. It lets a husband know that it's perfectly all right to touch you. In fact, if you combine it with the appropriate expression and body language, he may kiss you then and there, and take you in his arms."

"Do you think so?" Minette could so easily picture it. She'd dreamed it a thousand times. "So I must tempt and tease, and be seductive."

"Yes, mercilessly seductive. If you're having trouble getting into a seductive mood, think about stroking your kitty, and how pleasant it makes you feel. Better yet, do it in reality, just before you go to dinner, or the opera, or whenever you're going to be around Lord August. Men have a very good sense for when a woman is aroused. It tends to arouse them in turn."

"Oh. Why, that's so very simple. I've been too proper around him, I suppose, in an attempt to be a respectable wife."

"You mustn't be too respectable, my dear. It's the kiss of death when it comes to exciting your husband. You surely know that from your romantic novels."

"None of the people in those books are married. At least, not until the end, but by then, the story is already over."

Esme patted her hand. "In real life, your story is just beginning. Lord Augustine is a good sort of man, and I wish both of you much happiness. Just think in your mind that you are sensual and exciting, and that he excites you, and don't hesitate to show it. Can you do that?"

"Yes, I'm going to try." Minette tried not to blush. She must be bolder from now on, and not so prim and respectable. "I can't wait to try all these tricks you've told me. It might even be fun."

"Of course it will be fun." Esme gave her a genuine smile. "Now, would you like to borrow those books I told you about? I have a few that are much more instructive than a pamphlet."

Esme was teasing her about the pamphlet. Why, it was as if they were friends. Not that they could really be friends, society being what it was, but Minette was grateful for her warmth and encouragement. "I would love to borrow the books, if you think they will help."

Esme's brown eyes sparkled. "I think they'll help very much. Wait here, if you please."

The woman left the room and came back a short time later with four volumes, some slim, some a little thicker. She laid them in Minette's lap. "You see they are all illustrated, to make it easier to envision the author's advice."

Minette opened the top book and leafed through the first few pages. Oh my. She began to flush all over again. Why, the drawings went a bit beyond lewd into the realm of shocking.

"Perhaps it will seem disturbing to view such things and read more explicit texts, but I daresay Lord Augustine will thank you for it. I assure you he's read similar books, and all gentlemen are aroused by the acts depicted therein."

"Are they really?" Minette turned the book sideways, trying to figure out what the gentleman was doing to the lady in the picture. *Tempt and tease, and be seductive.* If Lord August craved salacious acts, then my goodness, she would learn about them for his happiness. No one could accuse her of not trying hard enough. She'd do anything to win his heart.

"Dear Esme," she said. "I hate to trouble you, but can you have these books delivered to Barrymore House later today? I don't dare bring them in the carriage. I was supposed to be at the milliner's, and my maid is waiting for me. Wrap them in paper, if you please, addressed to Lady Augustine, and then I'll have them delivered back to you once I've read them."

"That sounds fine. Include a note, please, about how your new tactics have worked, and if you have any more questions. I have a great fondness for Lord Augustine, and if you love him as much as you say you do, I can only wish you well."

Minette gazed back at the woman. She didn't want her to have a fondness for her husband, but she supposed it couldn't be helped. She wanted to beg her not to see him ever again, but that would sound silly and sad, and so she bit her tongue and gave her the address of the house so the books might be delivered. She'd taken far longer here than she intended. She was glad when she returned to the coach that the maid had been too lazy and cold to set out after her.

She was also glad the cold weather served as a believable excuse for the lingering redness in her cheeks.

As soon as they got home, Minette sent her lady's maid away, pretending to need a nap. Instead, she practiced her seductive expressions in the looking glass for nearly an hour. She came to understand it had very much to do with relaxation, with releasing tensions, and letting her mouth and eyes go soft. She thought of the scandalous pictures in the books Esme promised to send, and her insistence that August would find such interactions enticing. Minette would study those books until she knew everything and anything a woman could do for her husband's pleasure, and he would surely reciprocate by giving her pleasure too.

Why, he had given her pleasure that night at the Townsends', at least until the point he had thrust inside her and shocked her sensibilities. He had roused her so thoroughly that her body had shattered into ecstasy. She didn't admit it to Esme, but she did indeed stroke her kitty sometimes, when she remembered August kissing her and touching her, and licking her there. She peered into the looking glass and drew up her gown, and put her fingertips on that warm, sensitive place. She stroked it as he'd stroked it, with a light, teasing touch, as she gazed at her reflection.

Oh, it did make her eyes go soft and needy. She drew in a soft breath through parted lips.

A knock at the door had her pushing her skirts back down again. "What is it?" she called out.

"A message, my lady."

The books must have arrived. Minette went to the door and opened it to find a footman with a note, rather than a parcel. She took it from the man, broke the seal, and opened it.

I require you in the study at once.

A.

A for August. Well, a summons from her husband was even better than the books. She was eager to practice her seductive wiles. She'd just been touching her kitty, further fixing her in the proper mood. "Let him know I shall be down shortly," she told the servant.

August paced the floor of his study until he heard Minette's knock at the door. She knocked again then, a bit louder.

"Come in," he barked. "It's half open, and you live here, for heaven's sake."

He blew out a breath. He mustn't let his temper get the better of him, not until he heard her side of things. Although he didn't know what she might say to exonerate herself, since the books that had been delivered to his neighbor were wrapped in brown paper with her name clearly written on the front.

She came into the room with an odd sort of slow, fluttering walk. What was wrong with her? And did she have an eyelash in both eyes? She was blinking and staring at him in the strangest, gawking way. "Good afternoon," she said, coming so close to him that he had to take a step back. There was something unnatural about her smile, her expression. She stared at him, her mouth ajar.

"Have you been drinking?" he asked her sharply.

"No." She took another step closer. He tilted up her chin and studied her eyes. She wasn't drunk, no. He couldn't smell spirits on her breath, but she was acting damned peculiar. "You wanted to speak with me?" she asked.

He took another step back. "I most certainly did want to speak with you. Our neighbor has just brought over these books, which he nearly gave to his daughter, Lady Augusta. She is seven years old."

His wife looked at the plain-covered volumes and blushed, and swallowed hard. "Oh. That would have been unfortunate."

"Can you explain why this might have happened?" He thought he sounded very calm, considering the state of his angst.

"Well, I suppose whoever delivered the parcel must have mistaken our address."

He flung the books down on the desk. "Damn it, Minette. Everyone hates me enough for jilting Colton's daughter. You needn't add fuel to the fire by having these sorts of things delivered in my name to the wrong damn address." So much for keeping his temper. She was no longer standing very close. "Where did you get them? Where on earth would you procure such volumes?"

She started to say something, then stopped, then started again. "You will find this the most appalling story, August, and there's every reason you should, for I'm so ashamed to have done this. But I'm going to be perfectly honest and—"

"Where?" he interrupted in a thunderous voice.

"Dirty Esmeralda."

Now he was the one blinking and staring. He could not for the life of him process what she'd just said. "Did you... Did you just say 'Dirty Esmeralda'?"

She took another step back. "Yes. I know I should not have gone to speak with her."

"You went to *speak with her?*"

August grasped for calm. Minette could not know of Dirty Esmeralda or his visits to Garrett Street over the years, and even if she did know, she couldn't possibly have gone to see her. A woman of Minette's station would never acknowledge the existence of a courtesan, much less visit her. Would she? But this was Minette, who hadn't the least bit of sense.

"I don't want to say how I knew a-b-bout her," his wife stammered beneath his darkening regard. "Except that I was a rather petite child and it was easy to hide places and eavesdrop, and listen to conversations when you all didn't think I was listening, and so I knew that you and Dirty Esmeralda—"

"Stop saying her name," he snapped. "What I do with that woman is none of your damned business. It's nothing you ought to know."

"Yes, that's absolutely true," said Minette. "And I wish I had never eavesdropped or learned about her, or gotten the idea to visit her because I thought she might know a bit more about you than I know, since you two have been on intimate terms for quite a while longer than you and I—"

He put his hands over his ears. "Stop. Stop talking. Just stop." He covered his face with his hands. If anyone saw her at Esme's doorstep, she would be ruined. He would be ruined. Warren would eviscerate him. "You didn't go see her, did you? You didn't really go and meet with her."

"I'm afraid I did. But I can explain."

"There's no explanation you could give me that would make this all right. When did you go? Who saw you?"

"No one saw me," she said in a tone of reassurance. "I took great care to conceal my identity and knock at the back door. And she was ever so pleasant a lady, considering I showed up unannounced. I can see why you enjoy her company."

"No, Minette. You and I are not going to converse about Esmeralda and what a pleasant lady she is. Do you understand what you've done? You've paid a call on a courtesan. You borrowed lewd books from her."

"Yes, and I'm terribly sorry they were delivered to the wrong address. What a coil it would have been if little Augusta had cracked one of them open. They're not meant for children."

"*Not meant for children.*" He kept repeating her because he couldn't believe the words coming out of her mouth. He couldn't believe any of this was happening. She had paid a call to a courtesan—his courtesan. He felt outrage, shame, and a dozen other emotions he didn't really have words for. He could feel the flush rising in his face as she gazed at him with her wide blue eyes. "Come here, Minette," he ordered.

She gave him an assessing look. "I'm not sure I want to do that."

"Come here," he repeated with a great deal more heat.

"Why? What are you going to do?"

"I'm either going to spank you or wring your daft little neck." She could not continue with these irresponsible capers, not with all the other challenges of his current life. She had gone to visit Esme, his longtime paramour. He couldn't believe it.

He couldn't allow it to happen again.

She took a step back, and another. "If you would just let me explain why I felt the need to—"

"Come here," he said in a voice that was really very strident indeed.

"I don't want to come there," she replied. "I think I would rather go to my room, or take a walk in the garden. Shall we go and have a walk in the garden together? I believe you need it. Outdoor strolls can be ever so calming for choleric humors. You know, it's not a good idea to discipline a person when you're angry. My brother always waited until he calmed down before he punished me for something, especially if it was a serious offense. Or an irritating offense. Would you say you are more irritated or angry at the moment?"

And there it snapped, the last attenuated strand of his patience. He strode toward her with a growl, arms outstretched to grab her and turn her over his knee, and redden her bottom until it hurt even to look at it. By the time he finished spanking her, she'd wish he'd throttled her instead. She'd certainly wish she'd never gone calling on Esme.

With a squeak of alarm, his wife turned in a whirl of skirts and fled.

Chapter Nine:
Frustrated

Minette ran out of her husband's study and down the east corridor, past formal portraits and rich tapestries. It wasn't at all dignified for a lady to run, arms pumping and legs flying, but if she didn't run fast enough, he'd catch her before she could find a place to hide, and that wouldn't do at all.

She could hear August behind her calling her name. She ran faster, toward the grand foyer where there would be footmen, perhaps even the butler to intercede if she begged for his help. Her husband could spank her if he wished, but not now, when he was so clearly furious. So much for her plans of seduction. He'd ignored her wiles, confiscated her books, and snarled at her for visiting Esme. Her immediate future seemed bleak.

And then she saw a familiar face before her, and heard a beloved greeting. "Ahoy there, mopsy. My word, is there a fire?"

She threw herself into her brother's arms, burying her face against his chest. "Thank goodness," she sobbed, clutching him. "Thank goodness you are here."

"Whatever is the matter?" He gazed down at her in consternation. "Are you crying?"

August's roar echoed down the hall, along with his footsteps. "Minette! I'm going to catch you, young lady, and when I do—"

He stopped as soon as he saw her with Warren. She squeaked and took up a position behind her brother's muscular frame. She couldn't see Warren's face but she could see August's expression go wary.

"Come to visit?" he asked Warren in clipped tones.

"Something like that," Warren replied in an equally cold voice. "Care to explain why you're bellowing at my sister? And why she's hiding behind my back?"

Minette peeked out at her husband. August shifted and crossed his arms over his chest. "I'm not sure it's any of your business," he said, "but we've had a row over something she did."

"A row? She's running from you over a row? *What have you done to my sister?*"

It terrified Minette, the way he said these words. "He hasn't done anything," she said quickly, only so that dark, threatening voice would go away.

August said nothing, only held her brother's gaze. Minette let go of Warren, cowed by feelings of guilt that August stood there alone, accused, when she ought to be his support.

"Don't glare at him," she told her brother. "August has every right to be annoyed. I went to call on someone I shouldn't have called on, and borrowed improper books which were delivered to the wrong address, and a little girl almost received them, and now the neighbors are angry with August, in addition to the Coltons and everyone else." She took a deep breath, swiping away tears. "I've annoyed him while his father's ill, and his mother dislikes me, and he never meant me to be here anyway, and—"

"Minette." August's voice cut off her painful recitation. "Perhaps you will walk in the garden while I speak with your brother alone."

Anxiety made her face and ears go hot. "Are you going to tell him to take me away?"

"Do you want to go away?" asked Warren. "I'll take you this minute if you wish."

"You're not taking her anywhere," August said.

"Don't argue, please." She moved so she stood between her brother and her husband. "Don't fuss at August, Warren. I don't want to go. But after today's misadventures, I'm afraid he'll make me go."

Warren looked back at August. It was hard to believe the two men had ever been friends; there was such animosity between them now. *Because of you, impossible girl. All of this is your fault.*

How many times had her brother warned her that August wouldn't make her a suitable husband? She had thought she'd known better. She ought to have listened and saved everyone a great deal of pain. "I don't want to go," she said to August. "I'll behave better, I promise. I'll stop annoying you. I'll stay in my room and—"

"Minette, I'm not sending you away." August softened his voice and took her hand, just for a moment, before letting it go. "I'm not sending you anywhere, but I think I'd better have a word with your brother now that he's here. Don't you agree?"

She looked between the two glowering men. "Perhaps you and Warren ought to stroll in the gardens. As I said, it's very calming for choleric humors. And I can... I can go and find Mrs. Collins and arrange for some tea."

"Yes, why don't the two of us stroll in the garden?" said Warren. "And then we'll have tea. You were very good to think of it, darling."

The affection in his voice almost started her sobbing again. What a failure he must think her. August would doubtless tell him all her shortcomings and Warren would realize she was a terrible wife. Perhaps he would insist on taking her away for August's sake. What a muddle she'd made for everyone, all because of her sleepwalking and because she had pretended to be a servant girl when she wasn't a servant girl.

She was starting to suspect that servant girl was the only one who would ever experience August's tenderness and warmth.

August felt too tense to walk. He felt too tense to speak, and yet he must do both out here in his father's gardens. It was a cold afternoon, when one might walk more quickly to warm the blood, but both of them kept a slow gait. A cautious gait.

"How is your wife?" August inquired as they turned onto the path. "I pray Josephine is well."

"She's very well," Warren replied. "She plans to call tomorrow, when she's not feeling so 'jolted and jangled' from the trip."

"Minette will be happy to see her."

"Minette is generally happy to see everyone. Especially you, which is why I was shocked to arrive and find the two of you at odds."

At odds. Was that what one called it when a wife hid behind her brother to escape you? Sobbing, no less. "It's difficult to explain."

"Nonetheless, I would like an explanation."

August knew he must confess the dire state of their union. Minette was the man's sister. Warren ought to know that things weren't exactly rubbing along, and so he thought a long while about the best way to say it. "Your sister and I are not very suited to one another, as you have always known. We're different in habit and temperament, and with the history between us, what we have can barely be called a marriage. If you wish to begin annulment proceedings, I won't stand in the way."

Warren pursed his lips. "It's not what *I* wish, Method. It's what my sister wishes. Let's be clear on that."

Were they to attack one another with Christian names, then? Very well. "What your sister wishes, Idylwild, is not in her best interest."

"Not in your best interest, you mean."

They walked a bit farther in silence. As younger boys they used to tear through these gardens, beating one another up whenever possible, whacking one another with sticks, digging holes so the other might fall into it. Had they changed so much?

"We have not consummated the marriage," said August.

"Yes, you have," Warren snapped. "There will be no annulment. You're stuck with her."

"She's not happy here. She's restless all day, then walks in her sleep every night, wandering about in her shift. They find her in the library, the parlor, or curled up halfway down the stairs."

"I'm not surprised she's wandering in her sleep. I understand you're both unhappy. But she loves you." Warren stopped and turned to him. "She lives for you, and you very well know it. You're the sun in her sky, the only flower in her meadow. You always have been. I don't understand why you can't return that love. She's charming, she's pretty, she's well-mannered, she's cheerful—"

"She's perfect. I know. She's also been my sister as long as she's been yours. What do you want me to do?" *Sleep with her? Debauch her? Slake my lusts between her thighs?*

He didn't have to say the words. Both men heard them in his tortured tone.

"She went to see Esme," August said. "We argued because she went to ask Esme for marital advice."

He could see Warren was taken aback, as shocked as he'd been. "Did anyone see her there?"

"She says no, but who knows? Your sister doesn't think before she acts."

"She never has," Warren said.

"She wants things of me, husbandly things I can't do to her. Not yet. Perhaps not ever."

Warren began to walk again, avoiding August's gaze. "Is it because of me? Because she's my sister? If you need my permission... If it has to come down to that, you have it, man. She's your wife. You have to treat her like...your wife."

"I don't need your permission."

Warren gave him a sharp glance. "You need someone's permission, apparently. You have Minette's. You have mine, damn you. Who else's do you need?"

"My own," August said raggedly. "Try to imagine my situation."

"I understand your situation, but you've got to figure things out. Do what comes naturally. I don't imagine you need lessons."

"You know I don't."

Warren's jaw tensed. "God, I don't want to talk about this. I don't want to think about any of this. Can't you just make her happy? You slept with her once, which is why all of us are in this snarl. She might have been engaged to some other gentleman by now."

The idea rattled August. Yes, she ought to have been engaged to someone else, anyone else. "My father's getting worse," August said. "That's why I told Minette to stay in Oxfordshire."

"Not the only reason," muttered Warren.

"No, but a damn good reason. The closer he gets to the end, the wilder his fits. Mother is beside herself. My father's heart is as bad off as his mind, and the doctor says..."

A matter of months. The doctor had said it was a matter of months, but August feared he meant weeks. There was no comparison between the formerly robust Marquess of Barrymore and the thin, deranged man he was now.

"I'm sorry," said Warren. "I'm sorry about your father. I'm sorry everything's falling on you at once."

"I'll survive." He reached to pluck a dried brown leaf off a hanging twig. "But Minette shouldn't be here. I don't have the time or patience to be the proper husband she wants. I lost my temper today over this Esme caper. If you hadn't shown up, she would have been over my lap."

Warren sighed. "Look, I'm not going to judge you for spanking Minette now and again. I even gave you a paddle to do it. Sometimes it's the simplest way to teach a naughty wife a lesson." He stopped and kicked at a clump of dirt. "But if the lesson you're teaching Minette is that you don't want her, I take issue with that. Understand this, August: I won't stand by and allow my sister to endure a miserable marriage." He emphasized these words with quiet intention. "I don't care how you do it, but I want her happy."

"What if I can't make her happy?"

"That's not an option. Damn it, man. She's loved you for so long."

August leaned back against a tree and shut his eyes. He'd like to pummel Warren the way they used to. August had always been bigger and stronger, and had usually prevailed by brute and stupid force. He did everything by brute and stupid force, and now he had this delicate, perfect wife he was terrified to touch.

"I'm afraid I'll hurt her," he said, opening his eyes and looking at Warren. "I want you to take her away."

"No, you don't want me to take her away." Warren's sharp rejoinder crackled in the stillness of the garden. "You love my sister as much as she loves you. If you want to wait a while yet to"—he grimaced and passed a hand over his eyes—"to take her to bed with you, then explain your reasons so she doesn't believe she's at fault. But in the meantime you must find ways to make her happy. Tease her. Smile at her. Let her shine, and accept that she's going to be Minette sometimes, and drive you out of your mind."

"I'm giving her music lessons," August said. "The pianoforte."

"There you go. A nurturing and intimate activity. Does she enjoy them?"

She spent the entire time mooning and smiling at him, very much as she had when she was a child. "I suppose she enjoys them," he said to Warren.

They began to walk again. "You always loved your music," said his friend. "You were always the reclusive one, the perplexing enigma of our rowdy little bunch. I wonder if Minette won't be good for you in the end."

"She has enough personality for us both," August said ruefully. "But she ought to have gone to some other more animated chap."

"Be that as it may, she's gone to you, and you've got to make the best of it. Townsend and I didn't start out with auspicious marriages, you remember. They took a bit of work, and you've never been afraid of work, old man. How long have you been handling your father's estates? Seven or eight years now? Listen, you're a decent person, the sort of man I would have wanted for Minette, that is, if you weren't my friend, and a crashing sex fiend, and broody as a woman. Still." He stopped as they neared the house and fixed August with a look. "I know you would never hurt Minette, not if you could prevent it. I believe in my heart that you love her, and that you want her to be happy. You've picked her up too many times to let her fall now."

This encouraging talk was well and good. Warren was always a wonder when it came to words, like his garrulous sister, but in his heart, August still felt doubt.

"If I can't make her happy, do you promise you'll take her away from me?" he asked. "Even if I don't want to let her go?"

Warren crossed his arms over his chest and let them down, and scuffed his boot against the ground again. "Like I said, it all depends on my sister. Now, let's go have tea with Minette like civilized gentlemen. And if you don't smile at her at least ten times before we're through, I'll slap a glove in your face, and neither one of us wants that."

Minette felt very cross tonight, and so she worked at embroidery in her private sitting room, making a handkerchief for August, painstakingly embroidering it with an ornately swirling *A*. Whoever would have guessed an *A* would prove so difficult to craft?

She didn't know if it was the embroidery that made her cross, or whether she was naturally drawn to needlework when she was out of sorts. She only knew that she mainly plied her needle when she was angry, which perhaps explained why all her monograms came out looking a mess. She was angry at herself and August, and her brother, who had not solved anything the way he normally did. He had stayed for tea and made polite conversation, and then left her with a kiss on the forehead and a whispered admonishment to *"Be a good girl."*

"Blast," she muttered as her needle slipped. She fluttered the handkerchief in irritation so the candles guttered and almost went out. At the same moment, there was a knock at the door.

Minette turned as August entered the room. He was in shirtsleeves, with no coat or cravat. For the thousandth time, she thought of their night at the Townsends', and the way he'd looked in the morning before he'd hurriedly dressed. Broad shoulders and bronze skin, defined muscles, and that masculine part of him she couldn't forget. That was what he looked like all the time under his clothes, as much good as it did her. He hadn't come tonight to romance her. She could tell at once by his shuttered expression, and his rigid stance.

"May I speak with you a moment?" he asked.

She looked back at her embroidery. "Of course."

Now she felt cross *and* shy. And nervous. He peered at her design as he sat beside her on the chaise, being careful of her dressing gown.

"You need more light," he said.

"No, I don't. If it looks awful, it's a lack of talent, not candles."

Goodness, that had sounded very cross. And she'd just put in a crooked stitch because of his nearness, and the intensity of his gaze. She laid the handkerchief down in her lap and faced him with all the bravery she could muster. "I apologize once again for my behavior earlier. For going to visit your...well. I understand now that it was very foolish and ill-advised. She didn't really teach me anything, except to be sensual and open, which I am not very good at."

"You shouldn't have gone."

"Yes, I know. Although I am curious about the books."

"You're not going to read the books. They'll be returned to Esme tomorrow."

"Oh. I had rather hoped—"

"No."

She gave a soft sigh and pulled at the edges of the ivory silk square. "Very well. And I suppose you may still spank me if you believe I deserve it. I shouldn't have run away from you earlier. I'm a terrible coward when it comes to such things."

His eyes looked more black than hazel as he regarded her in the dim light. "Why didn't you go with your brother?"

"Go where?"

"Leave. Go. Why do you stay here with me?"

How impossible he was. Handsome or not, he was brainless. "I stay here because I'm your wife. I belong here with you. Everyone will talk about us if I go live with Warren and Josephine."

"Everyone's talking about us anyway."

She turned a bit away from him. "I'm sorry. I'm so sorry for everything."

"I didn't come to scold you again, or spank you. But Minette... Look at me." She somehow managed to raise her eyes to his. "There shall be no more visits to Esme, or letters, or correspondence. You're not to look at any more volumes of a lewd sort. It's not proper for a lady."

"Esme told me that you read them. That all gentlemen do."

"Minette." His voice held a warning note. "Do you understand? Or do you need that spanking after all?"

Hmm. If he spanked her, at least he'd be touching her. But oh, it would hurt. She picked up her embroidery and attempted to look adequately chastened. "I understand. No more lewd volumes. Whether you read them or not." She was poking at him. Pushing at him as clumsily as she pushed her needle through the fabric. "It doesn't matter anyway, what I know or don't know about such matters, if you see me as a sister and nothing else."

"I've asked you for time," he said. "I'm sorry if you're frustrated."

Frustrated? She'd loved him as long as she could remember, had enjoyed one night of passion in his arms—well, mostly enjoyed it—and was now trapped in a platonic marriage, taunted by his nearness, his sensual lips, his deep hazel eyes, his tall and virile body. Frustrated was not a strong enough word. She gripped her embroidery frame harder.

"It's nothing to do with you," he went on. "Please understand it's my own sense of discomfort. I do think of you as a sister, a young woman who needs protection from villains like me."

99

"You're not a villain."

"I can be." The way he said it gave her a chill. "I don't want to be. Which is why I wish to leave you alone for now."

"Forever?"

"I don't know." He leaned closer with an apologetic expression. For a moment she thought he might kiss her, but he only looked sideways at her work.

"What are you stitching there? Is it a dove?"

She grimaced. "It's supposed to be an *A* for Augustine. But it's become such a mess, I suppose I'll have to undo the entire thing and start over."

"If you do, make it a *B*. I won't be Augustine much longer."

Oh dear. His father's illness. "I wish there was a way to fix him," she said, looking up at her husband. He didn't seem sad, only resigned and perhaps a little closed off. Minette thought to herself, *I wish there was a way to fix you.* She stabbed the needle into the cloth just to have something to do, since she couldn't embrace him the way she wished. "I shall work a *B* for Barrymore, then. How strange to call you Barrymore instead of August."

"And you'll be Lady Barrymore, when you've just gotten used to being Lady Augustine."

She bit her lip, saddened by the dull acceptance in his voice. "Why must we lose people we love? I wish there was no sickness or sadness in the world, or hunger, or people who are in pain. I wish everyone might be happy and warm and well fed, and content. Sometimes I think I have a difficult life, but I don't. Your poor father, and you and your mother..." Her embroidery work blurred with the effort not to cry, and she jabbed her needle right into the pad of her finger with regrettable force. "Ouch." She hissed and shook the injured digit.

"Be careful," said August.

At least she believed that was what he said. She wasn't sure, because right afterward he took her finger and drew it to his lips, and brushed a kiss across its tip. His lips felt warm and soft, and his touch so infinitely tender.

And gone too soon.

He let go of her finger and considered her handkerchief again. "If embroidery is not your talent, have the servants do it," he said. "Or commission some monogrammed handkerchiefs in town, if you'd like them for gifts or whatever."

She looked down at her lap, feeling dejected and ashamed. "I wanted to embroider some for you myself. So you would have something of mine. Something special. Don't wives do those sorts of things? I mean, anyone can buy something already made." She shrugged and looked back at him. Thank God she had managed not to cry. "Perhaps I will go into town and find some grand ones embroidered quite perfectly. When I'm so awful at making things, I haven't much choice."

"Make me one with an *M*," he said in a rough voice. "For Method. I'll use it no matter what it looks like."

"Everyone will laugh at the clumsy embroidery."

"I don't care."

She couldn't tell if he was angry or joking or simply tired of her. His color was high, and his expression cloaked as ever. "All right then," she said. "I'll make one for you."

"Thank you."

"It shall make me feel very much like a wife. And I am happy to be your wife, no matter if you need more time to get used to thinking of me in that way. I'll try to be patient."

"Thank you," he said again, with curt formality. "I suppose I'll leave you to your embroidery and go to bed."

She stood when he did, and stared up at him with her frame and needle clutched to her chest. "Will you give me a good night kiss? You could do it as if I was your sister. I wouldn't mind."

He gave a strangled kind of laugh and rubbed his forehead, and gazed at her again in that mysteriously intent way. He had enthralled her with that gaze so many years ago, and he still enthralled her to this day.

"Please." She was not above begging. "I think it will help me sleep better. A chaste kiss and embrace."

His arm came around her. She could feel his muscular strength through the fine linen of his shirt sleeve. He smelled divine, like cologne and musk. "Don't stick me, if you please."

"What?"

He nodded at her hands. "The needle."

"Oh." Before she could pledge to keep him safe from any and all needle sticks, he brought his other arm around her and held her close, right against his chest. His thumb came beneath her chin to tip her face up. For a moment, he just looked at her. Minette licked her lips, trying to remember Esme's advice about being alluring and sensual. His mouth covered hers, a short, firm press of warmth. She hardly had time to enjoy it before he pulled away.

"Do you think that will do?" he asked. "To help you sleep better?"

She swallowed hard, trying to find her voice. "Perhaps one more," she finally managed to say. "I've been so restless."

She saw a glint of humor in his eyes, a small quirk to his lips. He kissed her again, and this time she was ready to appreciate everything about it. The softness of his lips, the teasing contact, the way his nose brushed against her nose. She concentrated on feeling and remembering, and it seemed to her that this kiss lasted longer, but perhaps it was only because she was trying so hard to imprint it upon her soul. Lord knew when he would hold her like this again. It might be weeks, or months. When he released her, she quaked inside at the loss.

"Thank you," she murmured, touching her lips. "Kisses can be very calming things for sleeping." She said this as her heart raced and her blood thrummed in her veins.

"I wish you good night," August said rather abruptly, then turned and strode out of the room.

Minette watched him until the door closed behind him, then collapsed back on the chaise, flinging the handkerchief onto the table. She'd take the stitches out later, and make him the *M* handkerchief he wanted. That would be the easy part. Patience would be harder, because he stirred her so.

At least he hadn't given her another spanking. My goodness, she didn't want him to see her as a childish, naughty wife. She wasn't going to settle for a lifetime of paternal interaction and platonic spankings, and no other physical connection between them. She wanted his arms around her, and his lips against hers. She wanted his body and his passions, that he might desire her above all others. She was going to make August fall in love with her, and want her. She would never, ever give up.

Chapter Ten:
Books

August went to see Esme the following afternoon, with her erotic books rewrapped in paper and tucked beneath his arm. He had sent a note ahead for her to expect him, but of course she expected him anyway. She wasn't a fool.

By some stroke of luck, there had been no gossip of Minette's clandestine visit. Apparently no one had seen her, and Esme wasn't the sort to talk, so there'd be no need for an ugly confrontation. He was only here to return the books, and perhaps lie down and lose himself for a while. He had stayed away from Esme's out of some sense of honor, but his honor was straining along with his sanity, and if he didn't relieve some of his sexual tension, he feared what he might do to Minette, and how he'd feel about it afterward.

When Minette had asked him for a kiss last night, he had thought, *how difficult could it be?* A peck on the cheek, or the forehead. But then he'd taken her in his arms and become aware—not for the first time—of her small waist and her large and beautiful breasts. She had always been small, but the last few years she'd grown audaciously feminine. Exquisitely so.

And so he'd been forced to realize that he didn't so much see her as a sister, but a sister he wanted to do carnal things to. Which was so much worse.

"Esme," he whispered to himself as he stood at the door. Esme would help him, as she had so many times before. Antha let him in, and he handed over his cloak, hat, and gloves. He kept the books and made his way to the parlor. Esme was curled in a divan with her nose in a novel, her black hair falling in a tangle across the back cushion. She looked up as he crossed to her.

"Lord Augustine. What a pleasant surprise."

There was some gravity in her smile that unnerved him. "Hello, Esme. I'm sorry to visit outside your normal hours."

"I expected you to come." Her gaze dropped to the wrapped parcel, and he held out the books.

"I've brought these back to you." He launched into half-hearted scold. "I wish you had sent her away. If anyone had seen her here—"

"Did anyone see her?"

"No. But if they had, it would have been a disaster. I would appreciate very much if you would not correspond with my wife or loan her salacious volumes. If I wish her to learn about such things, I can very well teach her myself."

Esme looked more bemused than ashamed at his lecture. "Sit with me and have a drink, my lord. You look as if you could use one."

August took off his coat while she poured him brandy, and tipped a bit into her tea. For the first time he could remember, he felt guilty in her presence, guilty to be standing in her parlor stripping off his coat and throwing it over a chair. It was an act he'd always done with great joy, and great anticipation of the pleasure to come. He couldn't think of pleasure right now. He kept thinking about Minette.

"I wish you hadn't spoken with her," he said again. "It's made things awfully awkward at home."

"Things weren't awfully awkward before?" Esme regarded him with one raised brow. "You haven't been to see me. I thought it was a good sign, although I missed you on your birthday."

Her smile was flirtatious. Her body language was not. Was that why he didn't move closer and touch her, and kiss her, and stroke her skin?

"Have you come to say goodbye?" she asked. "It's all right if you have."

"No." His terse answer sounded loud in the soft, pink parlor. "I haven't come to say goodbye. It's only that things are complicated right now. My father and mother... My wife... I've been very busy."

"Your wife is delightful."

He drew in a breath and pinched his lips together. He didn't want to discuss Minette. He wanted Esme to open her arms and draw him to her breasts, and let him do all the indecent, needful acts his imagination desired.

"I want to lie with you," he said in little more than a whisper. It was hard to get the words out.

"You don't, Lord August," Esme replied after a moment. "But that's all right."

"No, I have to." His voice gained volume, along with an edge of panic. "If I don't have you, I'll have to have her."

"That's rather what I hope, for your wife's sake. She loves you, you know. She'd do anything to make you happy. She told me so herself."

He made a dismissive gesture with his hand. He could never take Minette the way he took Esme. He could never find that release with her, never in a thousand years. He might eventually manage to make love to her tamely, to beget children, but to expose her to the passion and vulgarity of his lusts... "I would very much like to come to you tonight," he persisted, "if you haven't any time to spend with me now."

She reached to stroke his cheek with a wistful expression. "Dear sir, how I'll miss you. So many memories, all of them magnificent, but I can't see you anymore. I'm only glad I've had this chance to tell you in person, rather than sending a note."

August stared at her, aghast. "You don't mean that we are over...forever?"

"I'm afraid I do mean that."

"But why?"

Esme frowned. "Why? Because of the look on your wife's face as she poured out her feelings for you. The longing, the anguish, the desperation to secure your affections. I'll not allow you to come here and waste your passions on a jaded creature like me, when you've got a treasure like her at home pining in your bed."

"She doesn't sleep in my bed," he ground out.

"Not yet." Esme took a deep swallow of his brandy. "But when you get desperate enough..."

He straightened his shoulders and glared at her. "If I pay, you'll do whatever I like."

"August, dear, I know you won't wish to be ugly during our last visit together. I'm sure you feel frustrated and confused, but keep a civil tongue."

His glare deepened, not that it did any good. How strange, to be powerless with Esme, when he had always been the one with the power in their relationship. He enjoyed wielding power over women, holding them down, fucking them hard, controlling them with pleasure. Esme liked submitting to such power, which was why they'd always been such a capital match.

"I need you," he said in a gentler tone. "I need you now."

"Minette needs you now. She wants to please you and love you. She asked me to teach her what you preferred, so she might make you happy."

"My God. You didn't oblige her, did you?"

"It's not my place to teach her what you like, but *you* ought to try. You ought to show her your rough and passionate side. How do you know she won't delight in it?"

"Because she's too sweet, too innocent," he said, pacing away from her. "I could very well lose her affection."

"My affection has survived your tastes for years now," Esme said, following him. "I love your force and intensity. I love your lustful imagination."

"Minette doesn't have a lustful bone in her body."

"You think not? Because she's sweet and pretty, and childlike? She's not the wilting flower you imagine. She came to see me, didn't she? Do you know any other woman of quality who would go to such lengths to gain the attention of her husband? You have given her some attention since then, I hope?"

"Not the sort she wished for. I would have paddled her bottom for visiting you, if her brother hadn't shown up."

Esme shook her head. "You're a mess of seething, unsatisfied hungers, I see. Come lie on the bed. Take your shirt off and I'll massage you for a while to put you in a better temper before I send you home." She helped him undo his buttons in an irritatingly businesslike way. "Have you been releasing your masculine urges with adequate regularity?"

"Stroking myself, you mean?"

"Yes, to disperse some of this tension."

"Is that what you recommend?" he said with biting sarcasm. Yes, he'd been stroking himself quite a bit, and was likely to continue doing so, now that Esme wouldn't see him again. He could always go to Pearl's, but he didn't enjoy those women as much. With his father's illness, he'd developed a healthy fear of the pox, and a desire for some measure of exclusivity in his partners. He trusted Esme. Her fingers traced over his skin, kneading and soothing tense muscles.

"You ought to let Minette do this," she said. "Let her massage you and explore your body. I think she would enjoy it."

He groaned into the bed pillows.

"I don't understand the difficulty," Esme sighed. "If you can't be passionate with your wife—"

"She's not just my wife. She's my best friend's sister. She pricked her finger last night, and do you know what I did? I kissed it, because that's the sort of thing I did when she was eight years old, and I was a callow young lad who thought her the most precious thing."

"That's a sweet story." Esme laughed.

"Why do you think I can't—" He groaned again. "I can't bed her, Esme. I can't. I don't want to do those sorts of things to her."

"What things? The things that have brought me such exquisite pleasure over the years? The things that will bring your wife pleasure, that she is eager and willing to learn? Here. Sit up and look at me."

He obeyed in a sullen fashion, hunching over when she took his shoulders in her hands.

"Listen to me, my dear, gruff Lord Augustine. I'm going to miss you horribly, probably more than I've missed any other lover I've lost. But I have great hopes for you and your lady. It's entirely possible to kiss her finger better, and then overtake her in your ardent manner of unbridled lust. You don't believe so now, but you will come to think differently, and when you do, you must give yourself permission to act on both sorts of feelings. I promise your wife won't mind."

"I've known Minette for years," he said in irritation. "You spoke with her for how long?"

"Less than an hour, but I'm a woman, and I know love when I see it. I warrant I know it better than you."

August wasn't sure this was true. Maybe. Well, probably.

"Lie down again," she said. "You're crotchety as a three-legged cat these days."

"With good reason. My ladybird's just told me not to come back."

She dug hard into the tense knots of his shoulders. "Your ladybird wants you to be happy. Do you think I'm not every bit as put out as you?

Blame your Lady Augustine. If she hadn't come here and bared her heart, you and I might have kept on as we were before."

"I'll pay twice what I paid in the past, if you'll keep seeing me."

"No." Esme kneaded a hand up his spine, the heartless vixen. "It's over, dear August. You're not to darken my door again."

August didn't dare return to Barrymore House—and Minette—in his current mood. So Esme had cut him off, had she? And it was entirely his wife's fault.

By God, he'd like to spank Minette until she couldn't sit down. Perhaps he would, next time he saw her, which was another reason not to return right away. Husbands shouldn't spank wives. Wasn't that what she'd yelled at him in one of her tempers? It was awfully hard not to take out his frustrations on her bottom when she was ruining every aspect of his life.

He considered going to the gentlemen's club, but when he was there everyone always asked after his father. Worse, Colton might be there, scowling at August and muttering words of condemnation in any available ear. He went instead to Townsend's, and found his friend at home. The butler led him to the grand parlor, a study in marble and damask with a roaring fire. As soon as he was announced, Townsend strode over to greet him at the door. "August, how wonderful to see you. Is everything all right, man? You look put out."

August stifled a sigh. "Remember when Lansing cut you off from all your women? After you married Aurelia? I've just been to see Esme—"

"I should have told you," Townsend interrupted. "Warren and Arlington are here too."

His friend—ex-friend?—Warren shot to his feet on the other side of the room. "You went to see Esmeralda?" he asked.

"To return the books," August said quickly. "And to ask her not to meet again with Minette."

"Esmeralda met with Minette?" The Duke of Arlington's brows rose as he stretched out his long legs. "I've got to hear this story."

"Minette is here too, by the way," Townsend said. "She came with Warren and Josephine. The ladies are sitting by the fire in the library, talking about babies and nurseries, I suppose. Shall I send for them?"

"No," said the other three gentlemen. August scowled at Warren while Arlington asked again about Esme and Minette.

"Are the two of them fighting over you?" jested the golden-haired duke. Easy for him to joke, when he was the only one still unfettered by the bonds of matrimony.

August flung himself in a chair, feeling supremely out of sorts. "They're not fighting over me. If you must know, Esme has cut me off indefinitely."

"Good," Warren said.

"But how did Esme make Minette's acquaintance?" asked Arlington.

"She didn't," August said. "Minette went in secret to see Esme because she'd overheard someone, probably one of you, talking about our relationship over the years. She went to Esme to ask for...marital advice."

Townsend stifled a laugh. "And Esme gave her books?"

"Which were delivered to my neighbor's house in error," said August. "The garishly illustrated volumes were very nearly passed along to his youngest daughter. Needless to say, the man was not pleased."

Arlington and Townsend looked half amused, half horrified. Warren looked irate. "I don't care how Minette found out about you and Esme," he said. "I don't want her over there, and I don't want you over there either. You have to give her up."

"I don't have a choice," August retorted. "As I just said, Esme's given me up, not that it's any of your business."

"You married my sister. It's my business."

"Gentlemen," Townsend stepped between them and gestured for calm. "Let's not growl at each other. August, will you have a drink? Tell us, how is married life treating you? How are things at Barrymore House? Your father?"

"No change," August said shortly. He accepted a drink from Townsend.

"That's a shame," said Arlington. "None of the treatments have worked?"

"No. He suffers now from terrible disfigurements, great pains, and feral madness. When he escapes his keepers, he stumbles about the house, groaning like an animal. My mother can't bear to look on him, he is so grotesque." It was probably more than they wanted to know, more than anyone would ever want to know, but he could only confide such things to them, and so the words spilled out with a sort of relief.

"A sanitorium, perhaps?" said Townsend.

"It's too late for that. It's...too late."

"I'm sorry," Arlington said, a sentiment echoed by Warren and Townsend.

"And Minette doesn't know what to think," said August. "She doesn't understand. I'm sorry, Warren, but she's such an innocent."

"She *was* an innocent," Warren replied.

Arlington frowned at the blond earl. "They're married, Warren. You must come to accept it. Will you hold it against August his entire life?"

"Yes, if he makes her miserable, and continues to consort with courtesans."

"I was *returning the books*," August said through his teeth. "I didn't go with any intention of sleeping with her. For God's sake, it was three in the afternoon." Lies. He was lying. He'd desperately wanted to sleep with Esme, although he couldn't have managed it to save his life. It was Minette who haunted his dreams, Minette who fired his fantasies. It was Minette who felt smooth and voluptuous and perfect in his arms. "I am not making your sister miserable, either. You and Josephine weren't blissfully happy at the start, were you?"

Arlington barked out a laugh. "He's got you there."

Warren tugged crossly at one of his cuffs. "Wait until you marry, Arlington. You'll have the worst time of any of us, deservedly so, after all your taunting and holier-than-thou lecturing, which amounts to nothing whatsoever, since you've never actually had to wrangle a wife."

"Let's go join the ladies in the library," Townsend said, cutting in. "Otherwise I fear we shall come to blows. Will the lot of you be staying for dinner?" He frowned, glowering at each of them in turn. "You're invited if you can manage not to snap off one another's heads."

Minette gawked, staring over Josephine's shoulder at a spare drawing of a lady sandwiched between three astoundingly virile gentlemen. "What is she doing?" Minette asked. "Why is her head down there?"

Josephine giggled. "Oral pleasures."

"Oral pleasures? It looks like a lot of work to do with one's tongue." Minette held the book closer, but she still couldn't figure out where the lady's tongue actually *was*.

"There are all sorts of things one can do with one's tongue during love play," said Aurelia, as Josephine dissolved in more laughter.

"And gentlemen expect this? To be caressed by their wives' tongues?" Minette was rather taken aback by the drawings in Lord Townsend's collection of erotic books. She wasn't inexperienced. She wasn't a virgin, and she'd been kissed more than once, but she was puzzled by just about everything she saw.

"Gentlemen enjoy a great many things that would surprise you," said Aurelia. "Josephine, I wish you would stop giggling. This is important. If Minette is to capture August's attentions, she must—"

"Must what? View the most perverse collection of leaflets and sketches in the world? Honestly, where did Townsend procure these?"

Aurelia gave a sigh. "It's probably better not to ask. And don't think Warren doesn't have a collection like this also. Sorry," she added as Minette shuddered.

Minette knew her brother was no celibate—Josephine's giggling testified to that—but it was difficult to imagine him, or Josephine, or Townsend and Aurelia, or anyone participating in these carnal and abandoned acts. She turned the page, to find a couple teasing one another's sexual parts with ostrich feathers. The lady's expression was one of transported bliss. The gentleman stood ready to impale her with his massive shaft. Had August's been that grotesquely large?

"Are all gentlemen made this way?" she asked, pointing at the protuberance. "So thick and distended?"

"They exaggerate the size in these books," said Josephine. "Just as all the women are tall and voluptuous to an extreme." She looked at Minette in puzzlement. "I thought you would know... Well, I'm sure it's none of my business, but I thought you and August had already..."

"We did, once," said Minette with a sigh. "But it was dark, and I don't remember it very well. I mainly recall that it felt quite wonderful for

111

some time, and then all of a sudden hurt very awfully. I'm certain he didn't mean to hurt me, but he's not, you know, small, as small as perhaps a man ought to be, and so it was quite a squeeze to fit." She buried her flaming face in another book. How was she to entice her husband when any thought of sexual congress made her stammer and blush?

"It gets better," said Aurelia. "The first time is always an awful squeeze. But then you become used to that filled-up feeling and it comes to feel rather grand. Did he touch you other places, and make you feel warm and excited?"

"Oh, yes." Minette's cheeks were about to catch fire. "He knew just what to do. He was so much more confident than me."

"Well, he's had more practice," Josephine said with an unladylike snort. Aurelia gave her a silencing look, which Minette very much appreciated. She didn't like to think of August's other women, women like Esme, who were more sensual and experienced than Minette could ever hope to be.

"I think our encounter must have been awful for him, because he hasn't touched me since," said Minette.

"Oh, my dear," said Josephine, stroking her hair. "It has nothing to do with you, and everything to do with August's mixed-up feelings about you being a sister. Warren isn't helping, I'm sure, hovering over you like a protective hawk. August will do his duty eventually, and when he does, he'll be sorry he held you at arms' length for so long, because you are warm and beautiful and accepting and perfect."

"Yes, and you won't need to depend on a repertoire of lewd tricks to capture his heart." Aurelia turned to the next page, featuring another thrusting, exaggerated organ being serviced by an eager—and naked—servant girl's mouth. "I mean, they are nice tricks to know, and it's good to be informed, because men enjoy all sorts of abandoned things. Ladies too. None of it is wrong."

"No, none of it is wrong," agreed Josephine. "As long as you and your husband enjoy it."

On the next page, an amply figured woman sat on a gentleman's face, while she stroked another woman's quim. The man's thing was sticking up, thick and swollen, with drops coming out of the tip, and the one woman was pinching the other's breasts. "The thing is..." Minette narrowed her eyes at the drawing. "I don't understand how any of this makes babies."

Josephine erupted in another bout of laughter, so Aurelia was obliged to clap a hand over her mouth. "Josie, hush. Do you want them to come and discover us? We ought to put all these books away. Townsend doesn't mind me looking at them, but I'm supposed to ask his permission first."

"Put them away?" cried Minette. "But I still don't know how to make August want me."

"Oh, goodness, you didn't expect to learn that in *these* books." Aurelia took her hand. "Listen, dear. Marriages take time to sort out. You mustn't believe it's some lack in you that—"

The door swung open, and four gentlemen, including her husband, entered the library. All four regarded them, huddled on the floor around the open cabinet, with piles of bawdy volumes and drawings spread out in a scandalous display.

Townsend grimaced as if he meant to look stern but couldn't quite manage it. "Why, I believe the ladies have stumbled across my private collection of books."

"You keep them in the *library?*" asked Warren.

"You said they were talking about babies and nurseries," August accused. "And here they are, leafing through your illicit novels."

Aurelia hurriedly closed up the books and collected the drawings into a pile. Minette thought one of them ought to speak, and make some excuse, but what excuse could they make? They were handily caught in the act.

"Is that what those were?" said Josephine, pretending surprise. "Illicit novels?"

"Josephine Bernard!" snapped Warren. "Don't make it worse. It's obvious what the three of you were doing."

"Reading?" she said in an innocent tone.

"Help me put them away," Aurelia hissed to her friend.

Minette could say and do nothing. August glared at her from across the library. *You're not to look at any more volumes of a lewd sort. It's not proper for a lady.* He'd said that to her *yesterday*, and mere hours later, she was caught in the act. It was only that she'd confided to Aurelia and Josephine about her visit to Esme, and the instructive books that August had taken away, which led Aurelia to reveal that Townsend had just such a collection of books, although Townsend's books were more numerous, more visually oriented, and much more explicit.

"I don't think we'll be staying for dinner," said Warren, scowling at her and Josephine both. Minette might have pitied Josephine, who was surely going to be punished when they returned to Park Street, if she was not so fearful of punishment herself.

"I don't think we'll stay for dinner either," said August.

The Duke of Arlington watched all of this with haughty amusement. Minette had always liked Arlington, and wished he would intercede on their behalf. Couldn't a duke tell a couple of earls what to do? Perhaps forbid them to spank their wives?

From the look on Lord Townsend's face, Aurelia was in for it too.

"I apologize for the reprehensible smut your wives have been exposed to," said Townsend. "Aurelia, why on earth did you get it out?"

Aurelia slid a look at Minette. *Please, please, don't tell him it was my idea.* But otherwise her friend might be blamed.

"It was my fault," said Minette quickly, before Aurelia could speak.

"No, it was not," Aurelia insisted. "I suggested it. It was my fault."

"It was my fault," said Josephine. "It was entirely my idea. Neither of you is to blame."

Arlington threw back his head and laughed. "It's not the end of the world, chaps. So they were looking at some ribald drawings. All of us have done the same. Sometimes a lady's curiosity can get the best of her, eh?" He winked at the three of them, looking so much like a piratical Viking that Minette smiled.

Her smile faded as August's frown deepened and he crossed his arms over his chest. Minette wished she might go home with His Grace rather than her husband, who looked very irritated indeed.

"I didn't even know you were here," she said to him, with a touch of sullen pique.

"I'm here," he said. "Now, stand up and tell your friends goodbye. We're returning to Barrymore House."

Minette took Aurelia and Josephine's hands, squeezed them and whispered "I'm sorry." She got to her feet, smoothing out her dress so she didn't have to look at her brother as she walked to her husband's side. All of this was terribly embarrassing, but surely not as awful as what was to come.

Chapter Eleven: Disturbed

They arrived home in the midst of some crisis with August's father. Lady Barrymore was crying, the servants were running around trying to be helpful, and Minette was ordered to go to her room.

"Why can't I help too?" she asked. "Why am I always sent away?"

"Do not anger me further," her husband said tightly. "Go."

And so Minette went, slinking upstairs in shame. This was not at all how she had pictured a marriage to August, and nothing she tried seemed to make things better. All she wanted was a smile, an affectionate glance. Something besides lectures and sharply spoken orders to go to her room.

When he came to her an hour or so later, she searched his features for any tenderness, any husbandly regard at all, but there was nothing. Only irritation. She stood and faced him with her back to the wall.

"Well?" he said by way of greeting. "What have you to say about your activities at Townsend's today?"

She clasped her hands in front of her. "I'll begin by saying that I'm completely finished looking at lewd engravings. The lot of it is outrageous and not helpful to me at all. Why, some of it is patently ridiculous, not that I'm criticizing Lord Townsend's tastes—"

"I told you already that you were finished looking at it," he said, cutting her off. "Don't you remember?"

Oh dear. She took a deep breath. "Yes. I do remember you telling me not to look at any more naughty books. I can't explain why I disobeyed you. Perhaps because I've always been curious to a fault. I don't deny it, and it's gotten me into cartloads of trouble over the years." She took a step sideways as her husband approached her. "But I regret very much going against your command. I'm terribly sorry that all your gentlemen friends, including my brother, came upon the three of us behaving in such an unladylike fashion and looking at such...unladylike..." She dug in her heels as he took her arm. "Such unladylike literature," she spit out. "From now on, it's nothing but tracts on moral philosophy and...religion...and household management for me. Oh!"

She tried to resist as he pulled her to a nearby chair, but he was far stronger, and all too handily she found herself turned over his lap. He pushed her skirts up, exposing her bottom to the cool air. "Oh, please, I've said I was sorry." His thighs felt hard and unforgiving against her stomach. She reached to brace herself against the floor. "Please, I wish you wouldn't spank me."

"Last time you disobeyed me, I promised the next time you wouldn't be able to sit down."

"But...oh...*oww!* That will mean an awfully long and hard spanking."

His only answer was a growl.

Minette cried out as his palm rained down on her bottom. She had believed the paddle must hurt more than anything on earth, but she'd been wrong. His hand was large and firm and hard, and he walloped her in such a steady fashion she could barely catch her breath. The pain quickly mounted to an unbearable burn. She squirmed and tried to pull away, but he wrapped an arm about her waist and cinched her against his thighs.

Now she couldn't move an inch, couldn't do anything but kick her legs in helpless torment. "Oh, please. Ouch! That hurts! I'm certain you wouldn't want to leave me bruised."

"Hush and stop kicking."

Stop kicking? How was she to do that in the midst of this awful pain? "I did not even enjoy looking at those books," she wailed. "You're punishing me for something I'll definitely never do again."

"I'm punishing you for being disobedient, and embarrassing me in front of my friends." The spanks never stopped as he scolded her. He reddened the sides of her buttocks, the center, the bottom curves, over and over until her whole backside felt on fire. "I'm going to tell my brother," she said in desperation. "If you don't stop, I'll tell Warren."

116

"Warren is busy blistering Josephine's bottom right now, just as Townsend is doubtless spanking Aurelia. Because of *you*, I might add. You earned this spanking and you're damned well going to take it. Now keep your hands down, and if you kick your legs again, I'm going for the paddle and starting over."

Minette realized she'd dug her fingers into August's leg. She put her hands back on the floor but it was impossible to lie still as he punished her backside. Her whole arse ached with a stinging, wretched pain, but it wasn't as bad as the pain of knowing he disapproved of her so thoroughly.

"Please stop. Please, I'll do anything, if you'll just stop being angry. I'll do anything you ask, if you'll just..." *Love me.* Even in the throes of her pain and panic, she didn't dare say it. She didn't dare ask for his love because she was terrified of him saying no. "Ow. *Ohh. Please*, I want to be a good wife. I can't bear this. I don't want you to hate me."

His hand stopped. The arm at her waist loosened. She bit back a sob, afraid to look up at him while she was in this state. The throb in her bottom seemed to beat along with her racing heart. "I don't hate you," he said gruffly. "Why would you say such a thing?"

"I know you didn't want to marry me. I know you don't want me for your wife." She could barely speak through the emotion choking her throat. "I know you wish for a different wife, but if you'll only tell me what to do, I'll try to be... I'll try to be whoever you want. I'll be whatever you want if you'll only tell me. Because I don't know!"

His palm rested heavily across her bottom. Her skin was so heated from the punishment that his hand felt cool. With an abrupt movement, he lifted her and put her on her feet. She was relieved at the respite, but somewhere along the way she had completely lost her composure. She fought for breath, for calm, as she gazed into his eyes. He looked stern and displeased as ever.

"I'm sorry," she said. "I only want everything to be all right between us, and I don't know what to do. I wish I could be a pleasing wife, so you aren't always frowning and sending me to my room. That's why I talked to Esme, and Aurelia and Josephine, and looked at those books. I don't want you to see me as a child." Her voice rose in anguish. "I want to be your proper wife."

His hazel eyes narrowed as he leaned forward in the chair. "You think if you learn lewd sexual acts you'll be a proper wife?"

"Perhaps." She rubbed her bottom through her skirts. "I don't want you to see me as a sister, or some naughty child to spank over your lap. I want to entice you. I don't want you to go to Esme for...those things."

"I won't go to Esme anymore," he said, leaning back again. "Now that she's met you, she's fallen in love with you like everyone else and told me to find my pleasure elsewhere."

She let out a shuddery breath, staring at the fine knot in her husband's cravat. "I could give you pleasure if you'd let me. If you could bear to..." She couldn't look him in the face. "I'm sorry it's me you had to marry. But maybe, if you closed your eyes..."

"Minette, please." His voice sounded so tortured and miserable that tears filled her eyes.

"I'm not a child," she said through the blurry haze. Desperation made her bold. She thought of the drawings she'd looked at, the voluptuous women and the thrusting men. There had been spanking in the books too, with whips and birch rods. Was her husband one of the men who became aroused by such things? She'd take any arousal she could get. She put her fingers on the buttons of August's breeches, and he didn't stay her hand. Beneath the fabric, she could see the burgeoning outline of his manhood.

She said a silent prayer to the god of well-meaning wives, and freed the first button from its loop.

August felt curiously out of breath. Not from the spanking. He could have spanked her another hour, and probably should have, but then she had begun to sob, and speak of him hating her.

God, he'd made Minette believe he hated her. It was a horrible thing.

He hadn't been paying attention. He'd been so caught up in his own crises and misgivings that he hadn't considered how his actions would seem through her eyes. She thought he *hated her*. Now she was leaning over him, undoing his breeches, and he felt too guilty to make her stop.

Oh, but she ought to stop. She opened one button, then another. Her fingers brushed his skin through the thin linen of his shirt. His cock awakened with a vengeance, not understanding this was not the time, nor the place. "Minette," he said softly.

But he didn't tell her to stop, and so she unbuttoned his breeches completely, allowing him to jut out in full and flagrant arousal beneath the curtain of his shirt's hem.

"You don't have to do this," he said, and it sounded like a plea. Why was he pleading with her? He could button himself back up, stand, and leave the room, but for some reason he didn't do this. She got down on her knees in front of him and he stifled a groan. *No, no, no.* Not *no* that she would do it, but *no* that he wanted it with a desire like fire. He wasn't made of steel.

It excited him to see her on her knees.

He let out a long breath of self-loathing even as he reached to touch her hair. So soft, so fine. So blonde. So innocent. He screwed his eyes shut. *Don't think about that.* She was the one who told him to close his eyes, and he determined to keep them closed as she drew away the tails of his shirt and exposed his pulsing length. She stroked his cock gingerly, with light fingertips, but the contact almost had him bowing off the chair. His thighs tightened.

"What did you learn in those books, before you were interrupted?" His voice sounded rough. Uncivilized.

"A lot of things. More than you think."

"Show me," he said through gritted teeth, resting his hands upon his knees. Minette bent over him. He heard the rustle of her skirts, then felt the tip of her warm tongue trace a trail around and about his cock's head. If only he wasn't so damned sensitive, so overwrought from lack of release. She began to lick him like a sugar cake, with a maddening, tentative delicacy. He didn't want this—he *didn't*—but he couldn't stop her. It had been an endlessly frustrating day, and he was weak and hungry with need.

He felt her fingers grip him, not firmly, the way an experienced lady might handle a man, but with hesitant pressure. "Move it now," he said. "Move your hand along my cock."

She obliged him. "Like this?"

"Yes," he said with another groan. "You needn't be so gentle. Stroke it firmly up and down as you caress me with your mouth."

She tried, but like any beginner, did not do exceedingly well. He didn't care. He ached to be touched and caressed. The fact that it was Minette was an upsetting detail, but he didn't stop her, because her mouth was warm and her tongue was surprisingly deft. All that chatter, he supposed. Silly Minette and her chattering. Minette, who was stroking and licking his throbbing cock.

He sat straighter. He meant to stop her then but she sighed and tilted her head, and licked lower, to the base of his shaft. She made a tentative swipe at his balls. They drew up at the thrill, the heady pleasure. *Don't do such things*, he thought. "Yes," he said aloud. "That feels good. Don't stop."

She bent her head and attended to him, stroking, licking, kissing, a clumsy mishmash of erotic attempts that contributed to a marvelous whole. She was making him so hot he could feel the flush of pleasure in his cheeks and his chest. He moved on the chair, biting back a growl as she opened her mouth and slid her lips down his length as far as she could go. He gripped his hands in his hair, only so he wouldn't bury them in her hair and impale her mouth with his cock. One didn't do such things to one's wife. One didn't do such things to a young woman one considered a sister.

And yet some tension was growing inside him, some ebbing of control. Misgivings were grinding against bodily needs, and reason was giving way to unruly fantasies. He had taken her once, his birthday night. Why not take her again? He wanted to be inside her so badly, fucking her, pounding into her. He could always push her skirts up over her face so he couldn't see who he was violating. He could picture it. He could feel it. Rather than the tease of her lips, he could be enjoying the hot caress of her tight, wet pussy. He pictured her legs splayed out, and imagined tearing her bodice so her breasts spilled free—

Abhorrent fantasies. Violent lust.

"No." He was telling himself no, that he mustn't entertain such thoughts about Minette. She paused a moment in her oral exertions and looked up at him in question. He stared at her dumbly, too stricken to speak.

She bowed her head to caress him again. "No," he said more loudly. He put his hands on her shoulders. "No, no more." *No more, or I can't be responsible...*

"I don't mind it," she said. "I admit I was puzzled when I saw the ladies doing this in those books, but if it feels good to you, then I enjoy doing it too. There's something about, oh, I don't know, the lazy, wet, sensual abandon of it all."

"No, Minette. I have to go." He felt close to breaking down, like he might erupt into a frenzy of emotion even worse than the frenzy of lust pounding in his brain. She looked devastated. "You did exceedingly well," he said to reassure her, "but I think... I..."

I think I want to throw you on the bed and ravish you. And I shouldn't feel that. I don't want to feel that, not toward you.

He had to leave. He shoved his aching cock into his breeches and buttoned his flaps with frantic speed as he strode across her sitting room and fumbled his way out the door.

They did not take dinner together that evening. His mother was ill with worry, and August felt too guilty to face his wife. Minette's maid said she was asleep, and would perhaps like a dinner tray later. August couldn't imagine how Minette had felt when he fled during her attempts to behave as a "proper wife." He couldn't bear to think about it. He drank a regrettable amount of brandy and went to bed.

Now, hours later, a servant was nudging him awake. "My lord, forgive me. It's the countess again."

He sat up, wiping the sleep from his eyes. "Where?"

The servant brought his robe. "In the ballroom, at the piano. She won't be led away."

"I'll take care of it."

He accepted a candle from the manservant and made his way into the hallway. The house was quiet, still, a little threatening in the darkness. He'd been afraid of the dark as a child, afraid of so many things. He was afraid of Minette coming to harm in her nightly wanderings. She might sail off a balcony or fall down the stairs, or bed down too close to a fireplace when she finally came to rest. One more thing to fret about on top of everything else.

The footman shadowed him as he made his way to the ballroom. August heard Minette before he saw her, faint sobs and jarring notes on the pianoforte. He gestured to dismiss the servant before he passed through the door. His wife was scarcely dressed, wearing only a woolen night shift. The maid in the shadows must have wrapped the blanket around her. He dismissed her too and sat beside Minette on the bench.

"A-B-D and G," she whispered, taking no notice of him. "A-C-G and, oh. Bother. I can't even reach the keys."

She tried again, playing a raw, dissonant chord.

"Your hands are too small for Telemann." He laid his fingers over hers to still them. "It's all right. Don't cry."

She wiped her cheeks and then sat still with her hands in her lap. He wrapped the blanket closer around her in the chilly room. It felt oppressively dim, lit only by the moon and a single candle left by the servants. He leaned down to catch her gaze. "Dearest, are you awake or asleep now?"

"I came here to practice," she said, which didn't answer his question.

"It's very late to practice," he pointed out. "You ought to play in the daytime. You should be sleeping in your bed." She reached to play again and he stilled her hand. "It's too late to play, and you've chosen too difficult a piece, at any rate."

She resisted, fighting to move her hand. Groggy tears gave way to blinking awareness and finally, wakefulness. She rubbed her eyes, then sagged against his side. "I wanted to practice for tomorrow's lesson," she said. "I thought it was a dream."

"No. You're walking about again." He studied the music on the stand. "I haven't played this in years. You've been riffling through my music in your sleep?"

She squinted by the candle's light. "Schwang-en-gess-gong...?"

"*Schwanengesang*," he provided. "It's German, like Telemann. Do you know what it means?"

"My German is not very good."

"*Swan Song*. It's a rather sad concerto."

Minette stifled a yawn. He ought to carry her up to bed at once, but she felt so warm, and so close. "Swans are rather sad creatures. Or bad creatures, I should say. Very mean and given to violence," she said in a drowsily indignant tone.

122

Very mean and given to violence. August remembered how sternly he'd spanked his wife earlier, only because he'd felt frustrated and cross. He ought to apologize to her. He would, perhaps, tomorrow, when she was not half-asleep. She gazed up at him with a fetching smile. Minette never held a grudge, not like those nasty swans.

"I remember you telling me how unpleasant they were, and how you did not wish them at our wedding," he said. "Do you know what a swan song is? They say that just before swans die, they produce a lovely song, vocalizing as they never did in life. And so a 'swan song' has come to mean any final or grand gesture before...the end."

He didn't want to talk about endings and death, not here in the dark, with his father suffering a few floors away. The Marquess of Barrymore would have no swan song. He would die in horrible pain and agony, if the physicians were to be believed.

Minette touched one of the keys, sounding a mournful note. "Well, that rather changes my opinion of swans. Perhaps they are only misunderstood. I mean, how remarkable, to sing a lovely song in the face of death. I wonder what it sounds like."

August's throat felt tight. "I don't know. I don't know if anyone's ever heard one."

"But they must have, if such a legend exists." She tapped the music. "Telemann wrote this concerto about it. Will you play it for me? I'd like to hear how Telemann imagined the sound."

August dutifully leafed to the second part of the composition, the melodious swan's song before the adagio and the swan's death. He played the piece full out, there in the wee hours of the night, with Minette pressed against his left arm. When he finished, she laid her head against his shoulder and patted his back. "You are an excellent musician."

"Thank you."

"You haven't any problems with Telemann at all, particularly this Schwaner— Schergang—" She took another stab at pronouncing the German title, slaughtering it badly. "Whatever it's called. Say, do you remember when you gave me that porcelain swan? The one you found in France?"

"Of course I remember." They had all bought trinkets for Minette on their Grand Tour, since she had been left behind with her auntie and governesses. August had seen the delicate swan in pink and ivory, and gold leaf, and known he must have it for her. He somehow preserved it unbroken until they returned to England. When he handed it over, she had flown into rhapsodies over its gold flecked wings and slanted eyes, and the red lips painted at the end of the beak. It had been a silly thing, but she had been so delighted.

"I'm sure it's in one of my boxes somewhere. I kept everything you ever gave me." She sighed against his shoulder. "I thought those keepsakes were all I would ever have of you. But now I have considerably more of you than I ever expected."

"Yes." And here he sat, picturing his considerable girth surrounded by her lips. She must have done the same, for her features rearranged into a self-conscious mask.

"Why did you leave so abruptly this afternoon?" she asked. "Did I make you angry? Was I being too...lewd?"

In the dark, with her sad, plaintive questions, he could only tell her the truth. "I left because I was afraid of insulting you. Because I was imagining doing things to you that I didn't want to do."

"Why not? Why wouldn't you want to?"

"Because I fear you wouldn't like them, or that you wouldn't understand. I know you want to be a proper wife, an experienced lover like Esme, but Minette..." He took her hand and held it between his. "You're still so young and sweet. No. Don't pout. To me, you're still an innocent. And I am not."

"Josephine was innocent when she married Warren, and he was a terrible rogue, and they still managed to get along together."

"Your brother didn't know Josephine when she was a child. Your brother didn't bring Josephine a little swan and watch her pirouette around the room in short skirts. Please, I beg you, try to understand. When you're more mature—"

"How am I to mature when you persist in treating me like a child?"

"I'm trying to show you respect. I'm trying to protect you!" He bit off an oath. His temper was slipping again and she didn't deserve it. She was the wronged one, the neglected one, the one who walked the halls of his home in the dark like a wraith. He squeezed her hand and let it go. "What are we to do about your night-roving problem? You can't keep walking about in your sleep. You'll fall from a balcony or something, and your brother will kill me."

"I don't know." Minette pulled the blanket closer about her. "I don't know what causes it, or how to control it."

"What did Warren do to stop you wandering about as a child?"

"He slept beside me so he would know whenever I got up."

Damn and blast. Of course that was the most reasonable solution, to sleep beside her in bed. She'd be safe and secure, and he could sleep an entire night through without being awakened by servants. That is, if he could fall asleep beside her. Perhaps he could simply lock her in her room, or tie her to the bed...

She shifted beside him, still going on about Warren watching after her, and being such a wonderfully protective brother, and the very pinnacle to sleep beside, since he didn't snore.

August wondered if he snored.

"I suppose we ought to go to bed before dawn comes," he said, cutting off her rambling with a sense of beleaguered purpose. "Shall we sleep in my bedroom, or yours?"

She looked up at him in surprise. "You're going to let me? Aren't you afraid I'll disturb your sleep?"

"I doubt it can be any more disturbed than it's already been. We can sleep in the same bed, but I ask that you lie as still as possible, and not talk as I'm trying to nod off."

Minette laughed. "Warren had the same rules."

Blast Warren. Blast Minette and her sleepwalking, and her bright innocence, and her goddamned swans. "My bedroom or yours?" he asked, snuffing the candle with his fingertips. Smoke scented the distance between them.

"Yours," she said. "So you will feel less annoyed at the inconvenience."

As he lay beside her later, he felt more annoyed than any man ever on earth. She felt too warm and comfortable as she huddled against his body, and smelled too alluring for him to find any peace. His bed was not his bed with Minette in it, just as his life was not his life, and his mind was not his mind. "You're driving me mad," he whispered into the dark.

But for once, she was not chattering or questioning or making excuses for her irritating capers. Her breath came slow and even, her pretty features angelic in repose.

Chapter Twelve: Trouble

November turned to December, and the house made preparation for holiday callers, although there wasn't much cheer in the air. August put on a brave face, and provided a shoulder for his mother to cry on, and a body for Minette to sleep beside at night.

She didn't sleepwalk anymore. No. Instead she slumbered upon his chest, or his shoulder, or nestled her face into the curve of his neck and stayed there all night, barely stirring. He was happy she was able to find restful sleep at last, but he barely slept at all.

To be safe, he left off taking his usual drink or two after dinner. He felt he must be ever sober and on guard, lest he enact another Mary-the-Maidservant interlude, and debauch his wife half drunk, in darkness and sleepy confusion. He feared he would grasp her and press himself inside her with thoughtless, inelegant force, just because she was there and because he was so, so tired, and because he remembered far too well what it had felt like to be within her.

He ought to just take her. He told himself so every night, but when he reached for her, he would be assailed by poignant memories of her as a bright and trusting child. All his life, he had wanted to protect her, not defile her. He feared if he took her, their history would be lost, and he would never again be the object of her naive devotion.

And he wanted that naive devotion. Selfishly, jealously, desperately. He needed her devotion to make it through these dark days before his father's death. Now that she was here, he understood he could never again send her away. He enjoyed their dinners and he enjoyed their pianoforte lessons, where she made laudable progress. He approved of the way she spoke to the staff and won them to her side. He admired the graceful manner with which she disregarded his mother's numerous barbs. He enjoyed everything about his wife except that he must sleep beside her at night and shudder with unsatisfied need.

He watched her now from the parlor window with the best view of the garden, where Minette insisted his father take the sunshine on any passably seasonable day. The great Lord Barrymore lay slumped on his wheeled chaise, head to one side, eyes and mouth open, insensate and mute. Blankets and bandages shielded his mottled skin.

The man's remaining life could be measured in days, not months, and yet Minette insisted on reading to him, and blathering away as if he could hear her. She read books to him, and smiled into his staring, ulcerated eyes. His mother could not bear to be in the same vicinity as her husband, but Minette...

"My lord?"

August turned at the servant's voice, thinking, what now? But it was only a caller, the esteemed Duke of Arlington looking dapper in a deep plum coat and black breeches. Going to the theater? The opera? To visit some lady of the night? Arlington greeted him with a rakish smile. "How goes it, Augustine?"

August raised a brow. "Where are you off to?"

"Nowhere yet. I'm just back from the club. Warren and Townsend were there, and asked after you."

"How are they?"

"How are you?" Arlington rejoined firmly. "There is talk that you never leave the house, that you are put upon by your bride, or suffering a terrible illness, or escaped on a trip abroad, or a dozen other hypotheses you really ought to put to rest."

"It's nearly the holidays. I've been busy."

Arlington seated himself on a divan and stretched out his tall frame. "I thought you'd say something like that. Anyway, the fellows say hello, and wonder where you are, and Warren said for me to come here and tell you he hopes his sister is well. I imagine he wanted to visit himself but didn't wish to encounter you. When will the two of you settle your differences?"

August watched Minette reach to smooth a wrinkle in his father's blanket. "I don't know," he said absently. He really didn't know. Things hadn't been the same between them since that morning at Townsend's, and perhaps would never be the same again.

Arlington let out a long, slow sigh. "Are you all right?" When August didn't answer, his friend came to stand by him at the window. The duke noticed Minette sitting primly with her book, reading to his dying father. "The dear lady. How sweet she is."

"He can't hear her. He responds to nothing at all. I don't know why she bothers."

"She bothers because she's got a kind heart." Arlington caught August's gaze. "I'm afraid you're having a hard go of things, and reluctant to ask for help. Is there anything I can do?"

"You can assure Warren that Minette is fine. She is mostly fine." He looked back out the window, at his wife's curls peeking out of her bonnet. Now and again she tilted her head as if emphasizing some passage in the book. "She says my father must be in the sun. That he would not want to spend his final days in a dim sick room. She's reading him poetry, to soothe his soul."

"She's being very much like Minette, isn't she?"

"My God. Arlington." The words burst out, embarrassingly desperate. "What am I to do with the girl?"

"First of all, you've got to stop this nonsense about her being a girl. She's not a girl. She's a woman, and you've married her."

"She's like a sister to m—"

"She's not your sister," Arlington interrupted. "You've suffered enough guilt and self-denial, don't you think? And now you're making her suffer too." His friend leaned on the sill, as dangerously insightful as ever. "Your father will die soon, and his dark cloud of a legacy will be gone. Don't brew more storms in its place."

August pursed his lips. To liken his childhood to a "dark cloud" was rather inadequate to describing life as Barrymore's only son. His father had been angry. Stern. Violent. "I can't wait for him to die," he said.

"I know. And when he is gone, you shall be Barrymore in his place, with a kind and loving wife, and all your children, whom you will never browbeat or abuse."

August stalked away from the window. Arlington was too direct sometimes, because he'd been a toplofty, wealthy duke for more than half of his thirty-odd years.

"I'm afraid I'm just like my father," he said when he was safely across the room. "I'm afraid of hurting her."

"In what way?" Arlington asked. "In what way could you ever hurt Minette, whom you love so dearly?"

"I could easily hurt her. I have, and I could again. You saw the blood the first night I had her."

"Virgins bleed, August."

"She's so fragile. You don't understand. You've never held her."

"I have. I've hugged her and swung her around and rollicked with her the way all of us did before she was grown. She was strong as ever then, and I don't doubt she's stronger now. You're making excuses." August opened his mouth to speak, but Arlington held up a hand to silence him. "No. I don't want to hear any more about sex and Minette."

"You see? It's not only me."

"It *is* only you, because she's your wife, and *you* need to figure things out." He turned back to gaze out the window. "Look at her. She's a remarkable woman and she's all yours. Me, I've got to marry some Welsh stranger I've never even seen."

"What's this?" said August. "You're to be married?"

"A request from the king, but more like an order. Some favored border baron's got to be rewarded with a high-placed duke for a son-in-law."

"What a disaster," August said. "I'm sorry. When is this happening?"

"When the crown orders it to happen, I suppose." Nothing betrayed the duke's feelings on the matter, except perhaps the steady tapping of a finger upon the sill. "It's just as well. The rest of you have married. It's bloody boring to gad about all by myself. The women in Wales are pretty, aren't they?"

August hadn't any idea what women in Wales looked like. He imagined they looked rather similar to English ladies, at least he hoped so, for Arlington's sake.

"So you see," said his friend. "At least you've got a known quantity, a willing and eager minx who adores you beyond measure, whom you've known more than half of your life."

129

August wished he could explain what it was like, to lie beside Minette night after night, and want her and ache for her, and feel too conflicted to have her. It was a special sort of torture, one he had probably earned.

Minette made her way toward her husband's study after dinner, with ropes of ribbon and garland on her arms. The servants had decorated some of Barrymore House's rooms, but Lord August's study was not among them. When she asked why, they told her it was not normally decorated for Christmas.

Minette didn't care. She wished to brighten his quiet, private space. August spent a great deal of time at work in there, and she wanted it to look cheerful for the holidays. If she couldn't embroider a passable handkerchief, at least she could give him this.

She grinned at a footman as he bowed and opened the door, and then shut it behind her. Her husband sat at his desk, just where she expected to find him, but he wasn't working. Why, he wasn't even awake. His head was cradled on his pinstriped evening coat; the flickering candles reflected off his ebony hair.

She dropped her armful of greenery onto a chair and rubbed herself where the needles had abraded one wrist. She regarded August, feeling the usual fond fluttering in her heart. Or her stomach. Or somewhere down there. Even asleep, sprawled gracelessly upon his writing desk, the man was handsome as sin. She tiptoed closer, being careful not to wake him. She had long ago memorized every feature, every eyelash, every wave of hair upon his head, but that didn't stop her from staring at him daily, hoping to notice more.

How long and curved his lashes were, and my, how tired he looked. Perhaps it was only the shadow of candlelight that wrought dark circles beneath his eyes. His elegant hand still held a quill. It had nearly slipped from his fingers. She worried that his correspondence would be ruined if ink dripped upon it. She thought to slide the quill from his hand, but then became distracted looking at the page. Why, it was not correspondence. It was music, pages of it spread across the desk, each measure filled with notes penned by his own hand.

Her husband was a composer.

A cabinet door stood open beyond his shoulder. Drawn by curiosity, she skirted the desk and peeked inside, and found more pages of music, both loose and bound into volumes. This was not a recent lark, to jot down some song. Good gracious, there was so much!

Beneath the cabinet, a drawer was partly ajar. It was full of music too, in the same bold, heavy hand. Some of the bound pages had titles and dates. *Concertos One and Two, 1788. Sonata et Fugue, 1785. Etude in Red, 1777.* Why, he would have been only thirteen or fourteen then.

She stared at the complex arrangements of notes, wondering if her brother and his friends knew of this talent. If so, they'd never discussed it in her hearing. She tried to read one of the sheets as he'd taught her, analyzing it for tempo and tone. She wished to go play some of the music, even though most of it appeared too intricate for her modest talents. What a lovely motivation to get better. Someday she would play all of it, every single note. She opened the cabinet above to leaf through more of the handwritten music. If she could find some piece he'd written at eight years of age or so, perhaps she could perform that.

She took out a folio of work and the lined papers slipped from within, scattering over the floor. "Bother," she whispered. She didn't want him to wake, especially now, when she was snooping through his cabinets. She knelt to collect the scattered pages, but they were all out of order. She started to stand but—*ow!*—she knocked her head into the open cabinet door above her, sending it with a bang against the shelf. She clutched at the volumes of music to retain her balance and ended up knocking them over in a cascade of noisy thumps.

August startled awake and turned to her in alarm. "Minette. What are you doing?"

She might pretend to be sleepwalking. It would explain the mess she'd made of his music and exonerate her from blame, but she was too disarrayed to lie. She rubbed the back of her head. "I'm sorry I woke you. I was poking about where I should not be. I suppose I deserve this bump on my head."

He stood and smoothed the back of her hair, and inspected her scalp for injury. His light, seeking caress raised goose bumps on her arms and neck.

"I came to decorate your study for Christmas," she said. "I found you asleep over your music and I saw the open cabinet, and then I—"

"Then you started sorting through all my private papers and ended up flinging half of it on the floor," he finished in exasperation.

"Not half of it. And I intend to pick up what I've dropped and put it back in order for you."

She whacked her head on the cabinet again as she bent to retrieve the music. August muttered an oath and lifted her bodily away from the mess. "Go sit over there." He pointed to a chair on the other side of the desk.

"But I would rather help."

"I don't want you to help. I want you to obey me before you crack your head open."

He didn't sound in a pleasant mood at all. Well, she had woken him from a sound sleep and made a mess of his music, so she supposed she wouldn't feel pleasant either if she was in his position.

He shuffled the music heedlessly together, jamming it back into various folios. She wanted to tell him to take care, but was wary of irritating him further. The *WAR* paddle was in the desk's bottom drawer.

"I never realized you wrote music," she said instead. "And so much of it. What a fascinating hobby."

He made a grunt of a sound, shoving some folios back into the cabinet.

"I didn't mean to pry and disorganize everything, I only couldn't believe there were drawers full of it. If you like, I'll stay up and organize it for you, perhaps by date?"

"No," he said, and this time it was more like a growl.

"What sort of music were you writing tonight?" she asked, wishing to mollify him. "And how do you write it in here with no instrument? Why don't you write in the ballroom, at the pianoforte?"

He rubbed his forehead, rearranging a pair of pages. "I hear it in my head by this point. I know all the notes and how they sound in various combinations."

This was a brilliant talent, surely. How had she never known about his gift for composition when she had uncovered everything else about him, down to the name and direction of his favored courtesan? "I can barely believe how skilled you are, to play and write, and know all the notes in your head like some kind of musical savant. Why, you ought to be part of a show, a revue where people request a song and you instantly and perfectly play it, only by ear. I saw something like that once, I don't remember when, but Warren took me and everyone was so impressed and clapped for the gentleman, although he wasn't much to look at, or even a titled person—"

"I don't want to be part of any shows. I'm not some dancing bear."

The heat in his voice silenced her. She had truly angered him with her meddling. "I'm sorry. I never said you were a dancing bear. You look nothing at all like a bear, of course, and you certainly don't play like one. If it annoys you, I won't peek into your music cabinets again."

"I'd prefer that you didn't."

"But..." She was really pushing it now. She could see it in his taut expression. "Aren't you proud that you write music? Wouldn't you like to share it with someone? Perhaps you can play some of your compositions at our next dinner party."

"No, I don't think so." His voice softened at her crestfallen expression. "I suppose it's difficult for you to understand, but my music is a very personal and private thing, hence my decision to write it in here, privately, and not share it with the rest of the world."

"I only wonder if I might hear something you've written. I admire you so. I imagine it's wonderful music, but it's too far above my abilities to play it. Will you play some of it for me? Perhaps the one you like the best, your most favorite composition."

"I'd rather not. It's late."

It hurt her terribly that he wouldn't play his music for her. Did he dislike her so much? "Well, of course you needn't play for me if you don't want to," she said glumly. "I'll just put up a few decorations—"

"I don't want you to clutter my study. We don't decorate in here."

"Ever?"

His eyes fell on the pile of holiday trimmings on the chair near the door. "I'm sorry. The servants ought to have told you."

She didn't want to admit that they had, and that she'd disregarded their instructions. He was already irritated enough. "Perhaps just a bit of holly over the fireplace."

He thought a moment. "All right. If you want."

She went to fetch the prettiest, glossiest holly bough of the bunch. August sat and looked at the music he'd fallen asleep on, then shuffled it into a pile and turned it over. "Are you having trouble?" she asked as she returned.

He blinked at her. "Trouble?"

"With the music?" She smiled, hoping to fortify him. "It's so difficult to do anything at the holidays, with the calls and invitations, and gifts to purchase, and friends to have over for dinner." She arranged the holly carefully over the hearth. *Joy and peace*, she thought. *Bring them to him.* "Will we go to any entertainments this season?" she asked, turning back to him. "Perhaps it's insensitive to ask, with your father so ill. I ought to just leave you alone."

"Do you want to go to entertainments?"

He looked so tired sitting there at his desk. "No," she said quickly. "We don't have to. We shouldn't, I suppose."

"It's not your fault my father's ailing. You should go to some balls or dinners with Warren and Josephine. I'm sure they'd be delighted to take you, especially now that Aurelia and Townsend have left town for their country estate."

"You won't come too?"

"I might. It depends on the day."

Minette bit her lip. Warren and August were still not at ease with each other, so no, he probably wouldn't come.

Her husband stared down at the pile of pages before him. "Things will get better, Minette. Next year, next Christmas we'll have a great dinner and a ball. Would you like that? We'll have a house party in the country and invite all our friends, and have decorations and dancing, and a yule log in every room."

"That sounds very warm and wonderful."

He smiled, and a little of the tension inside her uncurled. He wasn't angry about the music anymore, only anxious and busy and terribly sad about his father. "Next Christmas will be better," she agreed. "Yes."

"Will you come and give me a kiss before you go?"

"You ought to come to bed too. You look tired."

"I'll come up soon."

Minette crossed to him. A hug, a kiss. She got them more now, but they were always the same—rigidly restrained and lacking in passionate desire. His arms came around her, embracing her as a brother might embrace a sister. Near the end, he brushed a hand through her hair.

"Is your head all right?"

"My head?" she asked.

"From the bump. Are you perfectly all right?"

No. I think I need a real kiss to heal me. But since that awful night when she'd had tried to pleasure him like a wanton, he'd kept her at arms' length, so much that she feared to be bold again.

"I'm perfectly all right," she said in a perfectly cheerful voice. "Everything is perfectly well."

"I'm glad. And thank you," he said, hugging her tighter. "For reading to my father and decorating my study, and for making me smile when I don't feel like smiling."

Minette smiled back at him, because she knew it was what she ought to do.

Chapter Thirteen: A Complex Melody

Minette put her fork down and looked around the table at her brother and his wife, and the Duke of Arlington.

"And then Lady Barrymore told me, in her ghastly warbling voice, 'I wish for you to bear many heirs, Wilhelmina. Many fine boys, and girls too, *if you must have them.*'"

Josephine and her brother burst into laughter as Minette related choice snippets of the conversation she'd had with her mother-in-law the night before. "What did you reply?" asked Josie, who sat beside her.

Minette waved a hand. "Oh, something polite and boring about not having a choice in the matter. One can never think of the proper cutting response until the opportunity has passed."

Arlington chuckled from his place across the table, poured himself more wine, and lifted a glass. "To Minette, for being polite and boring in the face of tiresome old ladies."

"Hear, hear," echoed Warren and Josephine.

Minette laughed at their silly accolade. She'd missed being silly. She'd missed these casual dinners with the Warrens, when all of them gathered around one end of the table and traded funny tales. It was good to be together again, although Townsend and Aurelia were gone to the country already to prepare for their baby, and August had been unable to attend.

It was such a relief to be away from Barrymore House that Minette felt she could breathe freely for the first time in weeks. A disloyal thought, but it was only one dinner, and August said she ought to go and take some holiday cheer where she may.

"I wish August might have joined us tonight," she said, as the footmen came to clear the ravaged dessert plates. "Lady Barrymore could not spare him."

"I imagine the truth is that he didn't wish to face me," said Warren. "What a coward he's become."

"He's not a coward." Minette frowned at her brother. "And the 'truth' is that he stayed back to be with Lady Barrymore because she's feeling poorly. If he doesn't want to be around you, perhaps it's because you've treated him badly when you ought to have been a friend."

Arlington arched a fine, bronze brow. "I believe you've just had a scold, Warren."

Her brother frowned back at her. She didn't wish to annoy him. She loved him beyond measure, but she loved her husband too and she couldn't bear to hear him disparaged.

"Do you really think I've treated him badly?" Warren asked.

"Yes, I do," said Minette. "I think you've made him feel defensive and ashamed at every opportunity. It wouldn't hurt for you to extend him an olive leaf."

"An olive branch?"

"Whatever. Branch, leaf. Whatever will make the two of you stop glowering at one another."

"Oh, my dear," sighed Arlington. "They glowered at one another long before you and August wed."

"I think I've shown admirable patience," said her brother, sitting up straighter in his chair. Josephine laid a hand on his arm, which he appeared not to notice. "Considering his behavior toward you, both before and after you married, I think I've exhibited a great deal of restraint. I ought to have called him out the very day he ruined you. I may still call him out."

Arlington looked heavenward and Josephine tsked. Minette bristled, standing from her chair. "You most certainly will not. If you do, I'll stand right in front of him so whatever you do to him, you can very well do to me first."

"You would take a pistol shot for him?"

"Of course I would."

Josephine broke into appreciative applause. Warren muttered to Arlington, "She is never polite and boring when she converses with me."

"But it's wonderful that she's in love," said Josephine, taking Minette's hand. "I find it very romantic that you should stand between your husband and brother and be shot, or run through with a sword, or whatever grisly method they chose to settle their accounts."

"There will be no settling of accounts," Minette insisted.

"Josephine, please, don't work her up." Warren held out a hand to her. "Minette, come here and give me a kiss."

She went to her brother's side, into his arms that felt so familiar. He kissed her on the forehead and then held her face between his palms.

"I won't call out your husband. As long as you're happy, I'm happy." He said this lightly, but his deep blue eyes searched hers. "Are you happy?"

"Of course I am." She looked away so he couldn't study her too closely. He'd mistake the tiniest bit of doubt as a very big deal. He turned from her and smiled at his wife, a smile which seemed especially...loving. Dear Josephine was only three months from having her baby. She was round and glowing and so pretty. No wonder Warren looked at her that way. If only August would stare at her so, with such admiration and longing. Perhaps if he was happier, more at ease in his life. Minette kept thinking about his musical expertise, and how much good it might do her husband to bring his secret talents into the light of day. Why, he would surely begin to feel more proud and content, and happier in general. Even better, he'd be grateful to her for giving him that wifely little push.

Minette cleared her throat and drew back from her brother's embrace. "I have a question for you, Warren, and you too, Arlington. Did you know August composes music?"

"I didn't," said Warren. "I knew he played, but I didn't know he wrote."

"He composes music?" Arlington asked. "What sort of music?"

"Concertos and symphonies and sonatas, mountains of them," said Minette. "He's written them all by hand, marking the notes and measures and various notations with his own pen. There are pages and pages of it at the house."

Arlington and Warren looked at each other, genuinely shocked.

"How difficult that must be," Josephine said, "to write entire concertos."

"I think he could be famous if he wanted, as famous as Mozart or Bach," Minette told them. "I've brought some of his work to show you, only a fraction of what's there. He's got cabinets full."

"Cabinets, eh?" asked Warren. "Wherever does he find the time?"

"He doesn't sleep much these days."

Warren and Arlington exchanged another look. Minette crossed to the side table to fetch the portfolio she'd snuck out of the house. Not that August would object to her sharing the music with his friends. Well, he probably wouldn't object. If only he were not so shy about his talents, when he ought to be proud!

"I was hoping you might play it for me and tell me what you think," she explained. "You know, whether it was good enough to be published by the music printers. August has been so tense and distracted lately, and sad about his father. I thought it might cheer him to see his music in the shops. Why, our friends might buy it, and play it in their parlors, and congratulate him on what a clever musician he is."

Warren looked doubtful, but when he opened the leather case and saw all the pages of musical notation, his expression changed. "Blast," he murmured. "This is a full bloody suite."

Josephine chided him for his language, but Minette felt a secret thrill that the dense display of notes had shocked and impressed her brother. "Arlington?" Warren said, looking up. "I never had a hand at music. Play it for us, will you?"

The duke took the pages, flipped through them with a rustle of lace cuffs, then headed through the dining room into the parlor beyond. He sat at the pianoforte, arranging the music as Josephine and Minette settled on the divan. "Turn pages for me?" Arlington asked Warren.

"Yes, Your Grace," Warren muttered. "If you can't be bothered to turn them yourself."

"Very good. I may be a bit out of practice," he said.

He began to play, and Minette thought that it sounded awfully fine, even if Arlington was out of practice. The piece began with lyrical stately chords, easy for the duke's long fingers. These soon transformed to a complex melody, a beautiful arrangement of notes. Louder, softer, slower, faster. Arlington smiled as he played a particularly dramatic bit.

"I say, this is grand." He paused as Warren was late turning a page.

"Do you know, he doesn't even write it at the pianoforte?" said Minette. "He hears it all in his head."

"Even with you chattering in the background?" teased her brother.

The piece lightened, notes tripping over one another in a dizzying cascade of harmony. Arlington stumbled, stopped, squinted at the page, and tried again twice before he got through the sequence. "Damn him," he said with good nature. "No pity for the clods who have to play it."

Josephine listened in awe. "It's amazing, Minette. You must be so proud of your husband."

Minette felt a flush of pleasure rise in her cheeks. It wasn't her place to be proud, for she hadn't written the music, but she was indeed very proud on her husband's behalf. When Arlington came to the end of the first movement, he stopped and cracked his fingers while Warren leafed through the rest of the folio.

"You say he has more like this?" asked Warren.

"Yes, so much more. I wish everyone could hear it."

"Indeed, it's a fine piece of music," said Arlington. "But it must be August's decision to share it with the world."

Minette felt the first pangs of conscience, that she had brought this music here without her husband's permission. "He doesn't wish to show it to anyone," she confessed. "I only hate that no one knows how talented he is. Why, I didn't know until I found him composing in his study, and he pretended it was nothing, a trifling pastime. I think he can be...shy."

"I think he can be stubborn," said Warren. "If he doesn't want to share his music, he won't."

"But he should."

"Yes, he should," said Arlington, looking back at the music. "It's a shame not to share such work."

"Poor Minette," said Josephine. "It's difficult when you don't agree with your husband. I also believe he ought to share his talents with the world, and perhaps one day you can convince him to do so. That's what makes a good marriage, you know—looking out for your partner and helping them become the most whole and full person they can be."

Warren sat on Josephine's other side and caught her in an embrace. "I've made you whole and full, haven't I?" he joked, smoothing a hand over her rounded belly. Josephine grinned back at him, her cheeks going pink in a spreading blush.

The two of them were so in love, Minette could hardly bear to look at them. Even Arlington, the rakish bachelor, seemed charmed by their display.

Please, Minette thought. *Please let August love me this way too. Someday. Some way. Let him make me whole and full, and let me make him happy.*

God, yes. Happy most of all.

Minette arrived home in a vexing state of delight mixed with devastation. She was delighted that she'd had a wonderful evening with her brother and her sister-in-law, and that Arlington had been kind enough to play some of August's concerto before he headed off.

She was devastated because August's music was even more beautiful than she'd imagined it would be.

Nothing seemed right in her life, although she ought to be happy. Why, she might be Lord Barrymore, dying of a horrible, painful disease that had rendered him insane. She might be Lady Barrymore, about to lose her husband. She might be August, about to lose his father, and married to an annoying wife. How selfish she was, to feel sad when everyone around her was suffering so much.

She must go to her husband and see how his evening had gone with Lady Barrymore, and inquire how his father fared, but first she must replace the music she'd taken before it was missed. She made her way to the study, the folio tucked securely beneath her cloak. She pushed open the door, finding the fire low and the desk empty. Thank goodness. She scurried over to the cabinet, opening the correct drawer and putting the music back exactly the way she'd found it.

"Minette."

She froze. August's voice drew out her name's two syllables in exasperation. She turned to find him frowning at her from a couch against the far wall.

"Why did you have my music with you?" he asked. "Why did you take it from this room without my permission?"

"Well... I was only..." *Think, Minette.* "I thought... I was going to look through it and perhaps find a passage I was capable of playing."

141

"You've been away all evening."

"I was going to...try to...play it at my brother's."

He looked at her in a very hard way. "I know you took it to your brother's, and I know you showed it to all of them. Arlington came to see me afterward. Imagine my surprise when he told me he'd just played some of my work."

"He did a very good job of it. Not a perfect job. He said he was out of practice, but I still thought it sounded wonderful."

"Oh, he had plenty to say about how wonderful it was, and how I ought to sell it to the music publishers, and put on concerts, and other such nonsense that sounded a lot like something you would say."

"None of it's nonsense," she said, sticking out her chin. "I knew you would never show them, and so I thought I had better do it for you."

"You thought that, did you?" he asked in a low and frightening voice. He stood and crossed his arms over his chest. "Even after I warned you to leave it alone?"

"You didn't really say so, did you? Not in so many words."

"Come here." His voice sounded very sharp now. Minette edged instead toward the door.

"I didn't mean any harm," she insisted. "I was trying to make you happier."

"Happier? You know what would make me happier, Minette? A wife who obeys me. A wife who doesn't lie and sneak about and go expressly against my wishes in order to do whatever she pleases. A wife who doesn't visit courtesans or browse my friend's lurid book collection or steal my music to show others. A wife who doesn't run from me!"

Minette nearly made it out of the room before he grabbed her and hauled her back. He kicked the door shut with a resounding bang and pulled her over to the couch.

"I'm sure you won't wish to punish me in such a tumultuous mood," she said, struggling to remain upright.

If only he were not so much stronger than her. He bent her over his lap and gathered up her skirts before she could catch a breath, much less plead her case.

"You wish me in a less tumultuous mood?" he asked, corralling her arms behind her back. "You're fortunate you weren't here earlier, when

Arlington visited and rang a peal over my head. *Why didn't you tell us? Why aren't you in the concert halls? Why don't you hold a recital next season at my house?"*

"I think that sounds like a wonderful idea."

August must not have agreed. He commenced to punish her bottom with a series of stinging spanks. "It is *not* a wonderful idea," he said. "I told you very clearly my music is private. If I wished to share it with Arlington and the Warrens, and all of bloody London, then I would have. But I haven't, have I? And I doubt I ever will." As he lectured, he spanked her again and again, sharp, firm cracks on either cheek.

"You are not being fair," Minette cried.

"I'm being entirely fair. You've behaved poorly and disobeyed me— again. How many times is it now?"

"But I only wanted—*oww!* I was only trying to do a good thing, so I think it is very cruel of you to punish me for it." He disregarded her pleas and dealt her a firm blow to the underside of her bottom. "Ow! Oh, please!"

She tried to shield herself but he caught her hand and held it in an unforgiving grip. "If you don't wish to be punished," he said, "then the solution is simple. Learn to obey me."

"*Ow!* Please, I hate that you are doing this to me when I only meant to do a thoughtful thing for you. You're not being fair. You're not listening to me."

"On the contrary, I think you're not listening to me." He righted her and set her before him, grasping her wrist when she tried to pull away.

"I meant to help! I was p-proud of you!" She forced the words out between sobs and tears. "I love you and I'll keep doing whatever my love prompts me to do. I don't care if you spank me a million times for it. I don't care if all you do is spank me for the rest of our lives. If that's all you'll give me, then that's what our marriage shall be. I shall do what I think is best and you can spank me forever if it suits you. I don't care!"

"I'm not going to spank you forever," he said, giving her a shake. "At some point I'm going to take you back to Oxfordshire and leave you there."

She slapped him. Hard. She hadn't meant to. In fact, she'd never slapped a man in her life, but she slapped August with tremendous force across his cheek and shouted, "Why won't you love me?"

He let her go, and she backed away from him, shocked by her own behavior. He scowled at her, holding a hand to his face. She felt as if she were falling to pieces. Tears flowed from her eyes, tears of endless angst and frustration. "Don't look at me like that," she shouted. "I've tried and tried, but no matter what I do, you look at me in that awful, damning way. It is very hard not to be accepted and loved for who you are. I'm your wife, and you won't touch me. Your mother won't call me by my name. You friends think I am ridiculous, a mere girl whom you were foolish to marry. I suppose you wish you had married perfect Lady Priscilla, but I cannot wish the same. I don't care if you hate me. *I still want you.*" Her voice broke as he glared at her. She could see the red marks of her fingers on his cheek. "I will always want you. I suppose that is the most depressing thing of all."

"Why will you not understand?" he yelled back. "I don't hate you. I'm trying to protect you."

"From who?"

"From yourself! From your misguided efforts to court my affections. You don't know the sort of man I am, not really. You see me as this figure of fantasy, this hero who doesn't exist. You don't know my darkness, my failures. You don't know the things I want to do to your body, the ways I want to possess you. You don't want me, Minette, I promise."

"Yes, I do."

He turned from her and strode toward the door.

"Don't leave me." Her anguished plea echoed off the walls. Minette could talk to anyone about anything, but she couldn't think what to say to make him stay with her. There were no polite and cheerful words to heal this agonizing rift.

"Please stay," she cried. "Please kiss me. Please hurt me. Spank me if you must, but don't make me live this way, cold and alone, when I am married to the man I love most on earth. And I do love you, Method Randolph. Do not dare say that I am childish and young, and that I don't know, and that I don't understand. I understand everything."

He turned from the door. "You understand nothing." He stalked to her and took her head roughly between his fingers. "I dream of you every night, and God, how I suffer for it. I dream of fucking you, holding you down and grasping your delicate little neck." As he said this, he gripped

144

her throat hard enough to make her gasp. "I dream of riding you so hard that you plead with me and cry out for mercy, and it fills me with such pleasure, to imagine how desperate you'd sound. I dream of tying you to my bed and invading every inch of your body as you struggle to get away."

She thought a moment, really thought about these fantasies and how she felt about them. She stared into his stormy hazel eyes and said, "I would never try to get away from you."

He ground his teeth. "Damn you, Minette."

"I wouldn't," she insisted. "Nothing you say is frightening to me. You can tie me up if you like, but I wouldn't try to get away from you. I want your passion and your torment. I already know what you're like, August. Why do you think I've loved you all these years?"

He pressed his forehead to hers and let out a long, haggard breath. "You're so foolish, so reckless. You don't know."

"If you keep saying that, I'm going to kick you."

He turned from her and went to the fire, and leaned against the mantel. He ran a hand through his hair so it stood on end, which gave him the look of a madman. Was she driving him crazy?

"The spankings are nothing," he said. "The intimacies I want are so much worse."

"Would you have done such things to Priscilla?"

"No. I wouldn't have wanted them with Priscilla. I want them with you." He passed a hand over his face. "But I shouldn't. I don't want to."

"But you do." Minette felt a warmth of joy spread through her body at the realization. "You want them with me. *You want them with me.*"

He gave her such a look then. A look of anger and shame, and restrained longing that burned to her very soul, burned even hotter than the fire dying in the grate.

"Minette—" His voice cut off as a crisp knock sounded at the door. "Not now," he yelled.

"My lord, please." The servant's voice sounded desperate. "You are needed at once."

"What it is?" He crossed to open the door.

The butler stood there, all color drained from his face. "I am so sorry, my lord. A thousand pardons for the interruption, but...it is Lord Barrymore." He swallowed hard. "My lord, you must come. You must hurry, before it's too late."

Chapter Fourteen:
Lost

Charles Ulysses Randolph, the eighth Marquess of Barrymore, took his last breath just after midnight. It was not a peaceful breath but a gasp choked with blood and vomit, as his father's body convulsed in seizures which could no longer be controlled. Only August and the physician were there to witness these last throes of agony, as his mother had taken a numbing dose of laudanum and retired in the care of her lady's maid. "Drape the house in black," he said to the servants when he emerged from the death room. "We'll make arrangements in the morning."

Then he went to the ballroom, sat at the pianoforte, and began to play.

Strange how, no matter his anxiety or sadness, his fingers could always play. Music soothed him as nothing else could ever soothe him, except perhaps Minette, but he didn't deserve her, not after he'd punished her tonight for the high crime of admiring his talent. What was wrong with him? Why couldn't he behave as a proper, affectionate husband when he loved her so much? He could make excuses about their past, and the pressures related to his father's illness, but now his father was gone. What was he to do?

For now, he would lose himself in music. He played for two hours without stopping, played dirges and dire, noisy, ugly things he'd written. *For you, father. Let me play you from this world with a bit of angry hate.* This instrument had been his first great love, the keys so soft and smooth, the vibrating sound of each note like an aural caress.

Minette was his second great love, and his most complicated one. He wanted her to stay the innocent Minette forever, at the same time he wanted to grasp and invade her, and fuck her to oblivion. She wouldn't resist him if he did. That was the worst part. She desperately wanted him to take her.

He left off in the middle of a song and began a new composition, one as light and complex as his wife. He added some blonde curls to the melody, to go with the deep blue undertone of her eyes. Some chattering chords and a bright sally of conversation to make him smile. It was still so hard for him to smile. His face would never be used to it. He stopped and played a section again, trying to commit it to memory so he might write it down later. Or perhaps he'd write something entirely different. A song about Minette ought to be a little different every time.

To amuse himself, or perhaps punish himself, he made up an accompanying song for himself. An August song, or, now, a Barrymore song, stark and grim, lacking any sort of beauty. Banging chords. *Don't touch my music, Minette, or you might manage to touch me.* He was mashing away at the keys like a peevish child when her voice came out of the shadows.

"August?"

He stopped and turned to find her in the darkness, looking light and pale as ever in a stark black dressing gown. In mourning already, was she? It seemed he had been in mourning his entire life.

"I don't know if you want to be alone," she said in a voice that was much more muted than her normal one.

He held out a hand to her. "Come."

She flew to his side and embraced him, and erupted in tears. They wet his cheek, reminding him of her tears from earlier. How miserable he'd made her ever since they'd wed. "The servants told me," she bawled. "They said your father has died. I'm so sorry."

He held her against him, wondering how she could weep so hard for a man she barely knew, when all he could do was play angry songs.

"Are you awfully distraught?" she asked. "What can I do to help you?"

"You ought to be asleep." He didn't know why he said such a thing. He sounded cold and emotionless, like a man with no heart. "I mean, it's very late. I'm not distraught, my love," he reassured her, wiping away her tears.

147

"I wish there was something I could do. I hate that lives must end and people must die." She bit her lip hard, as if trying to compose herself. "And the way you played...I was terribly afraid you were upset. I made this for you for Christmas but perhaps...well... I thought I would give it to you now." She produced a folded silk handkerchief from her pocket and pressed it into his hand. He looked down at the thing and spread it open, smoothing the fabric between his fingers. One corner had been painstakingly—if messily—embroidered with an *M*.

"The *M* is for Method," she reminded him. He could barely make out the letter's shape, but he didn't care. She had made it, and so he would always treasure it.

For him, the *M* would always stand for Minette.

"This is my most favorite gift I've ever received," he said, turning it over in his hand. "And it's a perfect gift for a sad night like tonight. The stitching is very fine. It must have taken a great deal of work."

"Not so very much." She pulled nervously at her dressing gown. "I thought of you while I was embroidering it, and bound some hope into the stitches. I wished you greater happiness, because you've had such a bleak time of late." Her voice trembled on the last words, and she began to cry again. "I'm so sorry for your loss. What can I do?"

Now that he had a handkerchief, he could more efficiently mop up her tears. He brushed at her cheeks thinking how pretty she was, even when she was tearful. "Will you sit with me while I play?" he asked. "And hold my new handkerchief so it doesn't go missing?"

"Of course." She accepted the dampened square of silk, pressing it to the corners of her eyes. "I'll stay as long as you need me. I love to hear you play."

He had always preferred to play alone, but now he was grateful for her solid warmth beside him. He didn't want to be alone tonight. As he began another piece, the ballroom seemed filled with a thousand ghosts, all of them his father, shouting and striking and stalking around. For once, Minette didn't chatter. He was the one who began to speak.

"I wrote this composition when I was very young." He did an elegant glissade. "I suppose I began to write music as an escape."

"An escape from what? All those sisters?"

"No." August's lips cracked in a smile. "My sisters were a trial, but nothing like my father. Barrymore had...rages." For a moment he felt like an eight-year-old boy again, that fearful, wary boy just coming to understand that his father was never going to change. "He hated me from the day I was born."

"I'm sure that's not true." Minette sounded horrified. "It was only his sickness."

"This was before...before his sickness. He was very selfish and full of himself, a gruff and unpleasant fellow. He was never happy." August punctuated this revelation with a series of minor chords. "I don't suppose you can fathom such a thing. Warren raised you so expertly. You have always been a very happy girl. Woman. Excuse me," he amended when she frowned. "Of course you are a woman now, but happy all the same."

"I try to be happy." She huddled closer and looked up at him. "Warren always said that was my gift to bring to the world."

"It is a gift," August agreed. "And not everyone has it. My father didn't. His gift to the world was anger and violence."

He didn't know why he said such things to her, when it would only upset her. In some way it was a confession. *This is what I come from. This is why I can't love you the way you'd like.*

This is why I'm so afraid of hurting you.

"It must have been awful to grow up with such an unpleasant person," said Minette, clutching her handkerchief tighter.

"Yes. Awful." Did he sound nonchalant? It had never been an easy thing, living through his father's rages. Music alone could mollify the bully. When August was at the pianoforte, Barrymore let him be.

"I remember the first time I saw him hit my mother," said August, starting into a more contemplative piece. "He was spitting out oaths, battering her with punches and kicks even though she was so much smaller and weaker. He caught her by the hair and backhanded her so hard she fell to the floor. It was the most frightening thing I had ever seen, then or since, and I thought..." He gritted his teeth. "I thought I ought to have stopped him but I was too little. Too afraid."

"Oh, August," said Minette. "Of course you were afraid. Did he ever hit you too?"

"Sometimes. Better me than my mother, or my sisters." He remembered fists, screaming, shouting, his mother's tears, his sisters' wide-eyed gazes peeking at him from behind nursery doors as his father punched and kicked him only for being his son. "It was easier to keep him

149

angry at me. As I said, he already hated me. I was never good enough, never smart enough or tough enough for the Barrymore title. He told me so many times that he wished he had another son, one who wasn't an utter and abysmal failure."

"Oh, no. I can't imagine," said Minette, clutching his arm. "He was terribly wrong to do such things. You're a wonderful person, a wonderful man."

August laughed, a short, sharp burst of laughter. Even as his father had taunted and battered him, and declared him an unfit son, August had begun managing the Barrymore estate to protect his mother and sisters' interests. His father could not do it. The man's rages were born of self-loathing and personal failure. By the time August left for school, his father was showing symptoms of the disease that would eventually kill him. The marquess had lost his life years ago to excessive drink and cheap whores.

"It was nice when I got big enough to defend myself, and them," he said. "And of course I had music to get me through the darkest days." He began to play another piece, a sorrowful melody he turned to whenever the hours were bleakest. "I remember the first time I hit my father back. Such a discovery, and such rage."

"Your rage?" asked Minette.

"No. His. He couldn't bear to be bested." He stopped playing, abruptly, in the middle of a sequence. "I'm so glad he's finally dead."

He hadn't realized moisture was leaking from his eyes until Minette dabbed at his cheeks with the handkerchief. Tears! This ignominious development both angered and befuddled him. He hadn't cried the entire time his father was alive, and now that the devil was in hell where he ought to be, he was sniveling like a child.

He forced the tears back, sniffed up snot and feelings and let out a sigh. "So you see, that's why music has always been an escape for me. And an obsession. It's also the reason I'm reluctant to share it with the world. There's a lot of pain and torment within those pages, more than anyone ought to know."

Minette put her arm through his and gazed up at him indignantly. "Why can't anyone know? They *should* know what you suffered. Why didn't you ever tell anyone what was happening within your family? They might have helped you. Does Warren know this? Arlington? Townsend?"

"It's not something you talk about. And they were boys, like me. What do you think they could have done? Warren had his hands full with you, and Townsend with his parents. Arlington was being groomed for his dukedom."

"You ought to have talked about it," she persisted. "Someone ought to have helped you. Your mother's family or friends, or the neighbors, or even the servants. Why, if I had known, I would have come over here and rung such a peal over your father's head. I would have railed at him until he stopped hurting you. And if he didn't stop, I would have gotten Warren's pistols and—"

August placed a finger atop his wife's lips. "This was the same man you insisted on making comfortable at the end of his life. The same man to whom you read novels and poetry in the garden for hours at a time."

She pushed his hand away. "Well, I didn't know then he was the devil. He was suffering so terribly."

"He suffered his whole life." August had realized this long ago, even if it didn't help him. His father had inhabited a miserable, dark existence, which he had taken out on those closest to him. "He was a devil, yes, but also a very tortured man."

"I wish he would not have hurt you." Minette's hand tightened on his arm and her lower lip trembled. "I wish I could have stopped him from hurting you."

August stared back at her, at her cheeks flushed with anger and outrage. She would have gotten Warren's pistols. He didn't doubt for a moment she would have. He wanted to say, *I adore you, and your words mean so much to me. I love you more than anyone else in the world.* But he didn't say that because he was afraid, and jammed up with a thousand emotions that had nowhere to go.

"The thing about my music," he said instead, "is that too many memories live inside it. That's why I got angry when you showed it to my friends. I shouldn't have punished you for taking that piece to Warren's. I regret that I behaved so unreasonably when I should have accepted your compliments with grace." He clenched her handkerchief between his fingers. "Will you forgive me?"

"Of course. I will always forgive you. I suppose you were very wrought up about a lot of things."

He didn't want her to excuse his behavior. There was no excuse. He had behaved exactly like his father this night, yelling at her and hurting her because of his own fearful weaknesses. Minette was always using those lavishly committed words...*always, everything, forever.* She loved him. She always had and she always would. By comparison, he was brittle and fragile and incapable of love. He feared he might break into a thousand pieces if she stroked his forearm again.

"You ought to go to bed," he said, turning from her to play another morose composition. "I doubt I'll sleep tonight."

She put her hands over his and stilled them on the keys. "Please, don't play anymore." She swallowed hard as she gazed up at him. "Come to bed."

She meant, *Come to bed and let me help you forget.* He could see it in her posture, in that slight tension. He let himself imagine it for a moment...losing himself, forgetting, releasing his angst and frustration all over her welcoming body. *No.* He dared not go to bed with her, not tonight. "My dear, I wish you would retire and get some rest. I won't be good company."

The light went out of her expression, so she seemed a disappointed angel sitting beside him on his bench. She could not understand his conflict, that he needed her to stay innocent and pure, because she was the only innocent, pure thing that had ever existed in his life.

"But...will you be all right?" she asked. "You will not be too sad? Oh, of course you will be sad. You've just lost your father, although he was a terrible man, from what you've told me. Even so, you must have all manner of feelings to sort out. And that's perfectly all right, you know. Mrs. Everly said she cried for weeks when she lost her first husband, even though she never liked him very much, although in her case I suppose it was more a matter of social incompatibility than any real emotional—"

"Minette." He took her hand to silence her chatter. "I'll try to come to bed in a while," he lied in a gentle voice. He could see in her eyes that she didn't believe him.

"Will you kiss me when you come?" she asked. "So I'll know you're there, and that you're all right?"

"Of course," he lied again. "Of course I will, my love."

Christmas had come and gone, but the decorations were still up, shrouded in black mourning cloth. For days, the house had been full of visitors. His sisters, with sobbing red eyes and screaming children, and their husbands and their families, and his mother's family and his father's relatives down to aunts and uncles and cousins far removed. Townsend had returned to town for the funeral, although Aurelia was too close to her confinement to accompany him. Warren and Josephine had come, and Arlington, and Minette's Aunt Overbrook, who had never spread gossip after all. His mother's friends came, doddering dowagers who shook their heads and clucked about how sorry they were. Sometimes it seemed a thousand people milled about Barrymore's dark halls and parlors as his father lay in state.

August did not know how they had managed to show hospitality to everyone, except that Minette awoke the morning after his father's death and calmly took everything in hand. She had been their saving grace, directing the servants and playing hostess while August flailed in a fog of numb emotion and his mother lay prostrate with grief.

Dear, sweet Minette. Where would they have been without her? She had told charming, heartfelt stories of her limited acquaintance with the marquess, until the ladies were in tears and the gentlemen all clearing their throats. She had put a publicly acceptable shine to the miserable character of his father, and brought brightness and order to the exhausting rituals of mourning. August was not offended by this fiction. He was grateful. As the next Lord Barrymore, he had an interest in maintaining the honor of the name. His mother and sisters, in fact, everyone who had criticized Minette after he jilted Priscilla, remarked how magnificent she was.

In one whirlwind week, Minette had won the *ton*'s regard, smoothed social snarls, and saved his father's legacy. This afternoon, when the last of the guests finally left, he noticed she looked thin and tired, and had dark circles under her eyes.

August was in love with her. He had been in love with her before this past week and all its challenges, but he was more in love with her now. It wasn't the careless, casual love he'd felt for her in years past. It was a new kind of love, fearsome, consuming, deep enough to drown him. This love suffocated him, pulling him under waves of confusion and self-doubt.

Now Warren sat across from him in the library, one leg crossed over the other, a befuddled frown on his face. "You want me to take Minette to Oxfordshire? Why?"

"It's her choice, of course," August replied carefully. "But I thought she might wish to be with Josephine during her lying-in. They've always been such close friends. You should present her with the option."

Warren snorted. "*You* should present her with the option. She's your wife. And as I recall, last time you stowed her in the country, she made her way back to you within the week."

"It's not that I don't want her here." At Warren's daunting look, August stood and began to pace. "It's only that things are in such disarray."

"There is no one better at dealing with disarray than my sister. She kept your household running all week."

"Yes," August said, turning back to him. "She's tired herself out. She'll always tire herself out, as long as there is work to be done, and endless visitors. There are so many tasks yet to be accomplished."

"Such as shunting your wife off to the country."

August sighed and moved to the window. Minette had mended some relationships this past week, but the rancor between him and Warren festered as painfully as ever. "It's not as if I'm trying to get rid of her," he said. "I love her very much."

"Is that so? Have you slept with her yet?"

"I won't discuss that with you."

"That means no," said Warren in a disgusted tone. "She must be going out of her mind, you heartless bastard. There will have to be children, you realize. Minette has always dreamed of children."

"Three months," August said, wondering when the fight had gone out of him. "Three months is all I ask."

Warren took a deep drink of brandy and put his glass down with a bang. "You're a liar. You don't love my sister."

August turned to fix him with a look. "Take care what you say to me, Wild."

Warren pursed his lips at the childhood name. "Help me understand then. You've always cared for her. I know you've a heart under all that bluster and scowling. If you loved her, you would try to make it work. You wouldn't send her away for a second time."

"Barrymore's dead and the house is in mourning. Why must she be here?" He hid his guilt and anxiety in mounting irritation. "She'll enjoy better looking after Josephine. She likes to be helpful."

"And who helps Minette?" Warren snapped. "She's not the same since she married you."

"Nor am I the same," August shot back. "Forgive me for my blundering failure. I wasn't ready to be married, not now, not to her. Forgive me if I haven't transformed into the perfect husband, like you. Like Townsend."

"You can send her off a thousand times, and she'll come back."

"If Josephine asks her to go to Oxfordshire, Minette will go. Three months," August repeated again. "You've been my friend for years, Warren. Help me. Take her with you until I'm better prepared to be her husband." He turned away from the man's grim scowl. "I ought to have spoken to Josephine instead. She would have been more sympathetic to my plight."

"I don't want you talking to my wife."

August turned back in shock. Warren looked surprised too, that he had said such words. But he had said them. This then, was the end of a twenty-year friendship. This judgment and hostility. This open scorn.

"Damn you, then," August said coolly. "Leave your sister here, or take her. Damned if I care."

A knock sounded at the door and Minette swept in, a smiling dove in the midst of two dueling hawks. "I wondered where you both were. Why, how dark it is in here, and both of you swilling spirits. The ladies would like your company, you know." She went to her brother and took his hand. "I know you'll be leaving soon, and I don't want to lose a moment of our time together. I'll miss you and Josephine when you go."

She came to August next and pressed her cheek to his. She was like the cozy, comforting warmth of the winter's fire.

"How pretty you look," he told her. She smelled like flowers. Like pretty lace kept in a scented drawer. "It's true that we're being unmannerly, darling. We ought to join you and Josephine. Has Mother retired?"

As Minette answered in the affirmative, Warren roused himself from his chair, draining the last of his brandy. "Yes, we ought to make the most of our last days," he said in a taut voice. "We'll be leaving by week's end."

"So soon?" asked Minette in dismay.

"Perhaps you'll agree to come with us, if you are not needed here. I'm sure Josephine would like your company as she begins her confinement. You know she's always been a restless sort, and you amuse her to no end."

"Come with you?" Minette slid August a look. He could see the conflict in that small glance. She was so giving—she would wish to help her sister-in-law. But she didn't want to leave him.

You should. You must. I need time...

Always more time.

What a coward he was. He forced a smile and pitched his voice to a light, casual tone. "Of course you must go with Josephine if she needs you. We'll manage here. The worst is over, and winter in London is so bleak."

"But I can't leave you. You'll be here alone."

"There's my mother to settle. And Arlington will be in town, he says. I'll miss you terribly, of course, but this is Josephine's first baby. If Warren agrees it would be all right, I think you ought to go."

Minette twitched restlessly at the front of her gown before looking up again. Were her eyes misted with tears? "What about my piano lessons?" she asked. "Without your help, I'll get terribly rough with my fingering. I may forget everything I've learned."

"I'm sure you won't," he assured her. "Your playing has progressed so beautifully, and Josephine will love hearing you play. Your brother too."

Warren stared at him with a deeply hateful gaze. He wanted to take Minette away now. "You needn't decide right away, mopsy," Warren said, turning to his sister. "We'll be a few days yet, packing up at Park Street. But I daresay Josephine would find you a comfort. Once the baby is born, you can stay a while longer, or return to prepare for the season. With Barrymore House so recently in bereavement, I don't think you'll need to do much."

"Goodness. It just seems..." Minette knit her fingers together, and looked back at August. "It seems so soon for you to be alone," she said meaningfully.

August had shown her a side of him, a tortured, ragged side no one had ever seen. Rather than feel repulsed by him, as any wife ought to, she wished to protect him. August wanted to haul her against him and disappear inside her brightness. He wanted to sob like a child against her neck. But he didn't, because he had to be strong.

"I'll be perfectly fine, if you think it best to go with Josephine," he said in a carefully steady voice. "I'll visit when I can, and we can write one another letters, of course."

If Warren glared at him any harder, he'd bore a hole right through his dinner coat.

If you don't want to be friends, thought August, *we won't be friends.* He had expected this, eventually.

He was growing grievously comfortable with loss.

Chapter Fifteen: Coming To Terms

Minette lay in her childhood bed at Park Street, a place she really ought not to be. Warren and Josephine were leaving tomorrow for Warren Manor, and Minette along with them. Everything was packed and ready to go, but her heart was not prepared.

Her heart wanted to stay here with her husband.

Josephine lay beside her, absently rubbing her rounded belly. Warren had gone out, Minette knew not where. To bid farewell to his gentlemen friends, and settle his accounts in town. His farewell to her husband earlier that evening had been unreservedly icy. She shivered now, remembering it.

"Are you cold, dear?" Josephine pushed more of the blanket toward Minette. "No, you must take it. I'm hot as an oven these days. The baby keeps me nice and cozy."

"I'm not cold." Minette eyed her sister-in-law's seven-month bump. "How does the baby keep you cozy?"

"I suppose it's like cuddling, to have a baby inside you. We're warmer when *we* cuddle, aren't we?" She eased closer to Minette, then took her hand and spread it against her waist. "If you wait like this, you'll feel the baby kick, or turn about. Warren talks to it sometimes in the evenings, and I swear the baby hears."

"He ought to tell it to stop kicking you."

Josephine laughed. "I like when it kicks me. I like to think it's happy and healthy in there, and that everything will go well with the birth."

Minette patted her bump gently. "I'm sure it will go well. And I shall care for you, and run to get you tea and cakes whenever you like, and keep the servants from tucking blankets around you if you're hot. I'm so happy to go with you to Oxfordshire, and help you and Warren with whatever you need."

Josephine gazed at her a moment, with far too astute a look. "You aren't really happy though, are you?"

"Whatever do you mean?" Minette looked away, lest her sister-in-law see the bleak misery in her heart. "I am marvelously happy to stay with you during your confinement," she said with manufactured conviction. "We shall become closer than ever. I've missed you, you know."

"I've missed you too." Josephine squeezed her hand. "But you don't have to come if you don't want to. I think you're sad, darling. I think you want to stay here with August."

"He's Barrymore now," she said glumly. "And there's no reason for me to stay."

"No reason? Why?"

Minette thought she felt a flutter of movement beneath her palm, but it may have been Josephine shifting position. How novel, to think a little niece or nephew was tucked so perfectly inside her friend. "Do you feel like it's a boy or a girl?" she asked.

"Don't change the subject, Minette. Why don't you want to stay with August, or Barrymore, or whoever he is now? You still love him, don't you?"

Minette caressed over Josephine's belly. If only August wanted her, she might have her own baby in a year's time. Their baby, his and hers, together in one blessed package. "I'm afraid it's never to be," she blurted out.

"What's never to be?"

"A baby. A child of our marriage."

"Oh, that takes time," said Josephine. "Sometimes it happens quickly, but sometimes it takes months, even years to conceive."

"No." Minette could feel her cheeks going pink. She ought not to have said anything, but the confession poured out of her. "There can be no possible way for us to have a baby. August won't touch me. Since that first night at the Townsends' house party, we have not... He will not... I have tried, believe me," she said at Josephine's shocked look. "I've tried to entice him, but nothing works."

"Oh, dear." Josephine sat up a bit straighter. "Perhaps he's only been preoccupied with his father's illness."

"Perhaps." Minette left her friend's side and sat on the edge of the bed, hoping Josie couldn't see her blush in the dim candlelight. "I think the real problem is that he never wished to marry me. The sister thing, you know. He's slept beside me only to prevent me sleepwalking, but he won't touch me in any husbandly way. I thought his father's death might bring us closer, but it hasn't. It's as if he's withdrawn even farther into himself. I suppose the truth is that we're not suited to one another, as much as I wished us to be."

"Oh, darling, he loves you. I could see it in his face when he kissed you goodbye."

"Perhaps he loves me in some honorable, necessary manner, but he doesn't *want* me. I irritate him and cause him all sorts of difficulty." She turned back to her friend with a rueful laugh. "When your husband has spanked you more times than he's bedded you, it's a terrible thing."

"He shouldn't be spanking you," said Josephine with a frown. "You should demand a proper honeymoon. No callers, no duties, no clothing whatsoever. Nothing but long hours spent together in bed."

Goodness, that sounded heavenly. Unfortunately, in their case, it was unlikely to happen. "Whenever I demand things," she explained to Josephine, "it puts him in a peevish mood."

"What about your peevish mood? If Warren went two months without..." Now Josephine was the one blushing. "Well, I think your husband's been lamentably derelict in his duties. You are charming and beautiful, and sweet."

"That's the problem." Minette stood and crossed to a low shelf, and opened a small trunk of her childhood keepsakes. "I think he would prefer some experienced woman of the world. He still thinks of me as a sweet young lady, too innocent to be besmirched."

Josephine laughed. "You're not innocent, no. Not since we browsed through Lord Townsend's private literature."

Minette's shoulders slumped. "August spanked me for that too. I suppose if he doesn't want a traditional sort of marriage, I'll have to let it go."

"Oh, Minette."

"No, it's all right. It's better for my heart if I just stop trying. It's become so painful." She sorted through ribbons and dolls, and a set of bells Warren had given her one Christmas. "We ought to take these to Warren Manor for the baby," she said, jingling them. "Your child should hear happy sounds when it's born. I remember how Warren used to sing silly songs for me, and play whatever instruments were around. And, oh goodness, this old doll. Warren brought her to me when I was ten or so. I begged my nurse to help me dress her as a bride, so she might pretend to marry August. There's a veil here somewhere..." She lifted a ragged fluff of lace and went still.

Beneath the scrap of lace lay a porcelain swan with a long, graceful neck. It was her French swan, ivory and pink and gold-flecked, with garish red lips. Her hero Lord August had gifted it to her, and oh, how she'd treasured it. How she had cared for it all these years, so it wouldn't be chipped or broken. *And here I am, already singing a swan song, letting our relationship die.*

"I can't..." she murmured, touching the delicate, curving neck.

"What, darling?"

Minette straightened and turned back to Josephine, holding the precious thing against her breast. "I'm doing it again. I'm not trying hard enough." She remembered so clearly when he had said that to her at the piano. It was one of her very worst faults. "I mustn't give up so quickly on our marriage. I can't sing my swan song already, when it's only been a couple of months."

"Your swan song?" Josephine looked perplexed. "What does that mean?"

Minette took to her feet. "It means I have to go back to Barrymore House right now and talk to August, and try again to make our marriage work. There has to be some way, if only I can find it. I have to keep trying to fix things until I do." She sat beside Josephine with an apologetic look. "Oh, my dear, I'm so sorry. I know I promised to help you with the baby, but..."

Josephine touched the swan and gave Minette an encouraging smile. "I'll have plenty of help with the baby. You're absolutely right, dear sister. It's too soon to resign your marriage to failure. You must go to your husband right this instant and show him that true love never gives up."

August sprawled in the front parlor, in the deep chair before the fireplace. He had an entire bottle of his father's finest brandy beside him, but he couldn't rouse himself to take a drink. He stared at the flames instead, thinking of his song for Minette. The notes came to him like all the other songs, in a persistent repetition, but instead of dark and heavy clamor, he heard phrases as light and lyrical as her soul. He heard her voice in the melody, the pleasing resonance of her chatter.

No, not chatter. He understood now that Minette didn't chatter. Everything she said had meaning, at least to her. She used words to soothe, to explain, to calm, to soften difficulties and make people smile.

August thought he ought to hurl the bottle of brandy into the fire. His mind wanted to do it but his body waited, stiff and unmoving. He was half dead in this body. His fears paralyzed him. *I will hurt her. I will fail her. I'm not worthy of her.*

I will become like my father one day.

"Come back to me." He said it to no one. To the fire. To the air. He didn't even really say it, only muttered it between numb, dead lips. For the thousandth time he tried to imagine himself as the husband he ought to be, cheerful and pleasant, with Minette smiling up at him in her vivacious way. She should not have become his wife. That Robert fellow, with the ginger hair, he would have made her a fine husband. Bancroft, Everett, any of the chaps who'd pined for her, they would have done better than him. Arlington, even. Arlington would have done everything properly and made Minette happy.

Come back to me. Out of all of them, I love you the most.

He fell asleep at some point, waking occasionally at a crackle from the fire. He hoped it would be easier to sleep without her in the bed. Folly. He could sleep better with some brandy. He turned to pour himself some and fumbled the glass, then thought better of things and put the bottle's neck to his mouth. Rich flavor burned down his throat. His father's brandy. His father's glass, embossed with a *B*. He flung the horrid thing into the fire with a satisfying crash. People were starting to call him Barrymore already. He had to make peace with it. He wished to become one of those cold, emotionless aristocrats who never smiled, who never betrayed the least hint of feeling. He'd be hard and icy as frosted glass, so no one could ever shake him. He intended to become that unflappable person, at least in a day or two, when he was finished breaking down.

His father was gone, buried. Why did he still feel his ghost in the room? He saw a motion out of the corner of his eye and gave such a start he nearly dropped the brandy. He put the bottle down and lurched to his feet. No, not his father's ghost, God save him. His wife stood in a black traveling gown with a box clutched to her chest. He felt disoriented, confused. He'd only had a swallow of brandy. She was supposed to be at Warren's, wasn't she, to leave for Oxfordshire in the morning? He had already kissed her goodbye.

"How did you get here?" he asked. "Are you sleepwalking?"

"No, Warren brought me." She took a few steps closer. "He said he wouldn't come in. He's angry, I'm afraid. Not at you. Well, perhaps partly at you, but mostly at me, because it's late and I made a big fuss and forced him to bring me here when he didn't want to."

"You're...not...?" He swallowed hard. "You're not leaving with them in the morning?"

"I know I ought to go for Josephine's sake, but I can't. I had to come back. I—I wanted to show you this."

She crossed the room toward him, becoming more and more real with every step. Minette was back. His heart's jubilation warred with dread.

When she stood before him, she pried open the box's lid. "I found it in my old bedroom at Warren's. I told you I still had it." She gazed up at him with a hopeful, almost desperate look. He had created that desperation, just as surely as he'd given her the porcelain figure nestled in the tissue paper. She took the swan out and held it right up to his nose, as if he might not recognize it otherwise.

My God, she'd really kept it all this time.

"I found it in my little box of treasures." He heard a wobble in her voice, a devastating note of misery. "I have loved you so long, August. I've loved you more than anything and anyone, except perhaps my brother. I've loved you more than my parents, because I never knew them. I loved you before I understood what love was, because there was something special about you."

163

Tears welled in her eyes. He couldn't bear to see them. "You ought to go back to your brother and Josephine," he said roughly.

"I can't. I love you. I never should have left."

"You didn't leave. I encouraged you to go."

"I'm your wife." Her indignant exclamation rang out in the silence. "You're supposed to want me to stay. I love you."

"You shouldn't," he groaned, turning away from her.

She was instantly at his side, tugging at his arm. "I love you, August. Until recently I never understood why, but now I do. There's a secret person inside you who's dark and hurting, who hides away because he's ashamed or afraid or unable to ask for help. But I knew about that person. Do you understand me? I think I knew about him even as a child."

The more she spoke, the more tears overflowed her lids. He stared at those tears, watched them drop onto the swan's glossy back and roll off the painted-on feathers. He wanted her to stop talking. He wanted to clap his hand over her mouth but he knew he'd never silence her. He pulled away instead, and put distance between them.

"I know you, Method," she cried. "And everyone has always said that I was put on this earth to bring brightness to the world, but I think I was put on this earth to bring brightness to you. Because you've lived long enough in this darkness and fear, and sadness, and loneliness—"

"Stop." He threw out a hand. His voice echoed off the paneled walls of the parlor. He turned away so he couldn't see her cry, or perhaps it was so she wouldn't see him cry. *Icy. Emotionless. Frosted glass.* "You don't belong with me," he said. "I have enough darkness inside me to eclipse us both."

"It doesn't matter. I'm not leaving. I'm meant to be with you, to bring light into your world. Don't you see, that's why we belong together, that's why I've always been drawn to you, even though everyone said we were so different."

"You've been drawn to me because you developed some childish fantasy when you were a girl." He spun back to her, eyeing the swan clutched against her chest. "And I encouraged you because yes, I was lonely, and yes, I only had big, mean sisters who taunted and laughed at me. I thought you were cute. A cute little sister. I still think you're cute. I think you're adorable." He said *adorable* in perhaps the cruelest way it had ever been said.

"You treat me like some fragile trinket," she said, advancing on him. "Like this swan, but I'm not a swan. I'm not fragile, I'm not your little sister. I'm not cute and adorable. I'm a grown woman and I want to be your wife. I want you to accept me and let me love you, and bring cheerfulness to your life."

"You can bring all the cheerfulness you want," he shot back in a hard voice. "It's not going to change our unsuitability for each other. It's not going to change who I am."

"It doesn't matter. I love you beyond all reason, beyond all meaning, whether we are suited or not. Why won't you love me back? I want you to love me. *I want you to love me!*"

Her voice had risen over the course of her speech to a level of hysteria, and on the last word, she raised her arm and flung the swan toward him in her fury. In the dismal space between them, it crashed to the floor and shattered into a hundred pieces.

For a second, two seconds, they both stared down at it. "Oh, no," Minette breathed. She rushed, weeping, to the pile of shards.

He hurried to her side and pulled her back. "Don't pick up the fragments. You'll cut yourself."

"It's broken."

"Don't touch it." He carefully extracted one of the larger pieces from her hand. "Don't. Don't cry. I'll get you another one."

She turned to him in a rage. "I don't want another one, damn you. I want you to love me." She pulled her hands from his and beat them against his chest. "I hate you, August. *I hate you!* I hate that you won't love me."

"Minette. Please." He struggled to contain her attack. "I love you. I do."

"You don't." She turned away from him, sobbing as if her heart had broken into more pieces than the swan. "You don't love me. You don't *want* me, and I can't *bear* it."

"Minette." He bore her down against the floor, covering her with his body to make her be still. She twisted away, looking over at the pieces of her broken swan.

"I've loved you forever," she shouted, crying through her anger. "But it hurts too much to be the only one in love, so if you won't love me, then

I'm going to leave you, and then you'll wish that you'd loved me, because no one else will ever love you as much as I do."

It was the truth. It was the raw and brutal truth, every word of it. He let her beat on his chest a moment longer before he captured her wrists and pinned them over her head. With his other hand he took her chin and held her face still, and gazed down at her. "No one will ever love you as much as I do, either," he said. She struggled as he pressed his lips to hers. They half kissed and half fought as he nudged her farther away from the glass. There were tears in her mouth, on her lips, on her cheeks. He licked them away between gentling kisses and nips with his teeth.

"I love you," he said against her lips. "Listen to me, darling. I love you, and you're not leaving."

"Yes, I am. I will." She arched beneath him and kicked, narrowly missing his balls.

"I love you," he insisted. "Until recently I never understood why, but now I do. There's a secret person inside me who's dark and hurting, who hides away because..." His throat closed up. He had hurt her so badly, when she'd understood everything exactly right. "My God, I need you." He gazed into her eyes and forced the words out past fear, past desperation, past suffocating dread. "Please don't leave me. I need you to light the darkness inside me."

She shook her head at him. "I can't be a child anymore. I won't be your little sister."

"No. You're too wise and strong to be mistaken for a child." He realized now it was never her innocence that had confounded his passion, but the fact that she knew so much about him, more than he had ever wanted to admit.

And she had always loved him, darkness and all.

His hands tightened on her wrists, as desire raced through his veins. *She knows me. She loves me. She's mine.* He kissed away a stray tear, and another. He pressed his cheek against hers, then raised his head to tease the corners of her mouth, wondering whether she was going to kiss him back, or kick him again.

She did neither, only gave a little moan and arched her hips. Just like that, his need for her overflowed his control. He took her mouth hard, with all the aching, lustful abandon he'd held so rigidly in check. If she understood his darkness, he prayed she would understand this too.

166

She opened to him with a sigh as he bit her lip and groaned into her mouth. He had bunches of fabric in his hand, bunches of her black gown that he was practically ripping off in his efforts to get at her body.

"I need you," he said. "God forgive me. I need you right now."

Minette sighed and clung to her husband's shoulders as he roughly pushed up her skirts. It was surprising, of course, to be passionately accosted in the middle of the parlor floor after so many weeks of avoidance, but she preferred this to some gentle and solicitous bedding that had nothing to do with his true self. He scrabbled at her laces in the back. She could feel him hard and ready against the front of her, and wondered why he bothered to undress her further.

"Oh, my," she said as he yanked her bodice downward and buried his face between her exposed breasts. That would be why. He kissed and suckled her nipples, creating a hot, wanting feeling even more intense than the first time they'd been together. As he kissed her, his fingers worked at her gown and petticoats, and stays and shift and stockings, pulling all of it away until she lay naked beneath him. When she pressed herself against his chest, he reared back and began to disrobe with frightening alacrity. He shed his coat, waistcoat, and shirt, tossing them into a pile on the floor. She hungrily drank in the sight of his strong, muscled body. *Finally.* Thank God she hadn't given up. His shoulders were so fine, his chest so sculpted, like a Roman statue. He worked at his breeches next, releasing his shaft. She had forgotten how outrageously large his male part was.

He looked down at her with a hungry look, the exact impassioned look she had dreamed of. She wanted to appreciate it, at long last, but she felt nervous and exposed as his gaze raked over her. She was afraid to show any shyness or cover herself, for fear he would snap out of this fit and tell her to go to bed or something, so instead she pretended to be fearless. When he lay back over her, she pulled him closer and pressed her lips to his.

"Minette," he sighed against her mouth. It was precisely the way she had wished him to say her name, all trembling and full of emotion. In the midst of their kiss, she felt his hand between them, positioning his rigid member against her quim. "No matter what I do, no matter how I try to control myself, I want to be inside you."

"Isn't that lovely?" she replied brightly. "Because I want you to be inside me. This will all work out perfectly well—"

Her voice cut off as his thick shaft poked against her center, a hot, hard reminder of his outsized virility. His lips fastened over hers as his hands roved over her body. "You're so beautiful," he growled as he pulled away. "So lush. God, how I've wanted you."

She was afraid—she was terrified—but she wouldn't have stopped him for the world. How long had she wished for this hungry sort of passion? This went somewhere beyond his love play with Mary the servant girl. There was a heightened intensity between them, a pressure as if a wave was cresting. His mouth mauled hers. His teeth nipped at her lips, then bit the lower one until she squirmed.

She did not feel like a child anymore. She did not feel innocent. She felt as if she might devour him alive. She bit his lower lip too when she could catch hold of it, and he gave a low chuckle and pressed his shaft harder against her quim. She moved her hips, trying to assuage the pulsing point of need just at the apex of her sex. She touched herself in that place sometimes when she thought of August. He made a hoarse sound and suckled her nipples again, then pinched them so her whole body moved and strained for his possession.

"Do you want me inside you?" The words were so terse, so low, she might have missed them if she were not attuned to his every breath.

"Yes. Oh, yes."

He spread her thighs wider, right there on the floor, pressing them apart with his hips. She craved for him to come inside her, and he didn't keep her waiting. He cradled her shoulders and drove forward with a commanding thrust. It was an invasion, truly, but her body was so wet she took him easily. He slid deeper and deeper until she was absolutely full of him.

"Ohhh," she sighed. She tried to reach for him but he was back to holding her down, which she found even more exciting. As he held her arms against the parlor floor, he pumped inside her, hard thrusts that made her feel helpless and taken and ardently desired.

"You feel so big inside me," she said. "Oh, you are making me feel very, very..."

She didn't know the words. She only knew that each time he pushed within her, it stroked some agonizing need. He ravaged her mouth, a rough, invasive kiss to go along with his rough, invasive strokes, and she struggled so he would kiss her harder. The truth was, he controlled her completely only by being inside her and stretching her open with his girth.

As she lay beneath him feeling held down and possessed, a surging sensation grew in her middle. She didn't think proper wives were supposed to enjoy this sort of unbridled lovemaking, but she couldn't get enough. *Tempt and tease.* That was what Esme had taught her, but Minette didn't want to tease him. She wanted to give him everything because he was giving her everything.

I need you. Dear husband, dear love, we needed each other all along.

If his time with Mary the servant had been a romp in the meadow, this was a raging storm, a bursting dam. A river overflowing its boundaries. She felt full and wild, enervated with erotic energy. She needed completion. She wanted the contraction, the pleasure, the rush.

"Please," she cried. "It feels so good. Please, help me..."

He reached between their bodies where they pressed together, and parted her with his fingers, stroking her most sensitive bud until she thought she must go mad. His shaft filled her, and her whole middle trembled as she tried to press on his questing fingers. He found the perfect spot to caress...oh, the *perfect spot*. She screamed "Yes! Oh, yes!" but then his hand came over her mouth so all she could do was moan behind his fingers.

"You like that?" he asked in a coarse murmur.

She tried to dislodge his hand, to say *Yes, yes, yes*, but he only stifled her harder as his other hand worked magic between her legs.

"Let go," he said. "Give me everything, now."

She arched her spine and lifted her hips, trying to press herself closer, although they were already closer than she'd ever been to anyone in her life. She supposed she looked like the very definition of a wanton woman, but she didn't care. Her climax came upon her like a lumbering thing, a hard, grasping contraction of such intensity that tears squeezed from her eyes. It was as if her tears, her heart, her blood, every part of her was connected to August and this violent closeness between them.

His hand left her mouth and settled around her neck as he shuddered atop her. His fingers tightened, choking her, thrilling her, drawing a few last pulses from her prolonged release. Was he feeling the same ecstasy she felt? She closed her eyes as his hand slid down to rest against her breasts. She didn't care if she was pressed against the hard, cold parlor floor. She didn't want him to leave her, not ever. His breath came in gasps as he rested his cheek beside hers.

"Minette. Dear love. Did I hurt you?"

"No," she said quickly. "Well, only in the most exciting way," she amended, since she must still have his fingerprints about her throat.

He stroked her face and kissed her eyes, and trailed his tongue down the column of her neck. As he leaned to tease her still-sensitive nipples, he moved a bit off her.

"Don't leave me," she said, clutching his shoulders.

"I'm not. I'm only giving you space to breathe." He smoothed her hair and looked to the side, at the remains of the shattered swan. His shaft was still half inside her as he moved her away from the mess and cradled her in his arms. "I was too rough with you," he said.

"No."

"I was."

She shook her head. "It felt marvelous, even if you were a little rough."

He lifted her face so she was forced to meet his gaze. Did he see everything she felt? The pleasure and relief, the tremulous adoration? The fear that he might still dismiss her as a child?

"Was I all right?" she asked. "You must tell me if anything was lacking. I'm eager to learn what you like best in these matters, if you would like me to be more vocal, or less vocal, or more active, or less active, or learn any sort of tricks that might add to your—"

He silenced her with a kiss. His leg came over hers and he drew her closer so his manhood nestled between them. To her shock, it was hard and stiff again. As he kissed her, he parted her legs and eased his way inside.

"Oh, you would like to...again," she breathed against his lips.

"Yes. Oh, God." He sounded like he was praying. "Absolutely. Again."

August came awake in the morning with a start, disarranging the cushions he'd piled before the fireplace. Somehow, in last night's passionate endeavors, they had never made it up to bed. A hearthside blanket preserved Minette's modesty as she slumbered in his arms, her head cradled against his chest. He hugged her closer before he realized what had awakened him. A tall, blond visitor stood staring at them just inside the door.

"Warren. Jesus." August angled his body to shield Minette from her brother.

"Everything's in order, then? Very well." Warren turned on his heel to leave. August's irritated exclamation had roused Minette to half-wakefulness.

"Is it morning already?" she sighed, wrapping her arms about his neck.

"No, darling. Don't wake yet. I'll be right back."

He extricated himself from his drowsy wife and jumped into his breeches, and chased Warren down the hall.

"You might have knocked," he said to his friend's back.

"I wish I had."

"What are you doing here?"

Warren turned. His eyes flicked with distaste to August's bare chest. "You're not dressed."

"Why are you here? What do you want?"

"What do you think I want?" he snapped. "I wanted to check on my sister. I wanted to ask her again if she wouldn't rather leave. And then I find you...and her..." His lips twisted in a grimace.

"You ought to be happy."

"That you bedded her in the front parlor, in the middle of the floor? You've always been such an elegant fellow. Just what I hoped for my sister."

August had made a mistake when he ruined Minette, and made a whole world of mistakes since then, but he was getting damned tired of Warren's contempt. "When are you going to forgive me?" he asked, throwing out his hands. "Five years? Ten years?"

"My wife is waiting in the carriage." Warren moved toward the door. August followed, disregarding the butler who stood holding Warren's gloves and hat.

"Will you never forgive me? It would be helpful to know. Talk to me, Warren. Out of respect for our friendship, talk to me."

"You want to know when I'll forgive you?" Warren said, turning on him. "I'll forgive you when I forget the look on my sister's face as you foisted her off onto me and my wife. *'Oh, it's Josephine's first baby. I think you ought to go.'*"

His unflattering mimicry made August's fingers curl into fists. "You're the one who encouraged her to go," August reminded him.

"After you begged me to do so. Let's not rewrite the bloody farce."

This was the frosted glass persona August had wished to possess, the persona Minette had stubbornly thawed last night. Warren had mastered it, and was freezing him to the bone. The man took his gloves from the butler and pulled them on with irritable haste. "I'm leaving my sister with you because she would want it. I'm traveling two days' journey away, to be with my wife and await the arrival of our child. But if I hear the barest whisper of suspicion that you are mistreating her, from Arlington or anyone else—"

"Arlington won't spy on me for you," August interjected.

"He already has been, you idiot. And if he reports that she's not chirpy as a goddamned summer lark, I'll bring her to Warren Manor and you'll never get her back. You'll never see her or speak to her again. If you're careless with her heart, if you extinguish in the slightest her brightness and *joie de vivre*, I'll make it my life's work to destroy you. Are we perfectly clear?"

His friend was quivering with barely restrained fury. August could feel it, if he couldn't understand it. Hadn't Warren noted Minette slumbering peacefully in his arms?

"We have come to terms, your sister and I," said August, crossing his arms over his bare chest.

Warren snorted. "'Come to terms'? Is that supposed to paint a picture of marital bliss? Because it doesn't, really."

"We're figuring things out," August insisted. "It's taken time, but we're finding our way. I love Minette and I'd never cause her hurt."

"You've done it plenty of times before."

"I'm changed. She's changed me because she...she knows me and accepts me for who I am. She's patient and understanding, unlike her brother," he added in a reproachful tone.

"It's true, my patience and understanding are at an end," Warren said. "I'd advise you to remember that, Barrymore."

With those cool and cutting words, he accepted his hat from the butler and stalked out the door.

Chapter Sixteen:
My Naughty Minette

Barrymore House's courtyard was astir with grooms, horses, and servants on the blustery, late winter morning. Minette wished she could think of some way to calm August's mother. The nervous woman hovered over the last of the bags, picking up one and setting it by another.

"Mother," said August. "Let the groom handle it."

"I don't want to forget anything," she fussed, trying to stay busy although there was nothing left to do.

"Everything is in the luggage coach. And if you've forgotten anything, simply send a note and we'll convey it at once. Royston Hall isn't so far."

Two months after her husband's death, the dowager was finally on her way to stay with Catherine, August's oldest sister, in Hampshire. The lady's health and energy had blossomed in the past weeks, and she'd become less waspish as a result. Like August, she seemed to be healing from Lord Barrymore's legacy of roughness and abuse, and in fact was looking forward to spending time with her grandchildren. But first, there was this emotional goodbye, this departure from the house where she'd endured so much grief.

"It's going to be fine, Mother," August said, embracing her. "I wish you wouldn't worry. Minette and I will take care of everything here, and at Barrymore Park."

"You have always taken care of everything, my son, and I bless you for it." Minette heard tears in her mother-in-law's voice. The lady pulled away from August, took out a clumsily embroidered handkerchief—

174

Minette's handiwork—and pressed it daintily to the corner of one eye. "I won't cry, or become maudlin."

"No, you won't," said August with a smile. "You are off on a splendid adventure."

"And you, my dear." She turned to Minette. "Take good care of my son. As you always have." She gave her a warm hug and released her. "Take care of yourself as well." She lowered her voice to a whisper quite loud enough for August to overhear. "I would like more little ones, you know. One can never have enough."

"But of course you will have more grandchildren," Minette assured her. "My nephews and nieces must have cousins to play with when they visit Barrymore Park. And you know, Lord Townsend and his wife have just had a baby daughter named Felicity, which means 'happiness.' Isn't that lovely? And my brother and his wife shall have their child soon. It's my dearest hope they will all grow up together and be lifelong friends."

Some emotion flickered in her husband's eyes, and she remembered that his friendship with Warren was terribly strained at the moment. If only Minette knew how to fix the rift.

"I shall pray for you, dear Minette," said the dowager, "and write to you soon." The woman gave her one more peck on the cheek and did the same to her son. *Dear Minette.* The haughty lady had finally left off calling her Wilhelmina, and become something more like the mother Minette had never known. Indeed, she would miss August's mother when she was gone.

"You must come and visit often," Minette said as August helped the lady up the stairs and to her seat. Her lady's maid had already settled into the other cushioned bench. "Try to stay warm. Would you like another blanket? Have you enough refreshments to last until you come to the first inn?"

"Minette, she'll be fine. Mother, have a safe trip." He squeezed her hand and stepped back to let the groom shut the door. His mother peered out the window and waved at them, her eyes alight with affection.

Yes, the dowager had changed a great deal. So much had changed in the two months since August's father had died. Everyone was happier, as if some dark and poisonous cloud had lifted off the house and set them free from their emotional shackles. They mourned Lord Barrymore in public, in the proper fashion, but in private August and Minette set about creating a new tone in the house, one of kindness and patience, and comfortable warmth. August began to write new songs with less onerous chords and more bright harmonies. It was as if they swept Barrymore's legacy from the corners, getting it out of the house like so much unwanted dust.

And now everyone called her Lady Barrymore, and August Lord Barrymore, except for Minette, who was still getting used to the transition. He said she might call him August as long as she liked, until they had a son to inherit the title. With the increased, almost frantic pace of their love play these days, she imagined a child would arrive very soon.

Making up for lost time, August said whenever he took her to bed. He would stay all through the night, every night, stroking and caressing her, and teaching her to please him in deliciously carnal ways. He pleased her too, doing things to her body she'd never seen in any of the books. She must write her own book one day, a romantic novel. The hero would be tall and reserved, with jet black hair and brooding hazel eyes. He would be a grand pianist and composer, who very much enjoyed debauching his heroine...

"Minette?"

She turned to her husband, and noticed she was still waving into the distance, although the carriage had disappeared from view. "Well, your mother is on her way," she said, dropping her hand and hiding her embarrassment by fussing at her skirts. "She will be happier at Royston, don't you think?"

"Indeed. The change of scenery will suit her well." He offered his arm and led her back into the house. "We finally have the place to ourselves, darling. What should we do?"

Minette thought a moment. "I suppose the parlors and hallways might benefit from an overhaul. A bit of brightening, perhaps some fresh paint and decorations. And now that we've moved into the east hall, we ought to do up our old rooms for guests, don't you think? And before too much time passes, we really must spruce up the nursery wing." She noticed her husband's arching brow, and the libidinous glint in his eyes. "Oh, you weren't talking about renovations, were you?"

"No."

"You meant...what shall we do...together...now that we're alone."

"Yes."

Minette gasped as he swept her into his arms. "Good gracious. Where are you carrying me?"

"To my bedroom."

"Oh, yes," she murmured. "That would be appropriate."

She clung to his shoulders as he carried her up the stairs, right past the statue-like footman at the top. It was the same footman who used to collect her from various places in the house when she roamed in her sleep. She never roamed anymore—too blissfully exhausted, once her husband was finished with her. Her cheeks burned, although the servant pretended not to see either of them. It was rather unrefined to be carried about by one's husband, especially straight to his bedroom, but in the past few weeks he'd proven himself an unabashedly ardent lover, and she enjoyed their private activities very much.

"Oh, my," she said as he set her down in the middle of his bedroom. Rather than move into Lord and Lady Barrymore's fusty old chambers, they had redecorated their own wing with adjoining rooms—and greater privacy. "How can you carry me so far without toppling over?"

He said nothing in reply, only set about removing her clothes. She tried to help as he untied and unlaced her, then watched in dismay as he tossed each garment on the floor. "Perhaps I should put them over a chair or something," she suggested.

"I'll put you over a chair," he replied. "Leave them." He lifted her shift above her head and tossed it down beside her gown and stockings and garter ties. She gazed up at him, thrilling to the hunger in his gaze. He pulled her closer, teasing the tip of her nipple as she arched against him. His buttons felt cold against her front.

"Aren't you going to undress too?" she asked.

He undid his coat only, and threw it over the back of a chair. "We've a rather unpleasant matter to take care of first. I can't seem to find the paddle Warren gave us. The one I keep in my desk drawer."

Minette swallowed hard, staring at the outline of her husband's muscular arms beneath his shirt. "Oh, dear. I suppose it has gone missing in the midst of all the moving. Perhaps it was mistakenly packed up with your mother's things! How embarrassing, for her to find it. What will she think? Oh, do you imagine she will take it for a bread paddle?"

"I don't think so." He unfastened one sleeve, and began to roll it up. "She'd know at once it was a disciplinary paddle, and with your initials carved into it, no less."

Minette put her hands to her cheeks to hide the rising flush. "This is terrible. Well, I guess we shall have to muddle on without it."

"Minette," he said, rolling up his other sleeve.

"I mean, you wouldn't want to ask her about it. It would be far too humiliating for everyone involved. I suppose we must count it a total loss."

"Not a total loss." Her husband turned to pick up an oblong, charred piece of wood from his clothes chest. "The servants brought this to me a couple days ago. Do you recognize it? They fished it out of the kitchen fire."

Minette stared at the paddle. Blast the kitchen servants. Why hadn't they let the thing burn? "My goodness," she said, because she couldn't think of anything else to say that wasn't incriminating.

"My goodness, indeed," August replied drily. "Those are your initials, aren't they? How did this paddle make its way from my study desk drawer to the kitchen fire?"

"I can't imagine." She bit briefly at her lip. "It must have been all the moving about."

He stared at her steadily, in a way that made her feel shamed and excited at once. Then he turned away and opened a drawer. "Luckily, I have an excellent carpenter on staff, who was able to replicate the paddle despite the damage. In fact, I believed he's improved it." He withdrew a shiny new implement, turning it over in his hand so she could see the *W.A.R.* carved into one side. "He's made it a bit larger, and thinner, to increase the sting and impart a stricter punishment. And he's promised to make a few more, in case one...or two...should go missing. A man of his talents can provide me an endless supply. Isn't that wonderful, darling?"

"I wouldn't call it wonderful," said Minette with a pout.

August smiled and tapped the paddle against his palm. She was glad he was feeling happier these days, but she felt anything but happy at this moment.

"I believe I shall keep one here in the bedroom," he said, "for punishing my naughty wife when the situation calls for it. For instance, when she steals a paddle—which was a wedding gift—and throws it into the kitchen fire, and then pretends she didn't do it."

"It was a horrible wedding gift, you must agree." Minette took a step back, and another. "I wish you would put that down, so we might get back to the embracing and kissing and..." She slid her hand down to the tuft of hair between her legs and caressed herself in what she hoped was a sufficiently seductive manner. "Don't you want to touch me?" she asked. "Touch me here?"

"Indeed I do. After I paddle your naughty bottom."

Minette stopped fondling herself and thought about the best way to escape him. Unfortunately, he was standing between her and the door.

"I only threw it in the fire because I considered that paddle a great detriment to our marital happiness," she cried.

"I disagree with your assessment. On the contrary, I think it rather effective at keeping you in line. Come and bend over this chair if you please," he said, indicating the one with his coat thrown over it. "Let's make sure you understand that you mustn't throw any more of my things into the fire."

"I won't. Oh, I most certainly won't. I understand completely. I'm absolutely finished throwing paddles into fires, even if they belong there." She searched her husband's features for some hint of softening.

He only gazed at her, unmoved. "I will give you the usual warning: the longer you dally, the longer your punishment will go on."

Blast. Well, she supposed it *had* been a wedding present, and she had snuck it out of August's desk without permission. She ought to know by now not to meddle in his things, especially when he was one of those husbands who had no qualms about spanking his wife. She felt very remorseful as she crossed the room and bent over the upholstered chair. She hoped he wouldn't make her cry, so she would drop tears all over his deep green coat.

"I'm terribly sorry I did it," she said, resting her palms against the cushion beneath her.

"I know you are." He rubbed a large, warm hand across her bottom. It felt rather pleasant, but then his caress was replaced by the hard wooden surface of the paddle. "Since I understand why you did it, there will only be ten strokes for your punishment. However, since I don't wish you to do such a thing again, each stroke is going to be firmly applied."

Minette closed her eyes. *Firmly applied?* He did everything firmly when it came to her bottom, spankings most of all.

"Ouch! Oh, no," she cried as he landed the first stinging blow. "Oh, please, that hurts!"

A second awful stroke followed on the heels of the first. Thank goodness he'd placed a hand at her back to hold her down, or she'd have fallen right off the chair into a pleading heap. This new paddle was much more painful than the last one. So much for her and her schemes. She pledged, as she always did in this position, that she would never, ever behave poorly again.

"Oh. *Oww...*" She wiggled her bottom after the third stroke, though she dared not reach back to rub it. She thought ruefully of her childhood spankings, which her brother had doled out on a regular, and deserved, basis. She'd thought marriage would mean the end of discipline, but she realized now that was not to be. *Because you're a hopelessly naughty woman...* She bit her lip for the fourth stroke, then the fifth brought a loud cry to her lips.

"We're halfway there," August said, relaxing his hold on her back.

"My bottom's on fire." She reached to rub it but he made a quelling sound.

"Leave your hands where they are."

"I'm trying," she said. "But you're hurting me very much. I wish you would touch me and stroke me instead."

He moved behind her and nudged her legs wider with the paddle, then eased the smooth side of it between her legs. The sensation was scandalously arousing. "Stroke you like this, you mean?"

It felt so wonderful she couldn't speak to respond. He turned the paddle the other way and slid the fine beveled edge just between her pussy's folds. She feared that she bucked against the thing in a very lewd way. "You do like to be stroked," he said in a low voice. "We'd better finish your punishment quickly, before you come off without permission."

"Please, no more," she begged. He'd awakened a heated, aching pulse in her center, and when he brought the paddle down on her arse— *whack!*—the need didn't go away, only built in magnitude.

"It hurts. Oh, it hurts," she said in her most pitiful voice, but he gave her the rest of the strokes, hard and stinging as ever. By the end, her parted legs trembled with the effort of holding still.

"There. Your punishment is over. For now." His voice was soft, rough, virile as he smoothed a hand over her burning cheeks. He slid the paddle between her legs again, so she felt hot pain and blissful pleasure in equal measure. He tapped it against her pussy, then eased it back and forth. "Tell me, Minette. This has your initials on it, but who does this paddle belong to?"

"You, my lord." She used the formal title of address because it felt right to do it. He was her lord in this, her unchallenged master when it came to marital discipline. She could feel increasing wetness where he pressed the paddle against her quim.

"It is *my* paddle, isn't it? For punishing you when you need it. You are not allowed to touch it, do you understand? Unless I've instructed you to bring it to me, for your own correction."

"Yes, my lord."

"God forbid it should end up in any more fires." She squirmed and gasped as he poked the tip of it right against her most sensitive place. "Have you learned your lesson, my dear?"

"Yes. Yes!"

"Don't move. Stay just as you are." He put the paddle down atop his wooden chest and began to disrobe. His clothes joined hers in a pile on the floor, then he returned to stand behind her, his stiff shaft jutting out. Her palms sweated against the seat cushion, but she didn't dare move them, or straighten. She flinched as his hands closed on her sore backside and squeezed until she whimpered.

"Your bottom's scarlet," he said. He sounded more excited than concerned.

"Yes," she whispered. "It's throbbing terribly. I suppose it's what I deserved."

He responded to this admission with a few more stinging spanks delivered to each cheek. She pressed forward against the chair, making complaining sounds, but in truth, she felt more wanton than ever.

"How naughty you are, that I must spank you to make you behave," he said. This time when he smacked her bottom, she rose up on her toes and made a sound that was not at all polite.

181

"I suppose it must be very frustrating to you," she said, arching her hips against his.

He squeezed her shoulders and then reached beneath her to pinch her nipples. She cried out, trying to pull away, but he trapped her, clutching her against his chest. "Open your legs," he commanded. "Give me your pussy, naughty girl, or I'll spank you again."

She obeyed as well as she could. Her wits had rather left her, gone fluttery at his lascivious words, delivered in a curt, stern tone. She didn't like to be spanked, but she rather enjoyed the aftermath, when he handled her like this. When she was positioned to his liking, he thrust inside her, all the way to the hilt. His size still shocked her, but it was a good kind of shock that brought pleasure and made her squeeze around him with her sensitive walls. "*Ohhh...*" she sighed. "How perfect you feel inside me."

He made a breathless sort of sound and withdrew, and plunged in again. She loved being taken like this, without couth, without civilized tenderness. She loved the heat of him against her back and the feel of his straining muscles as he covered her. She braced herself against the chair and moved with the rhythm of his thrusts. Every so often he delivered more smarting spanks to her bottom.

Yes, it was their house now, and their bedrooms, their place to play, and make love, and get spanked in this erotically charged manner. *I'll not take any more of his things*, she promised herself silently. *I'll be a perfect wife.*

Or an almost perfect wife.

Or...a sometimes perfect but really mostly mischievous and irritating wife.

Oh well. She was sure she'd get many more spankings, but she would have August's care and protection too, and his magnificent passion. It was everything she'd wished for her entire life.

She stilled her hips as the waves of pleasure crested within her. Behind her, August pounded against her sore, tender arse cheeks, as her pussy contracted in release around his rock hard shaft. Midway through her climax, he grasped her waist and pumped into her, filling her with his seed.

Perhaps they would make a baby this day. Perhaps they had already made a baby and she didn't yet know. She only knew that she wouldn't trade this gorgeous closeness for anything. His arms came around her and he pressed kisses against her cheek, her nape, her shoulder. "I love you," he whispered.

"Even when I'm naughty?"

"Especially when you're naughty," he said, laughing softly. "I adore you, my beautiful, naughty Minette."

August made his way to Minette's sitting room that night after dinner, with a tissue-wrapped bundle tucked beneath his arm. He knocked and pushed open the door, and located his wife at her writing desk. She looked up from her correspondence with a smile.

"August, you've come!"

She said the same thing every night, silly creature. Of course he'd come. If she ever locked him out, he'd break down the door to get to her. He looked forward with voracious longing to this private time with her, when he could bask in the warmth of her company. He lived for her smile, and her pleased adulation. She'd come to mean so much to him, in fact, that he'd developed a terror of losing her regard. Ridiculous, to fear such a thing when she'd adored him for years now, but the idea haunted him, unmanned him, disturbed his dreams.

"Good evening, darling. Are you at your letters?"

"Yes. Auntie Overbrook has written, and Josephine and Warren, and Aurelia, who says baby Felicity has dark hair just like her father, and that she doesn't cry too much, and nurses like a monster. Those were her words exactly, *nurses like a monster*, and how they made me laugh. I'm so happy for them. Isn't it delightful?"

"It is delightful." Minette's smile was contagious, like her ebullient moods.

She came from behind the desk as he walked to meet her. When she was close enough, he caught her in an embrace. Her sweet scent and closeness recalled that afternoon's dalliance and their playful bath afterward. It was all he could do not to tackle her to the floor.

No. You must control yourself. For a few more moments at least.

"What have you there?" she asked as they parted. "Is it a present for me?"

"Yes."

She clapped her hands as he led her to the settee before the fire. "How exciting. What is it for? The holidays have gone, and it's not my birthday."

"It's for your un-birthday then. Do you remember the talented carpenter whom I referenced earlier today?"

He smiled as she fidgeted on the cushion. "Your devilish carpenter, you mean, who has made it difficult for me to sit?"

"The very same. I asked him to make this for you too, and I think it turned out very fine."

He set the gift in her lap. She untied the bow and parted the wrappings, revealing an intricately carved and painted figure.

"My swan!" she exclaimed. "It's exactly like the one I shattered."

"Not exactly." He took it from her and knocked it with his knuckles. "You see, it's not breakable. It's carved of hardwood and will last forever, if you keep it from harm's way."

"If I don't fling it to the floor in a temper, you mean?" She tried to smile but her lips went wobbly. She bowed her head and ran her fingers over the swan's etched feathers and gold-leaf paint. "This is so very lovely. It's the grandest gift I've ever gotten."

"Even better than the first swan?" he asked lightly.

"Yes, much better." She cradled the figure in her hands and lifted it to her cheek. "It's better because we're better now, aren't we?"

Oh, my darling. You don't even know. He gazed at her, this blonde, be-curled angel who had changed him so thoroughly. "I've never been happier in my life. I'm so happy that it frightens me." He nudged the swan away and kissed her cheek, and then tasted her lips. "You're my own special swan," he said when he released her. "A little cantankerous at times, but still very pretty."

"What? Cantankerous?" Minette turned on him in feigned temper, pushing at his chest.

"Oh yes, swans can be violent," he said, capturing her hands. "Who told me that?" As she grappled with him, he pushed her back and kissed her. The swan fell from her hand and landed with a thunk against the floor. Both of them turned to look down at it.

"You see," he said. "Unbreakable." He kissed her once more and let her up to retrieve her gift, which was perfectly in order.

"I don't know where you've found this carpenter." She inspected the carving by the flickering of the fire. "There's such skilled detail. It's beautifully proportioned. He must be a master at his craft."

"He's very good, and very expensive. Fortunately, I've made a pretty penny from the music you made me publish. Perhaps it was a good idea after all."

Minette grinned at him. "Are you saying I was right? You're admitting, for once, that I had an intelligent, reasonable, and useful idea which was better than your idea?"

"Yes, little swanbrains. This once."

She attacked him again in her playful, ticklish manner, but he set her away and gave her bottom a swat. "Go finish your letters before you get me too worked up to control myself. Once I take you to bed, you won't be getting up for some time afterward."

Her impish grin widened. "Do you promise?"

"Letters," he insisted, ignoring her seductive gaze and the growing pressure in his breeches. He'd swept her away from her correspondence last night and didn't want to do it again.

He sat back on the settee and crossed his legs at the ankles, and let the glow of the fire relax him as he watched his wife. She looked so attractive when she was at work, whether it was writing letters or stitching handkerchiefs, or guiding conversations, or seeing to guests.

Or applying herself to tasks in the bedroom...

"August?"

"Yes, darling?" He pulled his coat down over the bulging evidence of his arousal as she frowned at the pages in her hand.

"I'm a bit concerned about my brother. He doesn't seem himself in this letter." She looked up, her expression clouded with worry. "I think we ought to go to Oxfordshire for Josephine's lying-in."

"Hmm. Do you?" August thought the last thing Warren probably wanted was for him to show up just as Josephine was about to have their child.

"I know you and Warren aren't on the best terms these days but... I don't know." She looked down at the letter again. "He seems rather at ends. I mean, he doesn't say so, but this letter sounds not at all like him."

"I suppose you know him best." He stood and crossed to Minette. "Why don't you write and tell him we'll be coming? If you like, we can leave at the weekend."

"May we?" She gave him one of her shining smiles. He'd face any amount of Warren's displeasure to make his wife happy.

"Yes, indeed, if you wish. Arlington's been making noises about escaping town and going to the country. Perhaps we could travel together."

Minette clapped her hands. "What a capital idea. I know Warren will love to see all of us, and Josephine will be happy to have me around to help with the new baby. Oh, I can barely wait to see them, and the baby, of course. I'll want to be one of the first to hold their child. It only makes sense, doesn't it, since I'll be the auntie?"

She spun off into ecstasies, making plans of what to take and when to go, and all the wonderful things they would do once they arrived. August was a bit less excited. He and Warren hadn't parted on pleasant terms last time they were together.

But for Minette's happiness, he would travel to Oxfordshire and put up with any amount of his former friend's scorn.

Chapter Seventeen:
Love

August sat as still as he could while Minette slumbered against his shoulder. He envied her facility to fall asleep in carriages; he had never been able to do it. Arlington sprawled across from them, his hat resting beside him on the bench. A rut in the road shook him awake, though Minette didn't stir. The disheveled duke seemed confused for a moment, his blond hair mussed where he'd lain upon it. "Where are we?"

August shrugged. "Somewhere near Maidenhead, I suppose."

Arlington ran his fingers through his disorderly mop and straightened his coat, and soon assumed his more typical refined air. His gaze fell on Minette. "Look at her. How does she do it?"

"I wish I knew. Put her in a soft, comfortable bed and she'll sleepwalk all over creation, but put her in a carriage and she's out for hours."

"Still walks about at night, does she?"

"No, actually. Not for weeks now." As soon as he said it, images of their nighttime activities crowded his mind, and a flush rose in his cheeks. His friend stifled a grin.

"I'm glad things are better. Minette seems happy."

"Our marriage is much improved." *Much improved.* What an inadequate description. He wondered if the depth of his feelings showed in his face. Probably so, judging from Arlington's smile. It was not the thing in London society to be enamored of one's wife. How they had teased Townsend when he fell for Aurelia, and then mocked Warren when he lost his mind over Josephine. Now August was the hapless husband caught in his wife's spell, hanging on her every word and living for her attention.

"Say, when are you going to marry that Welsh lass?" August asked, to wipe the teasing smirk off his friend's face.

"She's not a Welsh 'lass,'" Arlington replied with satisfying irritation. "She's a Welsh baron's daughter, whom the king is forcing me to marry."

"The king can't make you marry anyone," August said, to annoy his friend further.

Arlington shot him a withering look. "Warren can't make you marry anyone either, but we all know how that turned out."

August laughed for a point scored. "So have you learned anything else about this lady you're to marry?"

"I learned she's the youngest of eight, with seven older brothers. Imagine my delight."

"One hopes her brothers are not the protective sort."

"And she speaks the King's English, although I suppose I could make my authority clear to her without language, if need be."

August arched a brow at this assertion. "With a few sound spankings, perhaps?"

"Yes, if necessary. If I have to marry some Welsh aristocrat's daughter against my will, you can be damned sure I won't put up with any nonsense from her."

"With all those older brothers, she's bound to be a hellion." It was fun for August to tease Arlington for once, rather than the other way around. "Perhaps she'll come to the altar in war paint."

"The Welsh don't wear war paint anymore. They haven't for several centuries. Honestly, try reading a book some time, rather than sitting at the pianoforte all day."

"What's your hellion's name?" August asked.

His friend sighed. "Guinevere."

August tried—and failed—not to laugh. He clapped a hand over his mouth as Minette stirred beside him.

"What's so funny?" Arlington snapped. "It's a perfectly proper Welsh name."

"And I suppose you're to be Arthur in this tale, rather than Arlington."

"My given name is Aidan," Arlington sniffed. "And I'll thank you not to mock my future wife's name. We're to be married this October." He waved a hand. "I suppose I'll ride to the border and fetch her like some marauding knight."

"Like King Arthur?"

"It's wonderful that you find it funny."

August grinned at his friend. "In truth, I wish you the best. Marriage isn't as awful as we imagined it to be when we were wild, young rogues. Somehow Townsend and Warren and I managed to flounder our way to marital contentment."

"Flounder being the operative word," said Arlington. "How are you and Warren, by the way? Any thaw in the air?"

August glanced out the window at the black winter night. "No, not really."

"You've got to talk to him. By God, the four of us have been friends a long time."

August didn't reply. Yes, the four of them had been friends forever, and August would like to be friends with Warren again, but he couldn't undo the mistakes he'd made in the past few months.

"I say, we must be nearly to the inn now," August said instead. Arlington nodded and dropped the uncomfortable subject of his rift with Warren, because that was the sort of thing a good friend did.

They arrived to Warren Manor at midday, to find the courtyard in an uproar. Minette's heart jumped into her throat. She recognized the local physician in his dark coat and hat, carrying his bag into the main house. Her Aunt Overbrook's coach stood by the stables.

"Something has happened," she cried.

August grabbed her about the waist before she could open the door of the moving carriage. "Wait. Let them put the steps down."

"Something is amiss," Minette said. "The servants look terrified. Why is the physician here? What if something has gone wrong?"

"If something's gone wrong, they don't need you falling out of a carriage to make things worse," Arlington said, peeling her fingers from the door handle so August might pull her back to sit beside him on the seat.

As soon as the carriage stopped, Minette flew down the steps and ran to the front door. Inside the house, she caught one of the servants. "Has the baby arrived yet? What is happening?"

"Oh, milady, such a time," said the flush-faced girl, dropping a hasty curtsy. "Lady Warren is abed trying to birth the child, Lord Warren is pacing around in a panic, and the midwife's setting up a ruckus telling him to go away. Lady Overbrook is here, and the very best physician from Cowley, the one what saved the Atkins boy last year when he fell under that horse—"

"How long? How long has Lady Warren been abed?"

"Hours now. Since last evening."

"They are in the countess's chambers?"

"Yes, milady, but—"

Minette left the girl and ran for the stairs. She heard August call her name but she had to go to her friend and ease her suffering any way she could. When she reached the top, she followed the sounds of agony to Josephine's bedroom. She nearly collided with a maid carrying an armful of bloodied toweling.

"Oh, no," Minette breathed. "Oh, please, is she all right?"

August caught up to her and took her shoulders. "I'm not sure you ought to go in. You heard the maid downstairs. Things are in confusion."

"I must go to Josephine. If there is any way I can help, I must do my part."

She pushed open the door, to heat and noise and more panicked servants. Her brother stood by the physician, pleading with him to stop his wife's suffering.

"What in God's name do you mean, this is *normal?*" he shouted. "Is it normal for her to cry and scream and sweat for hours? Why aren't you *doing anything?*"

"Idylwild!" scolded Aunt Overbrook in her high pitched voice. "You are not helping. If you can't be useful, you ought to go away."

The harried midwife and her trio of assistants seemed to share the dowager's sentiments. The midwife actually pushed Warren aside to apply a cold cloth to Josephine's forehead as she let out another groan.

190

"Let me do that," said Minette, rushing to Josephine's side and taking the cloth from the midwife. She tried not to gawk at her sister-in-law's belly, which had grown enormous since she'd left town. "Oh, my dearest love. I'm so sorry to find you suffering."

"Minette, you're here." Josephine regarded her with an unfocused gaze. "I'm glad. But I'm afraid I won't be very—good—company at the moment." Her last word cut off in a grunt, followed by a ragged scream. "Help me get up," she said with breathless urgency. "Help me to my feet. I must walk."

Warren shook his head. "You mustn't try to walk, Josephine. Minette, how are you?" He acknowledged her arrival with a distracted kiss. "Mopsy, tell her she must rest in bed."

"What does the midwife say?" asked Minette.

"The midwife says she must walk," said Aunt Overbrook, "as any lady who's borne a child will know. I've worked in Women's Charities long enough to know what's what." She frowned at her nephew. "Help her up, Warren, and then be gone with you, so your wife can bear your child in peace."

Minette stared at her brother. She'd never seen him like this, wild-eyed and frantic, practically in tears.

The physician cleared his throat as Aunt Overbrook and the midwife labored to help Josephine stand up. "It's possible that your wife will find this easier, my lord, if you were to absent yourself and allow her to preserve her modesty. You might, er, retire to a distant parlor for a drink."

"August," Minette cried, hurrying back to the door. "Arlington! You must take Warren away from here and get him drunk."

"I did not say drunk," the physician corrected from across the room.

The two men peeked in, looking rather terrified as Josephine set up another wail. "Come along," said Arlington, beckoning Warren. "Why not leave this business to the ladies? I believe it's customary to do so, and they appear to have matters in hand."

Warren dug in his heels. "What if she needs me?"

"The servants will get you," said August. "Let's go have a drink, old chap."

"I'm not leaving my wife."

Arlington and August exchanged glances. "I'll stay here, just outside the door," said Arlington. "You go downstairs with Barrymore, and if the slightest need arises, I'll send someone to fetch you. I swear, I'll send someone on the spot, or come myself to drag you smartly."

"Go on with you," said Aunt Overbrook, prodding her nephew toward the door. "Let Josephine do what she must, without you fretting in the background. All her strength and attention are needed for this task."

Warren gazed in anguish at his suffering wife, now plodding back and forth in her shift, clutching her back.

"It won't be long now," said Aunt Overbrook. "Go await the news of your firstborn like a proper man should." The stolid dowager finally accomplished what the midwife and physician could not, and banished Warren from the chamber.

Minette walked beside Josephine, supporting her and sponging her forehead. "What can I do, dear Josie? Please, how can I help you?"

"I don't know. I'm so tired. I don't know if I can go on much longer. I'm... I'm scared."

"You must be brave. Aunt Overbrook says the baby will come soon. The midwife is preparing the bedding right now. Isn't it exciting?"

Josephine threw back her head and shouted, "I want it out of me."

"Of course you do," said Minette. "And out it shall come, although it's taking a terribly long time. You're right to be frustrated, and I think you ought to cry and scream as loud as you like."

"They say the first one is the hardest," said Josephine between pants. "And it's really, really hard."

"Perhaps, but you can do it. You've always been so strong."

Josephine went to her knees. "I need to lie down again. I need to lie down." She looked over at Minette, her pain-hazy eyes snapping to irritated focus for a moment. "Your brother did this to me, and I'll get back at him for it someday, mark my words. I'll punch him or something. Plant him a facer right on the nose."

"I think you ought to. He's definitely got it coming," agreed Minette. "I won't even warn him of your plans. Now take a deep breath, my dear, and rest for a moment on the bed."

Warren paced the room with such agitation, August could barely chase him down with the claret.

"Take it," he said, when Warren tried to refuse him. He put the glass in the man's hands and led him to a chair. "You're not doing your wife any favors, you know. Someone's got to be the calm and steady one."

"She's the calm and steady one." Warren sat heavily, and then jumped back to his feet. "She's been at this since yesterday with hardly a complaint, only that endless crying and moaning. You can't understand what it feels like, watching your wife suffer so."

August bit his lip. He believed he did know what it felt like to watch his wife suffer—since he had caused Minette far too much suffering—but it probably wasn't a good thing to mention now.

"She's going to be fine," he said instead. "She's an exceptionally strong woman. She grew up in the jungle, you remember, swinging from vines."

Warren made a strangled sound, downed his drink in one swallow, then sat and put his head in his hands. "I can still hear her, even with the door closed."

"Arlington will come if anything is wrong."

"If anything is wrong!" Warren said, looking up again in dismay. "My wife's been screaming for hours now. Everything is wrong. I'm never, ever bedding her again, I swear it. I'm not touching her. Nothing could make me do it."

I used to think that about your sister. Again, words better left unsaid.

August sat in a nearby chair, and rescued Warren's glass when it almost fell from his fingers. "Say, when did you last sleep?"

"I can't sleep," Warren said. "Jesus." He rubbed his cheek and stared at the fire a moment. "How is my sister, Barrymore? I barely said hello to her."

"She's fine. She was anxious to come. She had a feeling that you needed her, that you were not quite well."

"I'm not well. I'm damned terrified at the moment."

The words were roughly spoken, as if Warren's throat couldn't quite work. August reached to pat his shoulder. He wished he could make everything better for his friend, but sometimes one simply had to live through things. Survive until the bad times improved.

"Thank you for bringing Minette here," Warren said after a moment. "Josie will like to have her near."

"She's excited to be an auntie, and hold the baby."

Warren looked up at him. "Is everything still...better...between you?"

"Things are too marvelous for words." August could see some of Warren's agitation bleed away. A very little bit, but August was glad to give him some measure of relief. "As it turns out, we were always meant to be together. Minette only knew it a good while before me."

"She's devilishly clever." Warren rubbed his forehead, took August's glass, and drained it too. "All I ever wanted was Minette's happiness. For her to feel loved and secure in her marriage. I'm sorry if I behaved like an overprotective arse."

"You've always been that way about your sister. It's nothing to apologize for."

The men sat in silence for a moment. "Blast and the devil," Warren burst out. "This is so hard. Waiting is hard. Loving someone is hard. What if the baby dies? What if Josie dies? I'm so afraid of losing her."

August identified far too well with Warren. He struggled with the same fears, that Minette would come to harm, or somehow leave him. But the truth was, love was stronger than unreasonable fears or regrettable mistakes.

"You won't lose her," he assured Warren.

As if on cue, Josephine let out a hair-raising scream. August caught his arm but Warren was already on his feet, tearing out of the parlor and over to the staircase. As August trailed after him, he realized it was all right to be overwrought with love for one's partner. In fact, it was a wonderful sort of burden, one he'd be honored to shoulder for the rest of his life.

As they neared Josephine's room, Arlington held the door open with a smile. "You're a father," he said. "Congratulations, Warren. Go and have a look."

The men entered the room, which was now full of beaming faces. The previous hubbub had been replaced with quiet, broken only by an infant's vigorous wail.

"He takes after Josephine," Arlington quipped under his breath.

Josephine looked up at her husband from the bed. She appeared pale, tired, and decidedly wrung out, but she still found the energy to smile. "We have a son," she said. "He's gorgeous and perfect as can be."

"A son?" Warren walked toward the bed in a daze. The midwife tried to shoo him away but he wouldn't be turned off. He peered down at the bundle of his newborn heir, then knelt at his wife's side.

"Are you all right?" he asked, smoothing back her hair. "How magnificent you are, darling. I'm so proud of you, and so...so thankful." They put their foreheads together and started whispering to one another as the baby quieted between them, snuggled to his mother's breast. Love, thought August, was a very powerful and mysterious thing.

His eyes sought Minette's. She gazed back at him, a sweet smile tilting her lips. *I love you*, he thought. *I want to lie in your arms, and rest my head beside yours, and drink in your smile for the rest of my life.* And if the Lord blessed them with children, he'd be a conscientious father, patient and wise, and kind. He'd nurture his children and protect them from all harm, unlike the father who'd made him. He would be different.

Because of you, he thought, as he crossed the room to embrace her. *Because you taught me how to love.*

Chapter Eighteen: Epilogue

Minette snuggled closer beside her husband in Somerton's main parlor. It was Hallowe'en again, but this year there was no grand house party full of guests, no bobbing for apples on the terrace. This year, it was only the Townsends with their daughter Felicity, and her brother and Josephine with little Georgie, now nearly eight months old. And the Barrymores, of course, her and August and the little baby within her, too small yet to show.

"I say, it's not the same without Arlington here," said Townsend, bouncing his daughter on his knee as she drooled on a slice of apple. "I wonder how he's faring in Wales."

"Arlington does well at everything," Josephine pointed out. "So I'm sure he's charmed Lord Lisburne and his daughter. The lovely Guinevere is doubtless swooning over his sapphire blue eyes and magnificent mane of hair."

"I never knew you were so enamored of Arlington," said Warren, pretending to be piqued.

"I am not enamored," Josephine replied. "He's entirely the wrong shade of blond to suit my tastes." Everyone laughed as she ran her fingers through her son's light-blond hair. Little Georgie was even more tow-headed than his father. When his mother tickled him, his childish laughter set everyone chuckling again.

"I wonder what she'll be like," said Minette. "Arlington's new duchess. I've never met anyone Welsh before."

"Perhaps she'll be with us next Hallowe'en." Aurelia rescued a bit of apple from Felicity's chin. "Speaking of Hallowe'en—"

"We must tell ghost stories," Warren blurted out.

"No, it's Barrymore's birthday," said Aurelia with a smile. "And we've gotten you a gift."

"We have too," said Warren and Josephine.

Minette grimaced. She didn't want Warren giving August any more gifts, since the paddle he'd given him for their wedding—at least a copy of it—was still put to regular use. The past season had provided plenty of opportunities for Minette to try her husband's patience, resulting in numerous sessions over his lap.

"You're all too kind," said her husband as their friends delivered their brightly wrapped packages. Townsend and Aurelia had gotten him a collection of popular music bound in a handsome leather case, while Warren and Josephine had chosen a polished box and some smartly embroidered handkerchiefs with swirly letter B's. Thank goodness the man was to have some reasonably embroidered accessories. All her attempts still turned out a mess.

Minette handed over her present last. Now that he was a grand marquess, she had bought him a handsome looking glass of tortoiseshell with gold edging. Everyone exclaimed over it as they peered into the mirror together. August kissed her and told her it suited him very well, and that he had wanted such a mirror for some time. She hoped it was true. Even if he didn't love it, she knew he would pretend to love it because he was ever careful of her feelings.

"My wife is working on another gift for me," he said as he bundled up the wrappings, and passed a ribbon to little Felicity. "But it won't be ready until the spring."

Minette smiled shyly as a flush spread over her cheeks. Her husband smiled too and patted her waist, an obvious hint about her condition. Aurelia whooped, Townsend applauded, and Josephine rose to give her a hug. Her brother looked flustered for a moment, but then he smiled too.

"What perfectly wonderful news," said Josephine with a squeeze. "And a perfect birthday present, in my estimation, even if Barrymore must wait to have it for a while."

"Yes, and there's so much to do to get ready," said Aurelia. "The wait will fly by, and before you know it, you'll be holding your baby in your arms."

Townsend nodded. "And a couple summers from now, the lot of them will be tearing around the garden after one another, getting into mischief and pulling the roses from their stems."

"Congratulations, sis," said Warren, "and congratulations to you too, Barrymore. I hope you're ready to have a bunch of curly-headed chatterboxes underfoot."

"Warren!" Minette protested, but she could see the teasing glint in her brother's eyes. "Who's to say our children will be chatterboxes? Perhaps they'll have dark hair, and be quiet and brooding."

"Is that what you are?" Townsend asked August as Warren laughed. "Quiet and brooding?"

"More likely he can't get a word in edgewise," said Warren.

August pulled her closer and grinned at her peevish look. "Let them laugh. They're only jealous because they've never been able to brood as well as me."

"Brood, or breed?" asked Townsend, setting everyone off into more laughter. Warren shook his head, and then the two babies began to fuss.

Warren stood to walk about with George, while Aurelia cosseted Felicity, rocking her back and forth to soothe her. Minette was hardly much older when she'd lost her parents. In fact, she knew very little about being a parent, except that one must protect and love the little ones. She noted the way Warren whispered to George to calm him, and the way Aurelia tickled Felicity to make her smile again. She was glad her friends weren't the sort to banish their children to the nursery, or leave them to grow up primarily in a servant's care.

"Georgie always wants to walk about and play," sighed Warren, "only he's not capable yet, poor fellow." He set him on Josephine's lap, where the baby proceeded to kick his stubby little legs. "Say, Barrymore, play something, would you? Something to amuse the children."

"Oh, yes, do," pleaded the ladies.

"Of course I will, if Minette will help me. She's been taking lessons, you know."

"From who?" asked Townsend.

"From me, of course," August said. "And she's come a long way from last year, I'll tell you."

"Does that mean you won't be treating us to *Poggle and Woggle?*" joked Warren in a drawling voice.

"The children might like *Poggle and Woggle*," Minette pointed out.

"No, I've finished something else. A new piece." Her husband sorted through the music he'd been working on earlier, and propped open the pages. "It's called *Minette*."

"Minuet?" She could feel herself blushing again.

"No." A smile teased the corners of his mouth. "*Minette*. I wrote it for you, dear. I was going to call it Wilhelmina, only..."

Their friends erupted in more laughter as Felicity shrieked and waved her hands. "I believe the young lady wants us to commence with the music," said Minette. "In fact, she sounds insistent."

"You take the right hand. I'll do the left."

They seated themselves just as they had precisely one year earlier. She couldn't help thinking how much had changed since then, and how far she had come from *Flowers of August*, and Lady Priscilla's insults, and heartbroken tears in Josephine's arms. August didn't think her a child any longer, and he didn't dismiss her as a nuisance. He had even written her a song...

As they began to play the notes together, tears misted her eyes. The song was pretty, even merry, but with an underlying tone of wistfulness that saved it from sounding like some reckless jig. It was a song for her, or about her. Goodness, she'd soon become too teary-eyed to read the music.

"I like this song," she whispered to him.

"I'm glad," he whispered back.

"It's much better than *Flowers of August*."

"Anything is better than *Flowers of August*," he replied, hitting an especially resonant note.

Behind them, the children had quieted, entranced by the marvelous harmonies her husband was so adept at creating. The song rose to a bright and shimmering peak, a burst of happiness just like the happiness she felt in her heart. Her husband was so talented, and so amazing. She put her head against his shoulder. "Thank you, darling," she said.

He smiled and patted her hand upon the keyboard, then laced her fingers with his.

"Minette," said Josephine behind them. "How far you've come in your lessons. You must be very proud."

"Indeed," echoed Warren. Everyone agreed that she was ever so much more talented than before, but Minette thought she was still nowhere as talented as her husband.

"You must continue to play, so the babies will be entertained," she said to August. She hoped that would give her some time to compose herself.

A moment later, she was laughing with everyone else as August launched into a jocular rendition of *Poggle and Woggle*, silly lyrics and all.

August stayed up with the men for a while before he made his way to the guest chambers. He let his valet undress him and take charge of his clothes, then slipped into a night shirt and crossed to the bedroom.

He found Minette at the vanity table, brushing out her glossy curls. Her pale pink dressing gown gathered loosely at the waist, so he saw a hint of her beautifully curved bosom beneath her shift. He preferred to see her in pinks and florals, rather than black. After six months they had decided, with his mother's blessing, to have done with mourning and dress in colors again.

He walked over to her, taking in the furnishings and the great curtained bed with a rueful smile. "The Townsends have a jolly sense of humor, don't they? To put us back in this room?"

"Where else would they put us?" Minette's laughter rang out in the echoing chamber. "I have many memories of this room, you know. Most of them bad."

"Then we shall have to make better ones." August picked her up, sat down in her place, and deposited her in his lap. They peered into the vanity glass together, her light hair beside his dark waves, her blue eyes next to his hazel ones. The tortoiseshell mirror lay on the table before them. "Thank you for my present," he whispered. "Although I only ever see myself in you."

Minette touched his cheek. "What a poetic thing to say. If you start writing poetry in addition to composing music, you shall become too captivating for words. Honestly, I don't know how I could ever match up, with my poorly embroidered handkerchiefs."

"You're accomplished at conversation," he pointed out.

"Little good that does a person."

"Ah, but you're good at other things too." He cupped her breast and ran a thumb across her nipple to feel her shudder against his chest. As he fondled her, she lifted his mirror and angled it so both of them could look into it at once.

"There is an old wives' tale that if you peer into a looking glass on Hallowe'en night, you'll see your true love reflected back at you." She grinned at him in the glass. "If only we'd tried that last Hallowe'en, it would have saved everyone a lot of trouble."

"You're trouble personified," he said, giving her a pinch. "And you always knew your true love, didn't you?"

"Yes, I did. But you took some convincing. A mirror might have helped."

No, nothing would have helped him but to be forced into a marriage with Minette. Perhaps some Hallowe'en magic had been at work, or perhaps they'd always been fated for one another. He put her on her feet and nudged her toward the bed, and went about the room extinguishing candles until it was as black as it had been that night. The fire's muted glow disappeared completely when they drew the bed's heavy curtains.

Minette giggled in the black void and reached out to him, and nearly poked him in the eye. He found her shoulders and drew her close, and kissed her deeply in the darkness. "I can't see you," she complained when he released her. "I can't see a thing."

They groped about until they located the edge of the bed curtain, and pulled it open again. As soon as he saw Minette, he forced her back upon the pillows and divested her of her dressing gown and shift while she squirmed and giggled some more. When she was naked in the firelight, she turned her attention to his night shirt and pushed it up over his head. He gazed at her lips as she fondled his cock with maddeningly erotic attention.

"Taking my measure?" he asked.

"And an impressive measure it is," she answered in her adorable, shameless way. "It's too bad that first encounter took place in the dark. I couldn't see anything of your remarkable physique, only what I felt with my hands, and I was too shy to touch you very much. I remember so little! I honestly have no memory of how I ended up in your bed."

August pulled her closer, burying his nose in her hair. "I remember plenty of things. I remember how soft you were, and how lovely you smelled. If I wasn't half drunk, I would have realized you weren't a kitchen maid."

"Thank goodness you were half drunk."

He rolled her over and gave her bottom a spank. "Saucy little miss, aren't you?"

"But I can be as naughty and saucy as I like now that I'm breeding. Aurelia and Josephine tell me one of the great benefits of increasing is that they are spanked a lot less."

"I'll spank you whenever you need it. Don't test me in this, darling. Someone's got to make you behave." He caressed her rounded cheeks. "A paddle can impart a great deal of sting with very little harmful impact. So can a hand. Shall I show you?"

"No, you needn't," she said quickly. "I'll be good tonight, even if I wasn't on my best behavior last Hallowe'en."

"You were very naughty last Hallowe'en. A proper lady would have stopped me. She would have flown from the bed as soon as I began molesting her." August demonstrated this very same molestation, stroking her damp, hot pussy as she quivered beneath his touch.

"You didn't give me much opportunity, if you'll remember," she protested. "And you're the one who insisted again and again that I was naughty, all the while you did terribly naughty things to me. How shocking you were."

"*I* was shocking?" He pressed a finger inside her, then another. "Have you any idea how I felt when I woke up and found you in my arms? It was the shock of my life. And then your brother came strutting in and—"

Minette burst into laughter. "*Strutting in?* I hardly remember it that way."

"Because you were busy falling off the back of the bed as I was trying to put you to rights. Which was a damned waste of time, considering you'd bled all over the linens." In the end, he had to laugh along with her. "What a nightmare it was."

"Perhaps," said Minette, gazing into his eyes. "But somewhere along the line, it turned into a dream, don't you think?"

He didn't answer, only gathered her close and showed her how much of a dream it was every moment she was near. He kissed her belly where their child grew, and caressed her in all the places she most liked as she trembled beneath his touch. Then he covered her with his body and pressed inside her with aching slowness until she begged and clutched at him for more. He'd never been good with words, like Minette, but he could give her his love and longing, now and forever.

Minette was his song, his savior.

She was the music that had finally healed his heart.

THE END

A Final Note

I hope you enjoyed book three in my Properly Spanked series. If you've been following along, Aurelia had her grasshopper in *Training Lady Townsend*, Josephine had her tiger in *To Tame A Countess*, Minette had her swan in this book, and of course there's one more heroine (and animal) to come—the Duke of Arlington's Welsh bride, in *Under A Duke's Hand*.

I'm so grateful for all the readers who have read these new books and recommended them to others, especially those who don't normally read historicals. As always, your thoughtful reviews mean the world to me, as do your comments on Facebook, Twitter, and Goodreads. This journey is made more special because I'm sharing it with you.

As for the last book in this spankalicious world, you can learn more about the Duke of Arlington's upcoming story in the teaser below. You can also subscribe to my newsletter at AnnabelJoseph.com to keep up to date on book releases. For more frequent updates, follow me on Twitter (@AnnabelJoseph) or Facebook (if you like, shoot me a friend request!)

As always, I would like to thank my tireless beta readers, GC, Janine, Doris, Tasha L. Harrison, and my friend Tiffany, who pitched the whole "best friend's sister" storyline to me many months ago. Thanks also to Audrey, and Lina Sacher, my trusty and patient editors who provide invaluable help book after book.

Coming Soon: *Under A Duke's Hand*, the final story in the Properly Spanked series

A duke as wealthy and powerful as the Duke of Arlington requires, by matter of course, an elegant, perfectly pedigreed bride. Unfortunately, he must settle for the king's choice: Miss Guinevere Vaughn, the rough-edged daughter of a border baron. She's pretty enough for a Welsh hellion, but she hasn't the necessary polish to succeed in London society.

When Aidan explains that she'll need to improve her manners—and her disposition—he finds himself locked in a vexing battle of wills.

Gwen never asked to wed a duke. Her new husband is haughty, inflexible, and demanding, and makes no secret of his disdain for her upbringing. No matter how hard she tries to please him, she's never good enough. He disciplines her with an iron hand, and then expects her to submit to his vile whims in bed. Not that his whims are...completely...vile...all of the time. It's only that her husband doesn't love her, and she wants him to love her.

If only her feelings were not so complicated.

If only life was not so difficult *Under A Duke's Hand*...

A new steamy bodyguard romance from Annabel's alter ego, Molly Joseph:

PAWN, book one in the Ironclad Bodyguards series

High stakes chess competition has always been a man's game—until Grace Ann Frasier topples some of the game's greatest champions and turns the chess world on its ear. Her prowess at the game is matched only by her rivals' desire to defeat her, or, worse, avenge their losses. When an international championship threatens Grace's safety, a bevy of security experts are hired to look after her, but only one is her personal, close-duty bodyguard, courtesy of Ironclad Solutions, Inc.

Sam Knight knows nothing about chess, but he knows Grace is working to achieve something important, and he vows to shelter her from those who mean her harm. In the course of his duties, he realizes there's more going on than a simple chess match between rivals, and his fragile client is all too aware of the stakes. When she leans on him for emotional support, attraction battles with professionalism and Sam finds his self-discipline wavering. Soon the complexity of their relationship resembles a chess board, where one questionable move can ruin everything—or win a game that could resonate around the world.

Enjoy angsty, romantic intensity and hardcore alpha Masters?

You should be reading my Cirque Masters series:

Cirque de Minuit (Theo's story)

It's no easy feat transitioning from the disciplined arena of competitive gymnastics to the artistic whirl of the Cirque du Monde. Kelsey Martin finds secret inspiration in Theo Zamora, a dark, taciturn trapezist—until his partner dies in a tragic accident and he decides to leave the circus for good.

Theo doesn't understand why Kelsey reaches out to him, only that she compels him with her unique combination of innocence and recklessness. Before long the two are collaborating on an aerial silks act for a new production, the *Cirque de Minuit*. Theo's impatience with Kelsey's naivete is matched only by his passion for her, and the two soon become embroiled in a tempestuous, consuming romance.

But some still blame Theo for his partner's accident, and danger wraps up the two performers as inevitably as the scarlet silk of their act. Theo and Kelsey must find a way to connect and trust one another as he leads her deeper and deeper into a dangerous world of control and desire.

Bound in Blue (Jason's story)

At a small, struggling circus in Ulaanbaatar, a fearless trapezist fascinates Cirque du Monde talent scout Jason Beck, until he realizes, halfway through the act, that he already knows this exotic, blue-eyed beauty. Intimately. If he'd known she was part of the act he was here to recruit, he never would have done such basely carnal things to her the night before!

Torn by professional and personal desires, Jason invites Sara to Paris. She's thrilled to join Cirque du Monde, but her trapeze partner, Baat, is less cooperative. When tensions threaten the future of Sara and Baat's act, she finds solace in a sexy, consuming Master/slave relationship with Jason. His strict requirements match perfectly with Sara's desires to submit, to do whatever it takes to please her Master. Soon they're barreling toward deeper commitments, even love.

But circus life can be chaotic. Perilous. Cirque CEO—and brutal Master—Michel Lemaitre develops an uncomfortable interest in the submissive trapezist, and Baat becomes increasingly difficult to control. Fears and secrets, jealousy and uncertainties threaten to undo everything Sara and Jason have built in their intimate BDSM sessions. Hurt by lies, rocked by shocking revelations, the two must battle to remain bound together in love.

Master's Flame (Lemaitre's story)

In the sexually charged world of Cirque du Monde, CEO Michel Lemaitre reigns as king of depravity. He's a stringent, brutal Master who selects his slaves based on their ability to cope with strict handling and pain. He exerts rigid control over his chosen partners and they submit to him in all things—that is, until fiery Italian acrobat Valentina Sancia enters his life.

Valentina's known as *La Vampa*, the flame of Napoli, and her tempestuous personality and wild libido soar as high as her circus tricks. Michel finds himself drawn to the red-headed firebrand even as he tries his hardest to resist her. It doesn't help that the sensual beauty idolizes him and tempts him at every turn. He finally engages her in a one-month, no-holds-barred Master-slave relationship to prove their incompatibility.

And that's when the circus really begins.

The two become wrapped up in bondage, cages, physical ordeals…and an emotionally fraught battle of wills. He's never had a slave burn so bright, and Valentina's heart is set on pleasing her Master, no matter the torment and trials she must endure. Is there such a thing as too much passion? Michel's convinced there is, and he's determined to tame a billowing love on the verge of blazing out of control.

The Cirque Masters series is available wherever ebooks are sold.

About the Author

Annabel Joseph is a multi-published, New York Times and USA Today Bestselling BDSM romance author. She writes mainly contemporary romance, although she has been known to dabble in the medieval and Regency eras. She is recognized for writing emotionally intense BDSM storylines, and strives to create characters that seem real—even flawed—so readers are better able to relate to them.

Annabel also writes vanilla (non-BDSM) erotic romance under the pen name Molly Joseph.

Annabel Joseph loves to hear from readers at
annabeljosephnovels@gmail.com.
You can learn more about Annabel's books and sign up for her newsletter at annabeljoseph.com.

14575590R00117

Printed in Great Britain
by Amazon.co.uk, Ltd.,
Marston Gate.